Grims' Truth

Book 3: Chaos Theory

Arc 1: The Tainted

Isu Yin & Fae Yang

CHAOS THEORY
[Grims' Truth – Book 3]
2nd Edition Copyright © 2020 by Isu Yin & Fae Yang
(1st Edition Copyright © 2018 by Isu Yin & Fae Yang)

All rights reserved. No part of this book may be used or reproduced in any manner whatsoever, without written permission, except in the case of brief quotations embedded in articles and reviews. For more information, please contact publisher at Publisher@EvolvedPub.com.

SECOND EDITION SOFTCOVER
ISBN: 162253879X
ISBN-13: 978-1-62253-879-9

Editor: Lane Diamond
Cover Artist: Cindy Fan
Interior Designer: Lane Diamond (Images: Briana Hertzog)

EVOLVED PUBLISHING™
www.EvolvedPub.com
Evolved Publishing LLC
Butler, Wisconsin, USA

Chaos Theory is a work of fiction. All names, characters, places, and incidents are the product of the author's imagination, or are used fictitiously. Any resemblance to actual events or persons, living or dead, is entirely coincidental.

Printed in Book Antiqua font.

The GRIMS' TRUTH Series

Arc 1: The Tainted
The Spinner's Web
Conundrum
Chaos Theory

Arc 2: The Guardians
Prince of Shadows
Wiser
Soul of a Doll

NOTE FROM PUBLISHER:
The current publishing plan calls for an ultimate series of 20 arcs containing 3 books each, for 60 books in all, so please stay tuned for much, much more.

For those lost in the battle for balance.

TABLE OF CONTENTS

Map..0
Chapter 1 – Loose Ends..1
Chapter 2 – Topsy Turvy...14
Chapter 3 – Six Doors...17
Chapter 4 – The Plague We Spread...31
Chapter 5 – The State of Existence..44
Chapter 6 – Father...61
Chapter 7 – Ode to You...68
Chapter 8 – The Dreamscape...81
Chapter 9 – A Wistful Melody..91
Chapter 10 – Our Time..100
Chapter 11 – A Little Unorthodox..110
Chapter 12 – Amiss, Miss..119
Chapter 13 – Leihs ot Egas..130
Chapter 14 – What I Hold Dear..145
Chapter 15 – Solace..158
Chapter 16 – A White Lie..165

Chapter 17 – The Light of Time..176

Chapter 18 – A Resolved Riddle..186

Chapter 19 – The Eyes of the Universe..199

Chapter 20 – Out of Time...208

Chapter 21 – Only Time Will Tell..211

Chapter 22 – The Final Hour..219

BACK-OF-THE-BOOK EXTRAS:

Reference Guide

Book Club Guide

What's Next from Yin & Yang?

Acknowledgements

About the Authors

More from Evolved Publishing

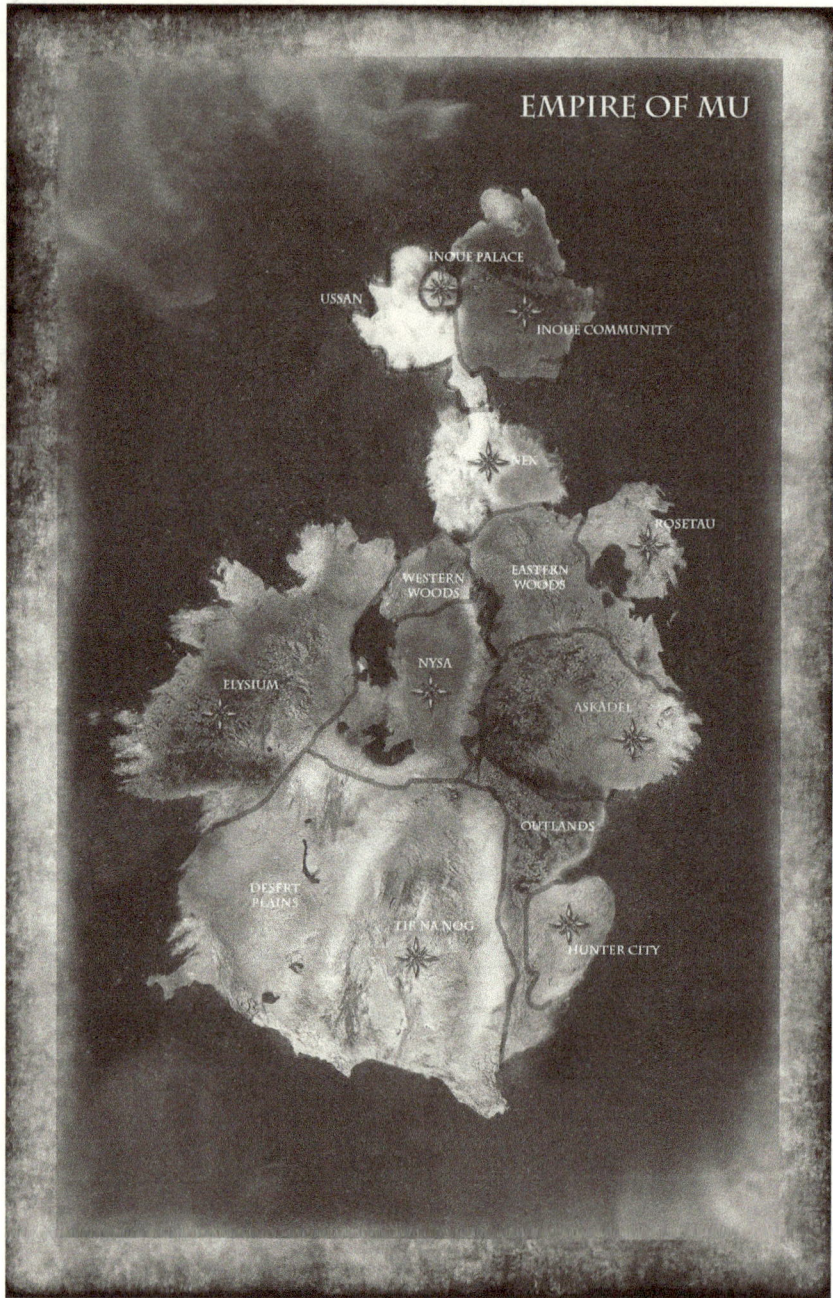

1
LOOSE ENDS

If life were a tangle of threads marking our beginnings and ends, I'd be a knot gathering in the middle. The more others try to untangle me, the harder it is to break loose. I'm Chaos – a means to an end that sweeps through, unaware of the innocents who have been caught in its wake. I can't be untangled, only clipped from the very fabric of existence. Be wary of the tempests, for they are blind to life – just like me.

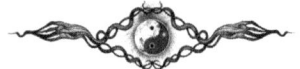

Hero stared out at the Ussan from the upstairs terrace in Inoue Palace. The large deck stretched out as though attempting to safely reach into the Ussan. The Royals often wished for things out of their grasp and, yet, the terrace seemed the closest to actual success.

He found peace gazing out over the crystal forest, listening to the chiming and whispers. It struck him as one of the only consistent things in Mu, as well of a reminder of past failures. Everything in the Universe came full circle, as stated by the teachings of Grim and of the Grandmaster.

While he viewed the shimmering branches, he muttered to himself. "Everything that has happened, is happening, will happen again."

In the nadirs of his mind, a voice whispered to him, *"You know what you must do."*

The door behind him creaked open, so he turned and faced a smiling Kyou.

"It's time," Kyou said.

Hero followed Kyou into the palace, tossing back the white cape that clung to his legs.

Kyou strode off quickly through the darkness, towards the stairway. "You know, they keep it dark to dissuade people from coming up here." He waited at the top, illuminated by the celebration from downstairs.

Hero delayed, glimpsing his reflection in a mirror on the wall. "The darkness never frightened me much."

Kyou cracked a smile and gestured down the stairs. "Me neither."

Finally, Hero left, keeping his eyes on the mirror until he'd stepped too far to view himself any longer. He hurried down first and snuck behind the crowd of Royals gathered before the viewing window.

Kyou joined him at the end of a red-carpeted aisle and waited for the High King and Queen to begin the ceremony.

In front of the window, a massive and intricate crystal bowl sat upon a small podium full of lotus flowers. This ceremony—the burning of a thousand lotuses—signified the flames of devotion, in which the strength and longevity of the fire reflected the bright future of the newlyweds, a ritual initiated during the rise of the Crystal Empire and one still practiced, as though to honor a tale of fated lovers.

Tori led Fate towards the aisle, the wedding gown glistening with silver and crystals as she stepped towards the High Queen. The silver and crystal headdress reflected the traditional flowers and swords of Thule. She embodied their hope for a united Mu.

Hero folded his hands front and watched her approach, reminiscing. Visions of a woman in a crystal crown danced before him. As Fate turned her head to smile at him through dangling crystals, he also saw this woman in her—Nuvem Fati.

He twisted his mouth at the memory of her.

Fate glowed blissfully in the Ussan's light as she intertwined her arm with his.

At times, her striking beauty made him question if he held genuine affections for her, but he refused to let it sway him. He quickly reminded himself: *All roses have thorns.*

The High King and Queen waited on either side of the carpeted aisle, holding two candelabrums to symbolize their support of the new couple. They handed their successors the lotus candelabrums, then lit the candles in the crystal pedestal bowl.

Queen Heqet cupped her hands around the flame of Fate's candle and beamed. "May the flame of your devotion burn ever bright, Caeles Fate."

Khnum nodded slowly at Hero. "I have high expectations for you. Ruling the Empire is a great responsibility... one that I shall someday leave in your hands. Do not let me down."

Fate and Hero bowed their heads politely and continued walking down the aisle towards the large crystal pedestal bowl. The guests clapped in unison three times, and then Hero and Fate lit the lotuses on fire. The flames soared and crackled with a blistering light.

The High King and Queen took the candelabrums as Hero and Fate faced each other for their final oath.

Hero gave his first. "I leave my soul in your hands. I shall protect you with every fiber of my being."

Fate held his hands tenderly. "It would be my honor and my privilege to use this darkness of mine to protect your light."

They resealed their pact with a kiss and faced their guests, hand in hand.

The ceremony turned out exactly the way Khnum had wanted... until Kyou shouted, "Let the festivities begin!"

Everyone cheered in agreement and reveled for the long night ahead of them.

Hero scanned the crowd, recognizing many faces—many of whom, in any other circumstance, remained at odds.

Navarriel of the Council stood beside the young Queen of Elysium, Bailee. Both grinned and applauded merrily. The union suggested a bright and peaceful future but he felt ill at ease.

Hero reflected again on the events of Undal and squeezed Fate's hand. Once again, the Council held them in an iron grip, and now had say in everything they did.

She leaned towards him. "What's wrong?"

He shook his head. "*Minua.*"

'Nothing.'

"I know when you're lying," she said, turning her gaze forward.

He frowned and regarded her carefully.

She understood me? You've been caught, Mistress.

Fate performed her duties perfectly and greeted each of the guests with a vibrant smile. The more she interacted with others, the more he felt certain that she hid a tremendous secret. Her aura radiated a certainty that it had previously lacked.

Hero said little despite the expectations placed upon him. By the end of the night, he just wanted to sleep in the dark to recuperate from all the festivities, for which he held little fancy.

They returned to the guest room after giving their final salutations.

Fate stepped out of her heels and placed them beside the armoire in her room. "They intend to celebrate longer, but we'll return home in the morning. Queen Heqet asked us to meet her in the conference room before we leave." She quickly dressed in a nightgown and removed the adornments from the wedding.

Hero tossed the cape onto a sitting chair next to the window. "We're leaving?" Both pulled back the covers of the bed and lay down, side by side, to get some rest.

"You seemed tired. I managed to convince the High King that it would do no good to pressure you after your trip. After all, how can you prove yourself as the future ruler if you're tired?" Fate flashed a coy smile as she turned over and pushed Hero's hair into place. "Get some rest. We'll have plenty of time to speak tomorrow."

He said nothing in response. Social events brought too much fatigue. In truth, the level of frustration brought about by the constant disruption to his plans wore not only on his energy but his nerves.

The exhaustion settled in, and he fell asleep.

In the morning, Hero dragged his stiff body from the bed and sluggishly changed out of his wrinkled dress shirt into a fresh one. He opened and closed his hands and counted the new black rings of Taint he'd acquired on his tour of Mu.

Fate moved about the room humming a tune far too old for someone her age to know.

He watched her reveal herself in a multitude of ways, all the while keeping his comments to himself. Even if he wanted to say something, the voice inside reminded him that such information was best kept to one's self.

He quietly followed her out of the room, down the stairs, through the long hall, and into the conference room to join Heqet. Although Fate treated him tenderly, his energy dwindled like the last flickers of a flame, until he could do no more than hold her hand.

A familiar feeling nestled into his bones, something he dreaded. If he guessed correctly, it would only get worse from here.

For all of the struggles they faced, at least the King had not rebuked them for deciding to leave. This simple fact most likely saved them a day's delay.

Queen Heqet sat with her back to the large window at the far side of the room. "Good morning."

Fate bowed her head, but Hero just took a seat across from Heqet and placed his hands on his lap. Everything in his body protested movement of any kind.

Chi, who stood brazen and focused beside Queen Heqet, glanced at him briefly as if to note his behavior. "Are you unwell?"

Fate maintained her poise while deflecting the question. "We're both just so drained from the festivities, though they were lovely."

Queen Heqet sat back on her chair. "Before you leave, I wanted to clarify some things about your new positions as the King and Queen of Nitor. First, Hero has been contained within Nitor Palace for some time. If this arrangement is going to change in any way, the Council has requested that he receive an examination. They will likely renew his seals."

Hero turned his head and looked out the window. No matter where he resided in the world, ultimately, he'd be imprisoned. "I can stay in the palace."

Queen Heqet and Fate stared on in dismay.

He continued. "Fate is more than capable of participating in the King's Committee. She has her own goals to achieve, and I believe we should give her the chance to move those goals forward. Mu deserves a just and intelligent ruler and Fate is exactly that. I, on the other hand, seem to instill concern in everyone—perhaps it's the stain. Either way, I've always been in the palace, so there's no point in forcing a change."

He knew the Council had intended all along for Fate to rule. Any unnecessary movements on Hero's behalf could jeopardize the Rebellion's plans and her goal of restoring balance to the Empire. Relinquishing his role as an active ruler gave him an advantage that no one had anticipated. It freed him from scrutiny, and allowed him to move freely about with the knowledge he'd acquired in the breaking of his seals.

Although Fate said nothing, she clenched her jaw. Clearly, his actions had even caught her off-guard.

Queen Heqet pressed a finger to her brow. "Well, I certainly won't argue if you've made up your mind, but I thought you wanted to be able to leave the palace."

"I *can* leave," Hero said. "That's all that matters."

"If you say so, I'll concede."

There seemed no need for further discussion. After Heqet excused Hero and Fate, they collected their belongings and boarded a carriage for the return home.

The carriage crept along the forest path and farther from the crystal trees of the Ussan towering in the distance. From the seat opposite, Fate scrutinized Hero with unrelenting skepticism.

He pretended not to notice and instead feigned interest in the greenery that passed by the windows. His actions earned him a most sour expression from his betrothed, and a menacing aura to match. He intentionally evaded her until the energy in the carriage swelled and the hairs on the back of his neck stood on end.

He pressed his hand on it and relented. "*Ye, mail'ou.*"

'Yes, my love.'

"*Muil'ou suu dei,*" she groused.

'*Don't* my love *me.*'

She continued her admonition. "I've told you before... I suspected they were deliberately trapping you inside the palace."

"Yes, to keep others safe from my condition."

"I thought you wanted to leave the palace, but now you're humbling yourself and accepting their imprisonment." She tapped the seat with her fingernails and exhaled through her nose.

He analyzed her for another long moment, recognizing Fati's temperament. It left him to question what had happened during his journey away from home.

She is awake... but to what degree?

She leaned towards him. "Do you really want to stay in the palace?"

He shrugged. "Why not? I never wanted to become King in the first place. You'll make a much better ruler." From the moment he'd met Fate, he had prepared himself for the changes she would bring. He knew to trust the Spinner's prowess, and felt confident that the Rebellion saw the same in her.

He learned that standing out drew fatal attention and that blending in meant survival, so he did exactly that. His only obstacle stared through him with her wise and primeval eyes. He wished to tell her everything he knew and observed. Although the curiosity often grew, he kept it buried and wrangled her into the Rebellion. Dealings with the Spinner might lead to complete victory, but only if you survived the encounter.

How much does she know? Dare I ask?

Fate caught him observing and twisted her head to one side with a hard squint. "What is it?"

He smiled. "You've really taken to the Language of Ages."

"Well, I can't stay in the dark. Only idiots choose to remain ignorant forever. I believe that all matters should be faced head on."

"My, how feisty you are."

His comment put a small smile on her face.

He said nothing more for the rest of the trip, and continued dwelling on her behavior in the past. Her temperament and behavior mirrored that of Fati perfectly. They aligned so well with the current events that he hazarded a guess at what might come next. Every move he made proved to be a gamble, but he excelled in deviance and odds, so the thought greatly improved his mood.

As soon as they arrived in Nex, Hero stepped inside and dropped his luggage on the entrance hall floor. He stood, taking in the abnormal quiet. With their marriage made official, this also made them the official king and queen, the rightful rulers of all of Nitor, minute compared to the size of an empire but a daunting job nonetheless.

Fate leaned forward to look at his face and raised her brows. "Are you okay?"

He stretched his arms and breathed in. "What should we do first?"

"You're asking me?" She faced the hall and viewed her surroundings. "It feels a bit strange to suddenly oversee all this. We've both been away for so long that it no longer feels like home."

He hummed in agreement.

The palace looked abandoned without the servants. Floors and furniture sat with a fine layer of dust, the chandeliers remained unlit, and the loss of the usual hustle and bustle gave way to an eerie silence.

Hero had heard the rumors of people fleeing from the Taint while the pair visited Inoue, but he'd hoped, in some small way, that his efforts to befriend them had produced more than this.

Fate muttered, "Where is everyone?"

As if in response, Firmus stepped out from the upstairs hallway and greeted them with a smile. "Welcome home. We didn't hear you enter." He hastened down the steps and collected their luggage.

Fate finally closed the entrance doors, perhaps equally surprised to find that no one had closed them. "We who? I didn't realize you had left the Capital."

Firmus shrugged slightly. "I'm not really one for festivities. I leave that to my siblings, thought it might be nice to come back to a clean palace given that everyone has....." He trailed mid-comment, seemingly aware of the misstep, and swiftly turned to take the luggage upstairs.

Fate glanced around and the disarray and chuckled. "So, I'm guessing you worked on the upstairs."

Firmus bowed. "It is a large space, and I am royalty, after all. You think Lady might spare some latitude."

Fate laughed aloud. "I have missed you."

Hero caught sight of a shadow moving on the second floor, looked up, and watched for whatever had caught his attention, but saw nothing more.

Instead, the doors of the throne room flew open, which seemed much to Firmus's relief.

Nigel perked up as he noticed everyone gathered in the entrance hall. "Oh! Back so soon? It's a good thing we got a head start. Sorry, we haven't prepared the entryway but it should be tidy before nightfall." He moved out of the doorway, looking back into the room.

The others waited for whoever kept his attention.

A tanned woman stepped out, her head covered by a scarf laced by golden coins. The sheer and flowing material of her attire seemed unsuited for Nex. "I always know when Hero has returned. It gets dreadfully cold."

Fate bent forward, her voice almost a whisper. "Fortuna?"

Fortuna shushed her pupil. "For your own safety, do not utter my name. I shouldn't be here. In fact, this will be the last I see you for—"

Fate rushed to the madam and embraced her. "I'm so glad you're well. I was so worried that something had happened to you."

Despite the warnings, Fortuna returned the affections with tears and a brittle voice. "I'm sorry. I failed you and your sisters. If only I...."

Fate shook her head and burrowed deep into her madam's bosom. "No, it's not your fault. I know you wouldn't leave unless you had to." She withdrew and took Fortuna by the arms. "What happened that day?"

Fortuna explained to the best of her ability. "There were rumors, the kind that could change all that we know and believe—the kind I had to see for myself."

Fate squeezed Fortuna's hands. "What are you talking about?"

Fortuna looked at Hero.

He lifted his head, surprised that she acknowledged him, though he found it preferable to remain unseen.

Her sorrowful expression faded into one of terror. "There's another Ghoul in Mu."

Fate glanced between them. "Another? Ghoul?"

Hero clenched his jaw. Mention of Ghouls brought back unpleasant memories of his late friends Luna and Syo. "You're certain?"

"I wouldn't be here if I wasn't."

He crossed his arms. "A Gishian?"

"She appeared as any normal Rahma girl, but everything about her felt off. Her very being struck me as unusual—stale even. She lacked a life force of any kind. There were only remnants of the person she used to be. I cannot say what drives those creatures but it is nothing natural, for certain. The moment I realized what she was, I fled. I couldn't risk the Rebellion's success on a gamble."

Fate inhaled through her nose as she mulled over the information. "Ghouls, like the legends, or more like a blood curse?"

Hero eyed Fate, wondering how far her awareness actually reached, and said, "One and the same. Legendary though they may be... we've been able to successfully track a few. This isn't my first encounter with a Ghoul."

Fate's focus trailed to some distant place. "The Elysium Royals. The family with the blood curse, no? That's what you were referring to when you mentioned the Gishian."

Hero squinted, taken aback by her forwardness on such a sensitive topic—another sign that he gazed upon Fati, and not the emotionally sensitive Fate. He wavered, taking in all the information he gathered through her actions. It just reminded him of how long they had been apart, and raised his curiosity about what had happened during their separation to cause such changes.

"That's correct," he said.

Nigel put his arm around Fortuna. "After the attack, we returned to Tir Na Nog. We were too late to be of any help here, and every moment brought us closer to discovery. I thought it best to disappear."

Hero pressed his fingers against his aching jaw. "You thought correctly."

Nigel lamented, "We recovered the documents and some equipment, but the girls...."

Fortuna patted his hand and spoke to Fate again, her voice cracking slightly. "I intend to disappear again, this time for much longer. There is nothing for me to protect here anymore, but I wanted to speak with you again before I left. Don't listen to anything you hear about me. Be strong, stronger than you have ever been. I'll leave you with everything the Rebellion knows about the battle for Mu, and what little information we've gathered about the Ghouls, and I hope you put it to good use. It's my belief that someone is raising them, but I can only imagine how."

Hero accepted the satchel containing the data. "Like necromancy?"

Fortuna replied, her voice tense. "What's that?"

He placed a hand against his throat. "Nothing any of us want or should handle alone."

"I see."

Fate gasped. "Do you think Mortis...?"

Hero moved only his eyes to look at her. It certainly had occurred to him before, but the matters of *who* turned Mortis and Lara into Ghouls still troubled him, and more so how they managed to acquire such a rare and horrific skill. Such a thing defied the entirety of the Ancient's philosophical views. He wondered if the perpetrator intended it as such, to erase or defile the basis of their existence — the Grandmaster's scriptures.

Rather than mention the correlation between Sally's appearance and the murders at the brothel, Hero avoided the more indelicate part of the conversation and kept things smooth and shallow on the surface. "Thank you for the information. We'll use it wisely."

Fortuna thickly replied, "I trust you will."

He used a soft smile to ease her nerves as he slung the satchel over his shoulder. "It seems like a shame for you to leave so soon. Why don't you join us for dinner and a few drinks?"

"Coy. I suppose there is no harm in staying a little longer." Her attention once again returned to Fate, letting on that she found it difficult to part from her.

"Very good." Hero noted the fact and wandered off to the kitchen to fix a meal. When he entered, he found an old man inside.

He looked the man up and down. By all rights, he appeared to be Rahma, but his aura suggested otherwise. Hero twisted his head, unfamiliar with why a sloppy-looking Ancient stood at the kitchen counter instead of his usual chef.

"Who the devil are you?" he demanded.

The man stopped chopping his vegetables and grunted, "Who do you think, boy? I'm the cook!"

Hero jerked his head back, alarmed by the man's tone.

Firmus finally returned from his tidying and stepped up to Hero's side to explain. "My apologies. I should have asked before inviting him. His name is Weimar and despite his chosen attire, he's the finest chef in Mu."

Hero made a quizzical expression before relenting. "Is he now? There is something familiar about you."

The old man scoffed as he continued cutting.

Hero knew well that the Igni viewed food as the last great conquest and held their chefs to the highest standards. "Uh, welcome to Nitor, Weimar."

Weimar pushed a tray of wine glasses and a bottle into Hero's hands. "Be on your way. Dinner will be served shortly."

Firmus took the bottle with a chuckle. "Isn't it nice to be cared for?"

Hero hesitated to leave the stranger in his kitchen, especially since he distrusted anyone with his food, and Fate's prior poisoning only intensified his feelings.

Firmus led him back to the entrance hall and steered everyone towards the dining hall. He returned to the kitchen after he completed his task.

After some hesitation, Fortuna sat down.

Dinner passed like any other gathering. They filled it with light and enjoyable conversation, each of them avoiding the unpleasant truths of the last turn.

Fortuna barely touched her meal but maintained a bright, well-rehearsed expression, although her gaze wandered the room as though searching for something.

Hero remembered the shadow he'd spied upstairs when they arrived. Something about the intruder perturbed him, so he rose from the table, using his usual smile to calm the edgy Fortuna once more. "Pardon me. I'm going to wash up and put this information someplace safe. Help yourselves, please."

Fate appeared unusually grave as she observed him, but she remained with the madam and their guests.

He hurried to the stairs with composure. Ever since he'd returned, Fate's aura seemed to have grown. He sensed that she noticed something amiss with him as well, and this made him uneasy. It took most of his focus just to keep her from seeing through him.

Mindful of the necessity of his masquerade, he hid his feelings and continued to the Right Wing of the palace, where he sensed the invasive aura. Whatever lurked in the shadows concerned him more than his wife at the moment. A tiny voice at the back of his mind warned that something had been watching him for some time.

Nothing appeared out of place. Each door remained fastened shut and faint light washed over the hall from the sconces that Firmus had left on.

Hero strode through the hall, touching each door to feel the energy in the rooms. As before, he felt nothing. Once he concluded his search, he spun on his heel to put away the satchel and return downstairs. The moment he turned, the hairs on the back of his neck stood on end. He stopped and listened for movement behind him—only the sound of static filled his ears.

There's no aura.

He spun again to look. Nothing. The static thickened but he neither saw nor felt anything aside from discomfort. One of the doors to his right rested ajar—the storage room. He touched the handle, once again trying to sense an aura.

As he stepped into the room, the static stopped. He uncovered each antique in the room—a worn piano, a wood dresser, flowery hatboxes, and an ornate oval mirror. While he contemplated, he stared at his reflection in the mirror, which appeared oddly distorted. His gaze trailed down the reflection to a small object now sitting on the floor behind him. He looked over his shoulder and crossed the room to get a better look. The moment he saw the object up close, he stiffened.

At his feet lay a small silver horse figurine.

He knelt and picked it up with a slight shudder. The object left him feeling vulnerable, as though the person who'd left it meant to expose him and say that they knew everything. He clenched his hand around the horse, gritting his teeth. Blood rushed to his face as he quietly tucked it into the cuff of his sleeve and exited the storage room.

2
TOPSY TURVY

Hero sat in his secret study, chewing the skin off his lip and mulling over the silver horse. Dwelling on it tied his stomach in knots.

Fate came down from the second floor carrying a book under her arm. She slammed it down on the desk hard enough to jolt him from his thoughts. "What could be so important that you left before dinner?"

He scrunched his brow. "A great many things are more important than dinner. Where should I begin?"

Compared to her past, malleable self, she acted inflexible. "Fine, I'll clarify. What could be so important that you left in the middle of dinner with my mother before I may never see her again?"

He exhaled and, feeling the heat rise to his face again, began to rap his fingers against the desktop. "It's none of your concern."

She huffed with an irritated laugh. "Is that a fact?"

He finally stopped his internal tantrum and placed his hand over hers. "I didn't mean it that way. It's complicated."

Her eyes shifted from his hand to his face.

He waited to see if she accepted this as an apology. If only he'd been able to seduce her, he'd possess a greater influence over her mood. The thought just added to his irritation.

Fate withdrew her hand and folded her arms, her expression stern. "Are Ghouls real? I thought that they were proven to be a myth based on the Gishian Blood Curse."

He exhaled again but with a quivering sound. Nothing had been going his way. As he answered her, he pressed on the bridge of his nose. "If Ghouls aren't real, how would you explain Mortis?"

"You think so too?"

He puzzled over what she meant to achieve by probing in such a way. Ever since she'd studied in the Capital, or since his departure, he found her difficult to read. He'd always relied on her transparency and now found it impossible. Memories of Nuvem Fati rose back into his thoughts, stirring a deep discomfort, but the woman that stood before him seemed to differ further still. He feared the possible answer, yet found it impossible to press her to discover the truth—fear prevented it.

The look on Fate's face reflected revelation.

What is she thinking about? Damn it.

He rapped his fingers on the desk again.

This time, she noticed and smiled. "Be at ease. Everything I do is for you."

The comment made his heart race. He questioned the implication of this and whether or not she knew something, or if she'd said it to elicit some kind of response, as she seemed to occasionally feign ignorance to gain information.

She sat on the edge of the table, caressed his head, and kissed his forehead.

The cloudiness in his mind washed away, as did all his concerns. When she released him, he pressed a hand to his forehead.

"I've thought of a way to cleanse the Plague. It should strike you as familiar."

His mind raced and all his thoughts scattered. For a moment, nothing made sense. "Huh?"

"I intend to return to Inoue Capital to aid Chi in cultivating the Ussan. I'm holding a conference to win approval for our project."

His voice strained, "Cultivate?" He blinked rapidly in succession, chasing away images of shattering crystal trees and millions of shards that sprayed through the air. "You mean to say that you're going to expand it?"

Her smile faded and one of tunneled focus took its place. "Yes."

His thoughts went blank.

She continued. "I want to restore the Empire."

His heart climbed into his throat, threatening to return what little of his meal he'd managed. His hands sweated. He wanted to ask, *which empire,* unsure if she meant Mu or the Crystal Empire itself.

"It'll keep you safe," she said, leaning hard on one arm and swinging a foot back and forth.

Hero gripped the arms of his chair and braced himself. "Are you awake?" They locked eyes, caught in a moment of silence and deliberation until a smile livened her face.

She poked the end of his nose. "How silly."

Their conversation left him in a state of bewilderment.

Fate hopped down from the table and straightened her dress. "Before I begin this project, I'd like to try Spirit Walking through your dreams. It's time for us to uncover the truth about the crimes in Mu, and I think that you have the answers." She examined him warily. Without uttering a word, she relayed her skepticism and left the room.

Hero sat alone for a time, though he lost track of how long. The world seemed so quiet that it almost felt as though time had stopped entirely. His thoughts, which always raced, were now silent, and not in a way he liked. He balled up on his chair. His stress stirred up the miasma coiling around inside him, and the stain reacted to his distress by fueling it.

She'd bested him. He fancied himself a strategist and skilled deceiver, but Fate played on an entirely different level.

How long can I keep up this façade?

Given that Hero lacked the Spirit Walking ability, he knew not how to filter his Dreamscape other than to somehow place an illusion over himself. Unfortunately, the seals made this impossible. If Fate saw anything that she deemed untrustworthy, he might lose her favor forever, a thing that must never happen under any circumstances.

As long as she continues to believe I don't know anything, it's okay.

3
Six Doors

Hero knocked on Fate's door to respond to the summoning she'd sent earlier that morning. Even after their marriage, she kept some distance. Not that he expected her to change after they had spent so much time apart... nor did he see their relationship as romantic, though it did mar his ego slightly.

Fate opened her door and ushered him inside, closing it behind him. "Thank you for coming."

"Sure." He glanced at a set of lilac-colored candles set up on her bed stand. *Daelia Quimora?*

Instantly, he knew what she meant to do, but found her knowledge of the plant peculiar.

Who taught her so much about Undal? Akira? No, she most certainly had awakened to Fati's knowledge.

Chills washed over him and he cleared his throat.

She said, "I'll be leaving for the Capital before we know it to comply with my duties. While there's still time, I'd like to peek into your Dreamscape."

He remained calm despite his inner panic. "Certainly." All of these references to Undal evoked memories of Ussan's fall. He pressed a hand over one of his eyes and frowned.

Fate carried on as though she didn't notice any of his tells, when, in fact, he knew her eyes missed nothing, that her skill surpassed his own.

She continued. "My goal is to break the Council's seals

without any repercussion. That is, if it's even true that you would normally die. I hope you'll trust in me."

He caught himself reminiscing and broke away from those thoughts. "At times like this, I must rely on you."

She smirked as she went to light the candles. "I wouldn't hurt you, not without good reason."

Smoke wafted from the wicks and filled the room with the aroma of flowers. It reminded Hero of the trees from which they blossomed. He braced himself for the upcoming side effects.

Fate simply observed, as if waiting for something, but he knew better than to let her perceive his thoughts. "Are you familiar with the flower Daelia Quimora?"

"Only from texts." He blinked hard and rubbed his head, overcome by a sudden haziness.

"Then you know what it's used for."

Hero rubbed his forehead vigorously. He now found it somewhat difficult to breathe. "It would depend on who's using it, no?"

She cracked a faint smile. "Indeed."

"Sorry. Um, I need to sit." He staggered to the bed as the room spun around him, and he grew clammy. As his gaze traveled the room, everything appeared to stretch.

Fate sat down on her knees before him and rested her hands against his legs. "Relax. It's just the effect of the candles."

He took shallow breaths. The fogginess heightened his anxiety, and he feared that if he lost clarity, he might also lose his ability to mask his thoughts.

She gently lay him down and pressed her finger to her lips. *"Shh. Remus, Leoht Miina."*

'Shh. Sleep, Leoht Miina.'

Hero opened his eyes, his surroundings spinning around him in his woozy spell. As the spinning slowed, he adjusted to his Dreamscape and the entranced feeling that came over him. He lay with the cold, white floor pressed to his cheek. Everything in this space shared the same smooth, white appearance, except for six colored doors that lined the glaring hall.

He staggered to his feet and found Fate waiting ahead of him. It seemed that she presented a more modest demeanor before his travels. Now, she behaved stoically and unconcerned with his physical condition, which made him both uncomfortable and slightly annoyed. However, he relied on her to break the Council's seals.

He wondered if the Council themselves knew this and hoped to use him as a way to determine whether the Spinner had awakened.

All the more reason to feign innocence.

He journeyed deeper into the hall, checking the doors. Each colored door donned a silver plaque of some kind. The green one held a plaque of two intertwined snakes, the blue one a violin, the red one a rose, the black one a raven, the white one a book, and finally, the purple one brandished a pocket watch.

Fate stepped forward and extended her hand. "At least one of these doors must be able to open. If we open all of them, we'll be able to reach the third seal."

"Are you sure?" He reached out and grasped her hand, following carefully.

"Don't worry. If you stick with me you'll be fine." She tried each of the doors; all except the green door had been fastened shut.

He understood the meaning of the symbol on the green door the moment he saw it—a crest with two intertwined snakes. This crest represented the notorious Gishian Family, that of his two late friends, Luna and Syo. He stared at a past he wanted to forget.

His fingers ran over the metal symbol with the faintest touch. As he touched it, an image of the burning Gishian Estate blazed before him. He clenched his eyes shut to fight against the stabbing pain that now struck the side of his head.

Another migraine.

Fate squeezed his hand. "Ready? I'm going to open it. Once we enter, you'll lose sight of me, but I'll be with you even if you don't see me. If you get lost, I promise I'll find you."

"I trust you," he said, and meant it.

The door opened and a flood of light escaped from the room beyond.

The competition known as the Astor Tournament commenced the same as all Royal occasions, with a meeting of the King's Committee. The High King summoned the rulers of Mu and their successors to the Capital's Conference Room to discuss his new plan to find a successor.

The King of Nitor had left Nex before sunrise without his son, so Hero traveled to the Capital with Isis, the Queen of Askadel, in a carriage. She sat across from him, tucking the excess fabric from her gown under her legs and brushing the loose strands of fair hair back from the window's breeze.

Hero had already grown used to his father's antics. Their status as Royals was their only bond. At thirteen turns, Hero was barely old enough to participate in the Astor Tournament, and his father felt that having him participate was the best way to stick beside the High King, Khnum, to keep his favor. As it was, Khnum already had his eye on a new power pair, the Gishian Twins, children of the treacherous, yet powerful, Queen of Elysium—Gishian Una.

In any case, everyone called her treacherous, but such things mattered not to the High King, whose focus had always been power.

Hero rarely paid attention to the affairs of the Royals, not caring about them or about succeeding the throne. He only respected Isis because of her unique perspective on Royalty, in spite of her being a Council follower.

She adhered to the original scriptures of her faith rather than embellishing, as the rest of her faction did.

Furthermore, instead of chastising him like his father, she simply questioned his state of mind that morning, when he expressed more consideration towards the citrus fruit in his grip than to the conference.

"You're making a funny face," she said, holding back a laugh.

"Isn't it bothersome that citrus is so acidic? If I eat this now, my fingertips will become stained with its scent for the rest of the day. Everyone in Mu will know I've eaten it, but somehow I can't resist the temptation of fresh fruit."

She laughed aloud this time. "There's never a boring day with you. I can always count on some unique insight that you alone seem to ponder."

"If these mundane conversations are enough to entertain you, I fear for what the rest of your day must be like."

Whenever Isis spent time with him, she seemed blissful. She was one of the few people that he could tolerate, and because of this exceptional tolerance he found in her, he obeyed.

He admired her as she watched the passing trees with refined posture and an amiable smile. Her grace seemed effortless, though she swore she took great pains to be regal.

She mused at his comment. "Your fears are in the right place."

He sank down onto his seat until he could press the soles of his shoes flat against the opposing seat. "How dreadful. People make royalty sound so extraordinary but, in reality, there's nothing great about it. Why not give the power to the people?"

Isis failed to conceal a chuckle.

"What's funny?"

"You know what the Elders would say? Your ways are very Caeles."

"Isn't that prejudiced?" He finally gave in to temptation and peeled the skin from the red fruit.

"Think of it this way: it's not an insult but an observation. If something is true, it doesn't have to be an insult, just a fact."

He nodded in acceptance and took a slice from the center of the fruit while examining it. "Nature asks for nothing but sunlight and nourishment. Yet, it bears fruit. Not only is it an exquisite design but a selfless one."

She rested her hand softly against her cheek as though in thought. "You seem to like nature in general."

"As long as it isn't trying to eat or maim me. Then again, nature was here first, so maybe we're the ones being intrusive."

"Interesting." She sighed lightly. "Now we really must get back to business, my dear Prince. I've heard that the High King is bargaining between you and the Gishian Twins. He's holding this tournament as a formality, but he already knows what he wants." Isis leaned forward, hanging her hands delicately over her knees as she prodded at Hero with a pleasant smile.

"But I didn't do anything."

"That's not true. You're brilliant and everyone knows it. Your father is only Rahma, so he puts your abilities to waste. This is a good opportunity for you to escape his grasp. What do you say?"

Hero shrugged again. "I guess. You know I don't care about this stuff. People can bicker as much as they want about the state of the Empire, but it's not going to change anything."

"Not everyone feels that way. If you don't care whose side you're on, why not join the Council's cause? I know you joined the Rebellion a long time ago, but you can learn more about us. I'm sure you are wise enough to see the reason in what I say."

"Yeah, I joined because of Kyou," he said, and averted his gaze.

"Don't be so naive," Isis warned. "Anyone can be nice when they want something. Besides, I'm not a fool. If it was that easy to win your favor, then I'd have you on the Council's side in a heartbeat."

"You have a point, but Kyou asked first. If I switched sides now, it would feel like I was betraying my father."

"But if you continue your allegiance with the Rebellion knowing that I support the Council, doesn't it feel like you're betraying your mother?"

Hero stopped as he was about to put a slice of fruit in his mouth, and stared at her for a long time as he considered the statement. It certainly put him in an awkward predicament. "I read somewhere that marital spats are unhealthy for children. They should be handled by adults with discretion."

"Marital? A Rahma term?"

"Ancients use it too."

"What kind of books are you reading? You always try to slip out of disputes with bizarre facts, you imp. Kyou and I aren't married, nor are we Bound, and for what it's worth, I'm not your mother and he's not your father."

This commentary troubled him even more. "Then, what are you?"

She smiled with gentle charm. "I'm not sure you're ready for me to answer that question. What am I to *you*?"

He lowered the fruit from his mouth and his mind drifted to some distant place. Sometimes this happened to him. He experienced this odd sensation, as if the world was pulling away from him and his soul was trying to recall something deeply buried.

Isis leaned forward again, tilting her head to one side. "Well?"

He scrunched his nose. "This riddle is beyond my current understanding."

She sighed. "It was worth a try."

"The Rebellion has Abyssus. I don't really care about politics, but his brain is really interesting... the kind I'd want to dissect. Though, if I did that, I'd lose something valuable."

She ran her hands through her hair. For the first time since the trip began, she seemed agitated. "Valuable? You like him that much? I'm surprised. I knew you two had been talking for some time, but I never realized how close you were."

"He's a lovable genius with the right amount of darkness."

"Darkness?" Isis's tone fell flat, appearing stoic as the delight faded from her expression.

The carriage pulled through the gates of Inoue Community, and they stepped down into the Centre.

As they took in the scent of the ocean air, Hero evaded Isis's disapproval and ran off towards Chi open-armed. "*Ch'ai!*"

'*Aunt Chi!*'

Chi embraced him tightly with a slight shake. "My little ball of sunshine and mischief! I am so glad to see you are well! Lady Isis, welcome back."

Isis bowed her head politely. "Good day."

"Thank you for bringing my troublesome nephew. I do not understand what that man meant by leaving Hero behind."

"Just trying to keep his head, I suppose. The Prince is good company. We do fine."

Hero mumbled. "*Better than the old man....*"

"Hey now...." Chi patted his side. "Be good! You need to be polite during the meeting, understand? The High Queen will be there as well. Be respectful."

He wriggled out from under her arm. "Quit nagging me."

Chi huffed, blowing a strand of white hair from her face.

Isis brushed the hair back from Hero's forehead. "Don't worry. I'll be there as well. He'll have to be on his best behavior."

"All right then," Chi relented. "Get going before you are late, and do not cause Isis any trouble." She gave a parting nod as Isis strode calmly towards the palace.

Hero followed, glancing at the Royals and successors who walked up the slope for the meeting. On the stairway, he met eyes with a dark-haired boy. He turned his head and stared back at Hero with bright green eyes. The boy's slit pupils retracted and then dilated with curiosity. Next to him, a smaller girl with the same snake-like characteristics peeked at Hero with the corners of her mouth turned up, making her appear even more snake-like. As they all locked gazes, he made mental notes—*the Gishian Twins*.

Their mother carried a black parasol and wore long dark clothing to protect her body from the sunlight. This fact made it hard to identify her, if not for her children following along like ducklings, and the rumored air of obscurity their family carried.

Hero recollected formally meeting one of the twins, Luna, at one of his birthday celebrations. She had suggested they marry for their own benefits, but judging by Syo's glare, her brother didn't approve of this idea. Not that it mattered; Hero had already rejected her proposal.

Some time remained before the meeting, so Isis patted Hero's arm and led him upstairs to the viewing balcony above the Palace courtyard. They regarded the glowing crystal trees of the Ussan, which shimmered in the sunlight across the channel.

Isis leaned her elbows against the white balcony railing as the breeze brushed against her hair. "As you well know, I'm the Queen of Askadel. There will soon come a time when I must return home to perform my duties."

Hero crossed an arm over his chest to loosely hold the arm opposite. He knew of this, as she often traveled back and forth between her kingdom and Nex.

"I also lost my parents when I was very young, and I've been responsible for protecting our kingdom and my siblings." She readjusted her posture to face him.

The way the wind caused her blonde hair to sway reminded him of a flower in a field. Her words held little weight, but she fascinated him nonetheless.

He cocked his head to one side, observing her. "And?"

"Your mother was a good friend of mine, so I might not be your parent, but I do feel a sense of responsibility to protect you." She approached and took his face into her hands with her usual gentleness. "Even if I'm away, I'll continue to protect you, so if you are in peril, just send for me."

Hero wondered if Isis's bond with his mother could be so important that she felt the need to dote after him. Surprisingly, he didn't hate it. She had always been there when he needed her and taught him a great many things. Plus, no matter how many times he tested her loyalty, she always proved herself.

He shifted his eyes in thought. "Isis, why did you move to Nex?"

Her smile waned momentarily, but shortly returned softer than before. "The High King asked me to monitor your father's behavior and decide if he is fit to rule. When I saw the way he treated you, I knew I couldn't leave you alone with him."

Hero felt strange about this but couldn't quite put his thoughts into words. It wasn't an unpleasant feeling. On the contrary, he may have been embarrassed.

Isis pulled her hands back. "Now, it's time to attend the conference. Come along, Hero."

"Right."

The King's Committee gathered in the Conference Room, greeting the High Queen at the door as they entered.

Queen Heqet always struck Hero as one with a traditionally regal appearance and demeanor. Her flowing clothes and willowy body made her seem softer than he thought possible, and she tended to whisper more than speak.

As Hero entered with Isis, Queen Heqet stopped and threw up her hands. "My sweet pupil! I'm so happy you've come. It gave me fits when I saw Niteo arrive without you!"

Abyssus leaned back on his chair, his expression lightening. "Oh, Hero's here!"

Hero wanted to go and greet him, but the High Queen had always been gracious, so he replied to her first. "I'll always come when there's a summoning. I can't let his irresponsible behavior influence me."

Isis beamed at his response.

The High Queen glanced at her husband and replied, dispirited. "I completely agree."

Hero bowed his head. "I'm sorry to be rude, but I'd like to step away and greet Abyssus."

"Of course! Don't let me get in the way."

Hero slunk past her and slipped onto the chair next to Abyssus, who flashed his usual dimpled grin and nudged Hero with his elbow. "Hey, friend."

Hero spotted a straw the same color as Abyssus' black sweater sticking out from his friend's sleeve, something well-concealed despite the notation. Hero lowered his voice to a whisper, "You shouldn't sneak food into the King's Conference."

Abyssus whispered back and winked. "It's not food. It's a drink. Besides, no one else has noticed."

Hero turned around on his seat and shone Firmus a nervous smile. "Hi...."

Firmus's golden eyes blazed behind his uncomfortably stoic expression. "Hello, Hero."

Hero still didn't know how to handle Firmus's intense gaze. He always got a little shaken up when their eyes met. In his attempt to avoid Firmus, he sat forward and looked directly at Gishian Syo.

This is worse. I should quickly look away before he strikes up a conversation.

The moment Hero switched his attention back to Abyssus, Syo narrowed his eyes and spat. "How rude. Our eyes met and you didn't think to greet me? Some future king."

"Ah...." Hero dreaded conversing. The blood drained from his face. "Me?"

"Who else?"

Abyssus chuckled.

Syo snarled. "What's so funny?"

Abyssus's face soured. "Hmm? I think my friend is cute. Does that somehow bother you?"

Syo snapped back. "Why are you even here? Are you even participating in the tournament?"

Abyssus checked to see if Niteo was nearby before answering. "I'm here to see Hero. These days, I swear I have to send a formal summoning just to get inside the palace."

Syo folded his hands, and his gaze softened as he glanced back at Hero. "You should be careful. I don't think the Prince of Macellarius is as innocent as he seems. He might be tricking you so he can steal the throne from you later. Those with brains have their own form of brawn."

Why is he suddenly warning me? Wasn't he just angry?

Luna seemed to sense Hero's confusion because she giggled and said, "Syo is more sensitive than he seems. Since you look naïve, he's just looking out for you."

"But I'm your opponent," Hero said, tilting his head.

"It's because you don't seem driven to participate."

She's right.

Abyssus gnawed on his straw. "Seems to me like you two might be the ones scheming. Mess with Hero and I'll show you just how strong I can be."

Luna mocked. "Ooh, so intimidating. You are simply eatable."

Una turned her head and lifted her lace veil with one finger. "Luna, Syo, don't play with your food. There will be plenty of time to do that later."

Food?

Niteo, who had been speaking with the High King, prepared to return to his seat, and jumped back as he saw Hero. "Praise be, when did you get here?"

"He's been here for a while now," Abyssus said. "Didn't you see Isis?"

Isis lifted her head as she heard her name. "Did someone call me?"

"Just explaining to Uncle that Hero came here a while ago with you."

Isis sat down at Hero's opposite side. "Yes, surely you noticed your son? Then again you did leave him at the palace."

Niteo straightened his neckpiece. "It's an easy mistake to make."

Syo made a throaty noise. "You forgot your own son?"

Una lifted her veil again and smirked. "My, my—and they call me cruel." She patted her daughter on the shoulder and released a haughty laugh. "Children, let this man be a reminder of the parent I *could* be."

Niteo's face burned with humiliation. Even though everyone except Hero commented, Niteo directed this rage at his son. Crimson in the face and trembling with fury, he sat down next to Abyssus.

Why do I always have to get the heat for everyone else? Just be quiet.

The rest of the committee took their seats, including the High King and Queen at the farthest end of the table. Khnum glanced around to see who had arrived.

Other than Isis, there was also the King of Nysa, Askelon, and the King of Rosetau, Lux Celo with his son, Baalis, and Firmus who represented Tir Na Nog. Another woman sat square across the table from Khnum, but a veil covered her face just like Una. Since all the other Royals were there, Hero deduced she was the Queen of Tir Na Nog.

Isis had also invited contenders from Askadel and Thule, but Hero neither recognized them nor cared to associate with anyone new. He did his best to ignore the unfamiliar faces of other royal children, certain that this would aid him in the tournament.

The High King began his announcement. "We have gathered here today to discuss the expectations of the Astor Tournament. I must choose a worthy successor for Inoue's throne, so I will be watching carefully to see who is deserving of this role. I do not wish to make any more mistakes. Listen carefully. The Tournament will begin outside Tir Na Nog. Contestants, your goal is to pave your way back to the Capital unscathed. I shall provide each of you with a sheet to collect stamps from every kingdom in Mu. How you do this is entirely up to you. Whoever remains will fight in the Capital Arena, and the winner shall earn the title of my successor. We begin in seven suns." Khnum shared a glance with each of the rulers. "Kings and Queens of Thule and Mu, you must return to your thrones during the tournament. Give your children guidance on their journey to become the future rulers of Mu. Each successor and their Bound may participate. Do you have questions?"

The room remained silent.

The High King is pitting me against the Gishian Twins. He already knows I don't have a mate. What is he trying to accomplish?

Cruentus Neco hadn't appeared on that day, though it still seemed probable that he'd force Abyssus to attend the tournament.

The High King dismissed himself from the meeting, which left the remaining members of the committee to discuss the tournament's details.

He could've sent a messenger to explain this. It's a setup. He wants us to strike a conflict before the tournament.

Abyssus nudged Hero with his head. "It's finally quiet. Do you think I'll be able to get into Nitor Palace anytime soon? I feel like I'm going crazy with boredom when you're not around to tease."

"Don't lie. You just don't want to be at home."

"True, but you're also fun to tease." Abyssus laughed while tousling Hero's hair, a well-known peeve.

"I'd tell you to come to the tournament, but I'm worried."

"Want me to go? I'll go for you. You'll get lonely without me, yeah?" He pulled out a piece of candy from his pocket and sucked on it before linking his arm around Hero's.

As he did this, Hero felt Firmus's eyes burning a hole into the back of his head, and grimaced. "Don't cling. Firmus is going to murder me in my sleep."

Firmus stood behind Abyssus's seat, resting his hands on the top rail of the chair. "I won't."

Hero attempted to smile. "That's relieving."

Abyssus took them both by an arm. "We're going to need supplies for the tournament. Let's stock up while we're here."

As Hero opened his mouth to respond, Niteo interrupted. "Hero, you must return to the palace and prepare for the tournament. If you spend any more time outside, you could risk spreading your miasma."

A silence fell over the Conference Room.

Hero glanced around at the other Royals, their cold and defensive stares piercing him. He lowered his head, feeling the full impact of Niteo's revenge for his earlier embarrassment. "Right."

At one side, the Gishian Twins looked at him with pity in their eyes, most likely from experiencing their own level of disdain from the others. Even so, they also avoided the Plague of the Stained Prince.

Abyssus blocked Hero with his arms. "Aren't you being too much?"

Isis drew Hero closer and raised his left hand in her own, exposing the black chord bracelets on his wrist. "Fear not. As a Council member, it is my duty to monitor his condition. I can assure you, he will not infect anyone during his short visit. So, as Abyssus has expressed in his own youthful way, isolating him is 'a bit much.'"

The other Royals and their successors murmured with an air of humor and the tension eased.

Isis managed to turn Niteo's blatant attempt to control his son back on him, leaving the Rahma King with a bright red neck and ears.

Hero wanted to stop his embarrassment and hurt but it dug deep. He rose from his chair and exited the room, each step quicker than the last. The room stirred more upon his exit, but as he reached the stairway, he felt a tug on his arm.

Isis followed closely, pulling him into the study at the top of the stairs. She had always been gracious to him, and now she gave a warm embrace. "I'm sorry. My intention was not to embarrass you further. I just can't tolerate the way he speaks to you."

Hero pried her arm away and backed up against the door.

She watched, dumbfounded, with her arms still open. "Hero...."

Hero rarely cried, so it surprised him that his eyes filled with tears. The Royals and their cold stares had already upset him, but Isis's announcement stung more. His face sweltered from the betrayal. "I feel extremely foolish to think I could trust you."

Isis blinked hard, as though struggling to process his words. "That's not...."

"You're just a Council delegate." He kept his gaze fixed to the floor and calmed his stance. "And I'm just the Stained Prince you're duty-bound to observe. You are more concerned about containing him."

Isis shook her head. "No, I was just...." Her facial expression rushed with realization. "The miasma. Hero, you're ill."

The door of the study opened and Kyou entered. He glanced between Hero and Isis with surprise. "Hero? What's wrong?"

Instead of answering, Hero left the room and ran down the staircase. He would return home alone, where he belonged.

I should have known. The foolish one is me.

4
THE PLAGUE WE SPREAD

Hero remained in Nitor Palace and tried to focus on his training during the days that led up to the Astor Tournament. On several occasions, he received a visit from Isis, but he locked himself in his room and ignored her attempts to seek forgiveness.

When he sat in front of his door, watching the handle rattle with desperation, he knew that he was being petty. There was no sense in torturing her for doing her job. Yet, when he thought of it that way, it upset him all over again, and he enjoyed watching her struggle.

He realized that this was likely because of his miasma poisoning. He just didn't care.

On the day of the Astor Tournament, he collected his supplies in a pack and boarded a carriage with Abyssus and Firmus for the checkpoint in Tir Na Nog. Once they arrived, they would need to trek across the desert sands in the blistering heat, a trip he dreaded. Any Caeles instinctually avoided the heat due to their natural inclination to the cold. He often wondered how the triplets managed their long stints in the winters of Nex.

It would be a dangerous venture for him, but also a necessary one.

Hero speculated why and how Firmus had wound up joining Abyssus in this competition.

As a royal of Tir Na Nog, the Council and the empire must recognize him as a contender but the logic left something lacking.

He decided to delve into the topic. "I'm amazed Firmus was allowed to tag along. I thought he wasn't allowed to leave Macellarius."

"Huh?" Abyssus gawped. "Oh, shit. Hero, you didn't know?"

Firmus whispered an admonishment. "Your language...."

Hero blinked in response, not knowing what they were on about.

"It's not really my business to tell," Abyssus said, glancing up at Firmus.

Firmus scratched his cheek. "I'd appreciate if you don't repeat this outside of here."

Hero nodded.

"My siblings and I were raised as Royals, but our parents banished me to Macellarius due to my condition. They thought it would be safer... for them."

Hero tilted his head, surprised to discover they had more in common than he previously believed. "Condition?"

Abyssus bounced on his seat.

After noticing his excitement, Firmus turned his head towards Abyssus. "Go ahead. I know you want to."

Abyssus blurted. "He's the next Heir of Fenix!"

Hero's eyes widened. "As in the last Emperor of the Ignis Empire?" He studied Firmus with new insight, not that there was much to observe. They had seen each other a million times.

Firmus explained with a sigh. "In our family, it's not uncommon for Fenix to be reborn every other generation. My grandfather, Ignis Velius, was the last heir. He died shortly after his awakening."

Hero frowned. "Was it because of his Bound, or something else?"

Firmus's aura seemed lighter when Hero probed him. He may have wanted to discuss his history in a positive light. "They say that it was due to the potency of his flames. For some time, the heirs have suffered due to something we call *anima sana*."

Abyssus chirped. "You can tell because the flame is blue."

Firmus sighed, allowing Abyssus to continue.

Abyssus pulled a leather journal from his pack, flipped it open, and passed it to Hero, pointing at a passage. "Anima sana is rumored to be a very intense form of *anima*. So, anima concentrate. Whereas anima is present in all living things, anima sana is only present in the ethereal plane, as it's far too potent for the mortal form to withstand."

Hero read over the writing, questioning Abyssus' plethora of knowledge. In order to obtain some of this information, Abyssus would need access to the Library of Records, and that required Capital approval. Since the Capital often needed Council approval as well, this seemed unlikely.

Either Abyssus had received such high recognition that the Council acknowledged his brilliance, or he was hiding something, and the latter seemed the more probable of the two.

"Fascinating," Hero said. "In this case, Firmus is quite powerful. I would very much like to spar sometime."

The corners of Firmus's lips twitched, and he turned his attention to the trees outside the window with a hum of agreement. He could be unusually shy for such an assertive person, but this habit of twitching always revealed his urge to smile.

The carriage rolled to a stop and the footman hopped down from his seat and opened the door.

Hero peered out of the carriage into the dry desert expanding out endlessly before him. Before him, the sun painted a blur of yellows, oranges and reds. A wave of heat washed over him as the air engulfed the now exposed cabin.

Of all the tasks he needed to perform during the tournament, the trek through Tir Na Nog posed the most danger.

Abyssus pulled his pack onto his back before covering his head with a piece of fabric. "I'm not up for a tan."

Hero chuckled but he envied the footman, who climbed back onto his seat and started the coach on its trek back to cooler temperatures.

They began their walk towards Tir Na Nog in the unrelenting heat. The dry clay crackled under their feet and nothing moved for what seemed to be miles. Not even the clouds in the sky appeared able to escape the discomfort.

Firmus kept water on hand to douse Hero whenever the temperature grew too scalding.

Even Abyssus seemed unwell. Although he didn't wilt as quickly as Hero, his gaze fixed to one spot in a struggle to keep steady.

It was Hero's first time noticing his friend's vulnerability to the heat.

Abyssus could no longer hide his moodiness but talked to fill the silence. "Are you still fighting with Isis?"

"We don't fight," Hero said, hoping to avoid the subject.

Firmus reflected on Hero's last encounter with Isis. "She seemed eager to make up. What made you so angry in the first place?"

Hero poured water on the white fabric that protected him from the sun and draped it over his head. "I'm not angry."

Abyssus narrowed his eyes. "What made you so butt-hurt?"

Hero raged. "I am not."

Firmus made a humming noise as he thought. "Is it because she said she's there to monitor your condition?"

Hero scowled. "Why would that upset me?"

Abyssus wore a calculating expression as he scanned Hero, twisting the ends of his dark hair between his fingers. "You seem pretty upset to me. I really wonder why."

Firmus generally kept to himself, but today he exerted his skills of observation. "He trusts her. After all, there are few people he can rely on in Nitor Palace. I know the feeling. When I lived at the family house, I was imprisoned. If you find someone you can trust, they become your ray of light and hope."

Hero didn't know how to describe his feelings but this seemed true.

After their conversation, he deemed Firmus more lighthearted than he appeared.

They traveled the rest of the distance in silence and didn't speak again until finally crossing into one of Tir Na Nog's outer cities. The heat had completely exhausted Hero, but he kept his strength as a Firmus lead them through the dusty, vendor-filled streets towards the palace.

Hero gawked at the multitude of faces both Ancient and Rahma, as well as the never-ending variety of animals and wares.

The clay buildings reflected the desert's colors, bringing more warmth to the boiling desert. Dust and sand clung to everything, making it difficult to breathe.

Firmus walked unhindered, empowered even, by the heat. His stride eased and his pace quickened until he noticed his companions struggled to keep up.

They approached a massive wall lined with guards clad in golden armor.

Hero watched as Firmus struck up a conversation filled with laughter and smiles. It seemed strange to him that Firmus was so friendly with the people that cast him out. Then again, the guards and the Royals were not the same. Perhaps it made sense in a twisted sort of way, and he thought he too should try it.

They passed through the gate and into the innermost part of the kingdom. The palace jutted up into the sky like a golden beacon of life in the ruthless heat of the desert. The street bustled with activity and the small group snaked their way up to the palace steps.

Much to Hero's surprise, foliage flourished on the other side of the palace walls. Long strands of bright red grass cushioned the base of long willowy trees with dainty orange and yellow blossoms. He leaned over a cart to catch a glimpse of a stream before following Firmus into the palace.

By the time they finally arrived in the throne room, the Gishian Twins had finished their business and passed them by at the doorway.

Luna glimpsed Hero as she exited with her head low and her lashless eyes fixed on him.

Hero suffered too much from the heat to falter at her attempt to intimidate him.

Fortuna, now in her role as Queen of Tir Na Nog waited patiently, her skin glowing in the light that radiated around the room. Her airy gown spilled over the throne and draped the floor in swirls of glimmering gold. She stood upon their entry, flashed a loving smile and approached with her arms extended out to her brother.

"I'm surprised to see you away from Nex," Firmus said, accepting his sister's warm embrace.

"Yes, well, the High King insisted that we all return to our posts for the tournament. Have you noticed the other participants? Several have passed through here already."

Chances were that the Gishian Twins would knock them down before he even noticed. They likely already had.

"We haven't seen anyone other than those Gishians," Abyssus said.

Fortuna sighed with a knowing nod. "I see.... They really don't stand a chance. Thulians lack the constitution to survive our extreme elements. It's a pity that lives are being wasted on this tournament. Might as well just put Hero and the Twins in an arena to fight it out, though I do wish you would show more determination to take back your power as a Royal, Firmus."

Firmus turned away from his sister. "If I'm with Abyssus, then I'm already regal enough."

She shook her head and laughed. "So you'd rather be his guard than the Family Master? I'm impressed." She leaned towards Abyssus, smirking as she studied him with her Cat's Eye.

He kept still even when she got right up in his face.

This only amused her more. "*Ma'ail so.* He reminds me of someone."

Hero adjusted his head upright in another attempt to regain stability. The room swayed around him and his shoulder blades throbbed. He virtually gasped as he spoke. "Madam Fortuna, I'm sorry. Can you give us your stamp?"

"I'm Queen right now, aren't I? At least call me Lady."

"Yes. Sorry. You're right."

"Oh!" Abyssus touched Hero's face and waved a bloodstained fingertip. "Your nose is bleeding!"

That was the last thing Hero heard before darkness enveloped him and he hit the floor.

Hero awakened again to find Fortuna leaning over him as he rested, still fully clothed, in a wash bin full of melted ice.

Fortuna held up a bloody cloth. "You've come to. I thought we might've killed you for a moment."

"How long was I unconscious?"

"Just long enough for Abyssus and Firmus to gather supplies. I've provided your team with weaponry and consumables. The true battle isn't about how quickly you arrive at your destination, but how many allies you can make along the way. It's probably best if you steer clear of the Gishian Twins anyway."

"*Ye.*" His skin hurt from heatstroke. "By chance, do you have confections that I can stash in my bag?"

Fortuna showed a quizzical expression. "You like sweets?"

He laid an arm over the side of the tub and sat up, aching all over. "They're for Abyssus... to quell his temper, I mean."

"I can have some made. I'm the Queen, after all."

"Thanks."

She grasped his arm and assisted him out of the wash bin. "Are you all right?"

"I'm alive, so sure."

"If it makes you feel any better, I was ill for at least a month after I started living in Nex. I've grown used to it now, but I still have to be cautious."

Water poured out of his clothing as he stood. Everything stuck to his skin—his hair, his shirt, his pants, his socks—but at least it kept him cool. "It's easier to warm up than cool down. I came prepared and I still couldn't do it."

"It's better that you made it here. If you'd fainted like that in the desert, you would've died. I'll send you back with an official and sufficient supplies. If your health suffers too much, you can rely on my brother. I know he sounds rude, but he's soft on the inside. He can always carry you with that brute strength."

"I'm already humiliated enough as it is." He dried off with a towel and sat on a nearby chair. "I'd change, but it's cooler if I don't."

Fortuna laughed in cruel amusement. "At least we know your nose bleeds before you faint."

He responded with a slow, dry chuckle, and listened to Abyssus's voice echo through the Queen's chambers as he made his way towards them.

Abyssus often spoke from afar, usually before he even made an appearance. His commentary about the spice in the palace food stopped as he poked his head inside and bellowed. "Our little Hero is awake!" He rushed up and squeezed Hero with all his might.

Hero choked out, "Your dramatics are stronger than my lung capacity."

"Oh, sorry." Abyssus released him. "We just met Fortuna's official, so we'll leave when you're ready. Don't push too hard though, okay?" Although Abyssus proclaimed himself to be weak and untrained, it was often his might that damaged Hero the most in times of weakness.

Abysuss smacked Hero's back once as he stepped out, causing a sharp pain up and down his spine.

"That child is a brute," Fortuna said, wincing. "He doesn't look it, but maybe that's what makes him scary."

Hero pursed his lips as he reached back to touch the throbbing spot on his back. "It's often the people you love most that have the greatest advantage over you."

"You speak the truth." She wrapped an arm around him and escorted him into her chambers, where the others waited. Long, sheer fabric hung around a canopy bed across the room.

Abyssus sat off to the right at a table made of stone, eating as Firmus watched him with overt adoration.

A tall woman had joined them at a lounge area under a colorful tile design on the Queen's wall. Her dark skin stood out amongst the sea of faces they had passed in Tir Na Nog.

Hero studied her quietly. To him, her appearance matched that of the notable yet lost clan of the *Si*. If his theory proved accurate, she would be as rare a person as he.

As this woman noticed Hero, she stood and bowed to him. "I'm Myrna. I'll be traveling with you across the desert."

Fortuna nodded in approval. She eyed Hero as though sensing his internal debate. "Though I'm sure it's hard to tell, she's part Callidae. She'll be there to ensure Hero's safety on your way back."

Part? A Half-Breed? A water elemental? How rare. Not as rare as a Si but still a fascinating companion to travel with.

Myrna tossed off the hood of her white cloak, revealing her voluminous dark curls. Her light-colored eyes glowed against her skin, like two golden jewels. "As soon as you're ready, we'll leave, but please take your time. The Prince's health is important for the future of his people."

Impressive.

Her facial features and dark skin differed from the Callidae, who generally had olive skin. Then again, she was only half Callidae, which gave room for his theory. Her attire accentuated her toned body, one honed for battle.

I want to fight her. Too bad I'm sick.

Fortuna smacked the side of his head. "Don't you know it's rude to ogle people?"

"Ow." He would've stricken her back if he were in a better condition.

"Oh, I'm so sorry," Fortuna said. "I was just joking."

"I think it's more accurate to say you don't know your own strength," Firmus said. "He just woke up. Don't knock him out again."

Abyssus trotted over and thrust a collection of fruit into Hero's arms. "Eat! It'll make you feel better."

That's his answer for everything.

Hero suspected that Abyssus' insatiable hunger had something to do with spiritual deficiency. Some people, even without the taint, emitted so much spiritual energy that it caused a rift in the soul. People like this were difficult to distinguish from the Tainted, as they exhibited similar traits of spiritual starvation and mischievousness. In massive outbreaks of the Plague, like the incident in the Ignis Capital of Chien, the infected people turned to outrageous solutions like conquest, rape, slavery, and massacre.

These traits were less common in the individuals who suffered from natural, spiritual deficiency, as they appeared more aware and in control over their behavior.

Abyssus was like this and seemed to prefer gluttony and violence to lust.

Fortuna waved a hand in front of his face. "Hero, are you still with us?"

Abyssus took back a piece of fruit and bit into it. "Don't worry. He does that all the time. He's just thinking."

"About what?"

Hero returned his attention to the group. "It'd take too long to explain. We'd better leave before we fall any further behind."

Abyssus gobbled down his fruit. "We got the stamps, so we can carry on right away."

"Thanks."

Firmus collected Hero's pack and slung it over his shoulder.

Hero cringed. "I've got that."

Firmus shook his head. "You can carry mine when we get to Nex."

"Fair enough."

Fortuna hugged her brother once more. "Take care of them."

He gave a quick nod and led the pair of princes of the palace.

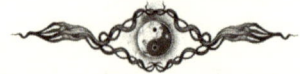

Hero still had a lot on his mind during the trek out of the desert. During those several days, he thought about the Tainted and the reason people feared and isolated his kind.

His gaze traveled over the dry plains as the group ventured into the outskirts of the massive empire. He thought of Chien, the once-great Ignis Capital that stood here before the fall of Undal. Although the Council-approved books claimed that Undal was nothing more than a myth, the faint shapes of ruined buildings could be made out if one knew what to look for. If one needed more proof, shards of melted glass lay scattered throughout the planes.

The books that he'd acquired told another story. One claimed the Caeles King Viro, the first Taitned, had caused the outbreak that ravaged Undal and swallowed Chien. Though it sounded fantastical and, with the unreliability of such old documents, improbable, he knew from his circumstances that the Tainted did, in fact, spread the Plague.

Myrna splashed him with water, jolting him from his thoughts. "Thank you."

She scanned him with her golden eyes. "You were looking a little peaked."

He took the bottle she held out in front of him and drank. His body temperature dropped and some life returned to him.

She pulled the hood off her head and pointed to the mountain range where greenery sprouted from the soil. "It should be easier for you from here out."

Abyssus glanced back over his shoulder with a grin. "You made it. Good job."

People like Abyssus gave Hero hope that there could be something more. Everyone loved Abyssus and got along with him, oblivious to the fact that he also had a natural condition. He had one, but he didn't suffer from it.

Hero envied him slightly. Being Tainted caused a lot of unavoidable pain and anxiety. If he didn't live in complete isolation, he had to live with being a danger to those he cared about. The majority of people in the Empire feared and rejected the Tainted. He just wanted to be around those he liked without the fear of hurting them—even at times when he felt more emotional than expected, like his pettiness towards Isis. It upset him that he couldn't seem to grant her forgiveness.

Abyssus eventually noticed the negativity radiating from Hero's aura and rubbed Hero's back. "Hey, are you okay?"

"How do I become emotionally strong like you?"

"I'm not sure there's a correct way to answer that, but I don't think it's necessary for you to change, either. You're fine the way you are right now. They say that suffering is just a part of existing and each person handles that differently. There's nothing wrong with being a bit soft," Abyssus said with a calm smile.

He had a way of seeming sure about his words. This confidence tended to ease Hero's nerves.

Hero sighed. "Because of the Taint, even small things seem big. A paper cut feels like an amputation. I can't seem to control that feeling of complete chaos and hysteria."

Abyssus stopped smiling, appearing contemplative rather than upset. "That's difficult since it's something that other people can't really understand. You see things that aren't really there though, no? Anyone would be frightened. It's not your fault."

Hero wondered how and why Abyssus managed to understand something that made no sense. Most people just thought Hero was dangerous, insane, or seeking attention. He exhaled, freeing the pent-up anxiety and turmoil before mustering a smile of his own.

Abyssus leaned and rested his head against Hero's, his smile renewed. "It's okay."

For some reason, even though he didn't provide any actual resolution, Hero believed that everything would be okay.

They continued to walk and things got easier, as Abyssus had said it would. They moved faster once they headed into the lush greenery of the mountains.

Hero unrecovered his head and basked in the cool breeze and the shade of the massive trees.

Abyssus ran up a hill filled with bright pink and purple flowers, pointing into the distance. "Hey! There's the border of Nysa!"

Myrna raised a hand towards Hero. "This is where I leave you. Would you like me to stay longer, or perhaps I should douse you once more?"

"I'm fine. Thank you for the help," he said.

"I hope we meet again. For now, I bid you well on your journey." She turned and started back to Tir Na Nog, her clothing catching the wind as she went.

Abyssus watched her and whispered, "She's really quiet."

Hero tilted his head. "More so than Firmus?"

"Firmus is not as quiet as you think."

Firmus pulled them along by their packs. "Come on, you two. We might not be racing, but we're not going to be in the High King's graces if we show up too far behind the others."

Hero and Abyssus faced forward and followed Firmus into the woods around Nysa.

From the border on, the scenery provided a much-needed change. A wide variety of trees, shrubs, and flowers sprung up from every possible surface.

Hero took in the display with a sense of awe. "They're like fireworks."

Firmus chuckled. "Yeah, Askelon is fond of that sort of thing."

This kingdom, though thick with lush green, parted and revealed a stone path that led into its city.

Hero stopped in his tracks and gazed upon the glory of Nysa. Everything he set eyes upon held the majesty of the Ancients. Anima coursed through the stones, plants, and water. Just standing before it, the weight left his body and the sickness that lingered from the heat of the desert dwindled and faded away.

The entire region around Nysa seemed to be at one with the palace and outwardly welcomed visitors.

Firmus pushed back branches that extended onto the path, allowing Abyssus and Hero swift passage.

The kind gesture made Hero think of the fact that Firmus was a royal, perhaps more so than he or Abyssus. "Firmus, why do you guard Abyssus if you hold such a high status?" He figured that even if Firmus's parents banned him, his status outweighed theirs. If he truly wished to take back his power, they could do little to stop him.

Firmus paused with his hand on the next branch and glanced over his shoulder. "Why do you stay inside Nitor Palace even though your father is only Rahma?"

Hero pursed his lips.

"We all have reasons for doing things. Some of them are secret. The moment you tell someone, it's no longer a secret. It's no mistake that I keep to myself."

Abyssus fanned himself. "Phew, am I the only one who's still hot? Let's keep moving." He pushed Firmus's back and the brazen soldier dropped his conversation. They soon continued their entry to Nysa.

Hero wondered why the pair behaved in such ambiguous ways, trying to remind himself not to be suspicious of everyone. The Taint stirred his thoughts and his paranoia. *Stop it. Not everyone is out to get you.*

5
THE STATE OF EXISTENCE

The small group entered an empty throne room and discovered the stamp secured to a note on a small table beside the throne.

Abyssus picked the note up and scanned it with a laugh. "King Askelon apparently had more important business to attend to."

Firmus threw his head back with a bright grin. "He must've received my gift."

Abyssus rested a hand on the much taller Ignis's shoulder. "You have excellent timing. Ah, the Feh...."

Hero stepped forward and used the stamp with a shrug. "No point in staying. We can make up some time this way."

Firmus scratched his eyebrow with a wince rather than responding.

The team made haste towards the border of Elysium. At their pace, they quickly found themselves in the depths of the Western Woods.

Hero knew when they had arrived because they stumbled upon a house that appeared to have been swallowed by the winding trees. He stopped when he saw it, as if caught by the sleeve. His gaze fixed to it. Somewhere, the tune from a violin played. The sound, which at first seemed harmonic, in time created a horrid screeching in his ears.

"Hero," Abysuss called and touched Hero's arm.

Hero gasped, breaking from his trance. He only now realized the cold sweat on his forehead.

Abyssus smiled and took Hero by the hand. "Keep close. These grounds are dangerous."

Hero continued onward in a haze, unaware that they had pulled him along to the heart of Elysium. After a deep breath and an alert look around, he glanced down at his hand and saw that Abyssus gently tugged him down what the locals might call a path... if anyone had bothered to use it in the last hundred turns.

He caught himself looking closely at Abyssus's gloved hand and running his fingers across the leather. "Abysuss, why do you still wear gloves?"

"This again? I keep telling you... it looks cool."

Hero squinted. *Liar.*

Firmus walked along beside Abyssus, occasionally glimpsing over his shoulder at Hero. "He's not a child, you know."

Abyssus clapped back, taking on an uppity tone. "He may not be a child but he has a childlike quality that I find rather endearing." Then his eyes turned dark as night as he glared at Firmus. "In other words, mind your own business."

Hero always found it mysterious that Firmus never got upset no matter what tone Abyssus used with him or how harshly he responded. Their relationship seemed decent enough despite these occasional moments of tension.

Firmus walked on seemingly unaffected. "Yes, you're right. My mistake."

They walked in silence, except for the whispers of Taint that only troubled Hero. Eventually, the whispers faded and Abyssus curiously released Hero's hand.

Can he hear them?

In all of their time together, Abyssus never said anything about the whispers, yet he always seemed to know when to comfort Hero.

If for no other reason, which he had many, he allowed Abyssus close, even to touch him when others were not afforded such a bond.

"There's the Gishian Estate," Abysuss said, pointing at the tangle of ivy and branches just ahead.

Hero slowed his step, trying to comprehend what his companion referred to until he saw the building, wrapped up in its leafy cocoon.

Abyssus surveyed the terrain. "It's quiet, isn't it?"

Firmus crossed his arms. "Eerily so."

Abyssus led them through the mess of vines and into a vast open space.

Hero took in the overgrown yet lavish courtyard, which clearly must have been from Mu's earlier turns. He studied the property certain that it had gone ungroomed for longer than he'd been alive. Between the vines of hellish ivy, white stone hinted at handiwork from the Ancients who'd built Mu. The Gishian family appeared to have quite literally buried history, though, he considered the lack of people and wildlife more concerning. They lingered in the courtyard until it became awkward.

Hero titled his head at the estate. "Maybe they're inside."

"Let's tread lightly," Abyssus said, walking ahead.

Firmus rushed after him. "Don't say that and rush in."

Abyssus approached the entrance first and opened the door, allowing it swing open fully without putting a foot inside. He waited for a while, listening. Rather than continue onward, he backed into the courtyard and looked upward. "Let's enter from the second floor."

Firmus hurried to a tree beside the estate, leapt to grab the branch, and swung himself up closer to the window. From his vantage point, he tried peeking in through one of the upper windows.

Abyssus moved closer to the tree to speak to him. "Can you see anything?"

Firmus shook his head. "Either the windows are just that filthy or it's at an inconvenient angle. There seems to be a latch on the inside. It would be best to enter without making any noise."

Hero grumbled under his breath. "We're already making noise."

Abyssus reached into the pack strapped to his leg and retrieved a wire and a hook. He connected the hook to the wire by a loop on the end.

Firmus let out his hand and pulled Abyssus up onto the branch.

Once Abyssus reached the branch, he took a rope from his pack, attached it to a loop on his belt, and gave it to Firmus to tie to the tree. He then took the hook with the wire and tossed it to the window across.

At that point, Hero realized the magnetized nature of the hook, as it stuck firmly to a metal panel just below the window. *How did Abyssus deduce that he would need these things? And how did he figure it out so fast?*

Abyssus removed a rod from a pouch strapped to his left leg, and extended it between the tree and the opposing wall. He tested its stability and placed his feet on the wire.

Firmus raised his head. "Are you going to be okay?"

"I haven't forgotten. How could I?"

He nodded. "Hmm."

Abyssus crossed the wire, one step at a time, until he reached the opposite side. With one hand still on the rod, he took a blade from a strap on his thigh and popped the window's latch.

Hero climbed the tree to join Firmus, unable to see what happened after Abyssus jumped inside the estate.

A pile of ropes flew out from the window, and Firmus caught them. He tied the ends to the tree, untying the other cord that had been hooked to Abyssus's belt. As the ropes tightened, they formed a bridge to the window.

Hero deemed it more mysterious that they be so well prepared for this specific instance. Nevertheless, he crossed the bridge with Firmus into the dark hall on the other side. Once there, he saw that Abyssus had tied the opposite end of the rope to a pillar inside.

Is this smart or is it something else?

Abyssus sheathed the blade. "How strange. There's no sign of activity at all. No sign of traps. It's almost like she wants you to come."

Hero proceeded down the hall toward the throne room. "Then that's what we'll do."

Firmus sighed. "That was a lot of work for us to just walk in."

Abyssus shrugged. "You never know. I somewhat suspected traps on the first floor but this floor seems unusually safe."

Firmus scoffed. "Safe. I wouldn't call Una 'safe'."

"Smartass."

Hero reached the end of the hall and placed his hand on the door. "Shh!"

Una spoke from behind the door. "Why don't you come in?"

The small group exchanged glances.

"Yes, I know you're there," she said.

Hero opened the door and let it swing all the way open until he spotted Una across the room.

She waited on her throne, one leg crossed over the other, and her eyes closed. "Finally, some entertainment." She looked both regal and relaxed as she reclined on her throne. Her excessively exposed skin and long silky hair nearly blended with the roots protruding from the wall behind her.

Hero turned his head towards what he thought sounded like a creak, but instead discovered thick tree limbs crawling on the walls. Numerous slain contenders lay across the floor and pinned behind the roots. "We came only for the seal."

Una opened her eyes, exposing her slit pupils.

Abyssus pulled his mouth to one side and rifled through his pack. He pulled something out, hiding it before Hero noticed what he held.

Una rose from her throne. "If you want my seal, come and fight for it."

Hero drew his blades from the straps on each side of his legs. "It can't be helped."

Una raised her hands with a malevolent grin, and the estate rumbled. Water coursed up the walls, across the floor, gushed into the room from all sides, and crashed into the team.

The force knocked Hero to the ground. As soon as he regained his bearings, he froze the water and directed the ice back towards Una, catching her in the middle.

She used the metal plate on her gauntlet glove to deflect the ice before it impaled her. With a laugh, she swung her hip out and placed her free hand upon it.

Hero stood, careful not to touch any of the roots extending into the water below, then readied his blades once more and charged. As he closed in, he kept a close watch on Una's movements with the hope that she may reveal a strategy.

Instead, he sprinted up to her and thrust his blade, piercing straight through her abdomen. Blood spurted from her wound and her mouth and he retreated with a gasp.

She didn't defend? Did I just kill the Queen of Elysium?

Hero's body seized up as he puzzled over Una's behavior. He fixated on the steady flow of blood that poured from her body, spilled out onto the floor and trickled into the water.

Una flashed a sinister grin and gripped him by the wrist with alarming strength. Her blood extended out from her body like arms and jutted towards him.

Abyssus ripped Hero back by the shirt, using his own dagger to slash open Una's side as he wrenched Hero from her grip. "Damn it!"

Hero stumbled backwards before he finally caught his footing.

Abyssus kept close to Una, careful not to fall victim to the numerous traps she laid. He dodged the tentacles of blood, her attacks, and the water with the agility of a wild animal.

Hero looked for an opportunity to break in but their deadly dance moved far too quickly.

Abyssus dodged and Hero caught the glimmer of the glass plate in his hand.

The attacks continued until Abyssus looked at the blood on the glass plate. "Firmus!"

Firmus pushed Hero out of the way and waved his hand to conjure flames. The sea of fire set Una ablaze.

Finally, her cockiness stopped, and she screamed as her skin seared from the biting heat. Water sprung from the floor and lashed out like a whip, trying to take form and put out the fire.

While she screamed and collapsed to the floor, Firmus swooped through the room, collecting Abyssus on one arm and Hero on the other. He raced out so fast that Hero almost slipped from his grip.

As Firmus sprinted out of the throne room, Hero watched her. She put out the flames with the water she'd manifested and gestured large with a swing of her arms. The estate shook again, this time more violently, and the waves surged after Firmus.

Hero held on tight, feeling his instinct to withdraw, though he could do nothing more.

Abyssus fixated only on his sample as he pressed another glass plate to the first and sealed them together, his excitement rivaling that of Una herself.

The waves crashed at Firmus's heels just as he reached the window and sprang outside. He leapt down to the first floor without looking back and continued dashing into the woods until they were completely out of sight.

Once breathless, he stopped, placed the boys down, and did his best to recover.

Hero awed despite the vague terror left from Una's attempt at murder. "You're so fast."

Firmus clenched his fists, shaking furiously as he turned to Abyssus. "What were you doing?"

Abyssus frowned. "I've obtained a unique sample... not that you would understand."

"Understand? Did you go in there just to get that sample?"

Hero ruminated as he played back the fight in his head. "Did her blood move? Is the blood curse real? It really moved, didn't it?"

Abyssus hurried to show Hero his sample. The blood inside the sealed dish writhed and tried to take different shapes. "Something this small could teach us more about people with the blood curse. It could be the precursor to new regenerative medicines." He put the dish in his pocket. "Or, you know, just a way to learn how to cut the head off a snake."

Firmus growled. "You're an engineer, not a doctor, or a scientist!"

Wow, he really managed to make Firmus mad this time.

Hero did his best to focus on the task. "Let's find the Twins. I don't think we'll have much luck getting a stamp from Una."

Abyssus agreed. "Sure. Firmus and I are dropping out after this round, anyway. We only need one sheet. They've already been to Tir Na Nog, so if we take it now, we'll have done well."

Firmus adjusted his bag. "I say we make our way out of the Western Woods and camp along the outskirts before dark. We didn't get what we needed from Una but I'm certain her children did— we can take one of their sheets. We should only be a couple of days behind. If we hurry, we can catch up."

Hero ran ahead and beckoned them along. "Then let's hurry. They're moving fast and it'll be dark soon."

They moved through the forest until the sunlight faded.

Firmus looked up at the twinkling stars. "We should set up camp for the night."

Abyssus dug through the pack on Firmus's back. "Are you sure it's safe to camp around these woods? I've heard a lot of rumors about people being snatched away or eaten."

Hero moved farther ahead. "I'm not tired. If you two are good, we should keep moving."

Firmus planted his feet into the soil and crossed his arms. "Pushing too hard will lead to disaster. Besides, Una will need time to recover. We'll be safe here."

"I'm sure they're well on their way to Askadel. They would have come here after Tir Na Nog, then cut through to Nysa, and they will have to pass back through the Eastern Woods to get to either Nex or, more likely, Rosetau then Nex, before finally heading into the Capital." He had spent his entire childhood training as his father asked and, though he had no desire to be king, he couldn't allow all his hard work to be wasted by the Gishian Family.

Firmus raised a brow. "It's a good idea to breathe sometimes."

Hero's frustration strangled him but he saw little point in continuing the struggle.

Abyssus set up a tent he had stuffed into Firmus's bag and lit a lantern. Once cozy inside, they engaged in their usual activities: reading, eating, and observing.

Abyssus still hadn't noticed the confections Hero had stashed, so he ate fruit. "Hero's right, we should be able to catch up with the Gishians in the Eastern Woods.

Hero rested the book against his chest and reviewed lore about their location. "If the Twins pass through, they'll be cautious, but if for some reason they decide to avoid it and pass through the Western Woods, we'll notice that from here."

"You seem sure of that."

"I've met Luna before. As much as she may try to hide it, she cares for her brother. Too many people have said the Eastern Woods are dangerous. Even if she's obstinate, she won't put Syo in danger by running through them in the middle of the night."

Firmus sat up. "Didn't she try and persuade you to marry her?"

"For Syo, mostly. You've seen their mother and heard the rumors. I'm sure they're having a hard time. I mean, how would you feel if you had no choice but to succeed, and someone with no interest in ruling kept getting in the way? The way they see it, they were born to be rulers. There's no other choice."

Abyssus offered Hero a piece of fruit. "You're always surprisingly aware of other people's feelings."

"Even if I don't want to rule, it's a king's job to be aware of other's feelings and circumstances. One day, I'll be king of Nitor whether I want it or not, so I thought it best to pay attention."

Firmus rested back, using his pack as a pillow. He kept everything close and always remained on guard. "Abyssus, I sincerely hope that stunt you pulled earlier brings more good than harm."

"If the only one I endangered is myself, isn't it fine?"

"But you didn't. What if Hero jumped in to try and protect you?"

Abyssus spoke tersely. "Firmus." After he set a tone of authority, he paused for a long time and didn't continue his thought until Firmus readjusted himself. "...if not for Hero's well-being, then why do I do these things?"

"That's a good question," Firmus said. He dropped his façade of anger and sighed deeply. "I'm just worried that something will happen to you."

Abyssus sank down, also used his pack as a pillow, and propped up a leg against his knee. "It will. It always does. No point in fretting about the inevitable. To exist means we're perpetually in a state of dying. If we're constantly afraid of it, we'll never be able to truly live. At the same time, if we aren't at least aware of death then life bears no meaning."

Hero turned a page in his book while listening to the dispute. He'd thought they got along rather well, but began to see underlying tension that, perhaps, he'd simply ignored in the past. *Or maybe I just didn't understand it.*

A cold wind swept against Hero's face and the conversation stopped. He looked up from his book to find that everything had frozen in time. A figure stood before him, wrapped in static darkness. His mouth fell open as he watched it.

It watched him too.

A voice spoke through the static, making the intonation difficult to perceive. A man? A woman? He couldn't tell because of the interference. "You've finally come. Why do you dilly-dally in needless memories?"

Hero remained frozen in place, unsure if he should respond. He considered asking who they were but it seemed like a pointless question. Not to mention, he wasn't sure he *could* move.

"You don't suffer enough," the figure said with a shake of their head. They knelt and stretched their hand towards Hero's head. "You have forgotten something important and you must retrieve it."

Hero closed his eyes as the hand reached him.

Abyssus patted Hero's head with a morning call. "Hero, wake up." He prattled on to Firmus while trying to wake Hero. "He's sleeping hard today. I wonder if the stress did him in yesterday."

Hero quickly awakened, rubbed his eyes, and began collecting his things. "I'm sorry."

Abyssus smiled as usual. "It's okay. I don't mind waiting, but I'm sure those twins will be on the move."

Was that a dream? I don't want to go back to the clinic.

They closed the tent and returned it to Firmus's pack, then started through the woods towards Askadel. Even though Isis would be more than pleased to invite Hero inside, the trap struck him as unappealing.

Abyssus had always advised against siding with the Council due to their view on the Tainted. He spoke about them with disdain, which rarely occurred without a valid reason.

Hero glanced at his friend, pondering. *But why do I trust Abyssus when I don't even trust myself? What makes him trustworthy?*

Abyssus caught him staring and grinned. He felt like someone Hero had known forever, someone who had already proven trustworthy. However, Hero relied on Abyssus so much for balance that it made him fearful of ever losing him.

His thoughts broke as a gentle hand patted his head.

Abyssus spoke to Hero softly, the way Hero expected one might speak to a frightened child. "I don't know what's on your mind lately, but I'm here if you need me."

Hero nodded, his thoughts racing with troubling suspicions. *What if Syo was right? What if I trust someone who means me harm? Did he stab Una knowing that she could manipulate her blood? What is he trying to do with that sample?* He rubbed together his clammy hands.

Firmus also watched Hero and, though he said nothing, his gaze reflected distrust.

Abyssus hurried off into the brush and left an awkward silence between the other two.

Hero fidgeted, driven to a state of paranoia by his thoughts.

Firmus pushed branches out of his path and sighed. "If Abyssus wanted to hurt you, he would've done so."

"Huh?"

He sighed again, this time with a slight growl. "His love for you is unfounded... at least that's what I want to say. He's a strange person, don't you think?"

"Strange?" Hero watched Abyssus excavate herbs from a patch on the forest floor.

"It's almost as if he knows something we don't."

Hero agreed. He trusted in this sense of authority and wisdom without knowing much about Abyssus or his thoughts. It made him laugh to know he felt so suspicious. "You're also a strange person, Firmus."

Firmus tipped his head and gave him a sideways glance. "How so?"

"You came all the way here to guard him, which also seems unfounded. He's always doing reckless things but you still tolerate it. You could go back to your kingdom and rule, yet you remain here as a guard under a Rahma's rule."

Firmus peered up through the branches and ruminated. "I don't know if that makes me strange or an idiot."

Hero chuckled. "Just strange. Abyssus is openly strange but you're a bigger mystery. That makes you more interesting to me."

Firmus seemed to understand that Hero meant to imply he knew something more and wouldn't say, because he plodded along with a clenched jaw. His aura created a wall as if to keep Hero out. "I don't serve the Rahma. I serve Abyssus." He walked off towards Abyssus. "Hey, we need to pick up the pace. Are you done collecting your samples?"

Interesting. Hero and his taint shared a common interest this time. *I want to dissect him and pull out all the hidden treasures.*

Firmus gestured him closer. "Come, Hero."

Hero joined the other two as Abyssus finished collecting his herbs. "Yaui Oldeus?"

Abyssus beamed. "Good job! We use a lot of this in the palace."

Firmus cringed. "You mean *you* use a lot of it."

"It's an herb, not a drug. Don't make it sound like I'm an addict."

Hero rested a hand on his chin. "Caffeine *is* a drug, though."

Abyssus whispered, "Whose side are you on?"

After their brief pause to excavate, they trekked through the day, camped once more, and rose early in hopes of catching up with the Gishians. As they traveled, the forest of blossoming trees and lush foliage gave way to a darker, more treacherous path of twisted roots and vines. A heaviness settled into the air, making the path all the more stifling. Orbs of golden light rose in small clusters, drifting into the sky. It all gave substance to the myths of the Eastern Woods.

Firmus grew deadly quiet, even his footfall barely made a sound.

The group slowed and time seemed to hang.

Hero caught a glimpse of something reflecting in the light, and swiftly altered his focus. Before the other two noticed, he slipped behind the foliage, took the dagger from the sheath attached to his leg, and dove through an opening where the sunlight had penetrated the dense trees. He pressed his dagger against Luna's throat as he came up behind her.

He ordered, "Lower your weapon."

Syo spun fast, drawing a rapier with a snake grip. "Release her!"

Hero noted that the reflection stemmed from the sunlight hitting Luna's bow and arrow, which she still pointed at Abyssus.

Hero pressed the dagger harder against her throat. "Drop your weapons now."

Syo set his rapier on the damp grass.

Luna started to place down her bow but released her arrow at the last moment.

Syo kicked his weapon up and struck. He and his sister moved in unison—as her bow hit the grass, she drew an identical rapier and spun, using her momentum to push Hero back.

At a wave of Hero's hand, ice shot up around Syo's rapier, trapping it in frosty branches. Both princes stopped upon hearing Luna's shrill scream.

Hero clenched his teeth at the sound and checked his side. Beside him, shadowy tendrils wrapped around Luna's body, squeezing her until she could no longer scream or resist.

Syo reached out and struggled to free her.

Her attacker, Abyssus, approached with his arm raised and his hand clutching the air. The shadows tightened as he closed his hand.

Syo dropped to his knees. "Please stop!"

You should've just stopped when I told you to.

Abyssus demanded, "Hand over your sheet!"

Syo patted down his clothing and gave his sheet to Firmus, who inspected it for Una's stamp. "Please let her go. I'll do anything."

Hero sheathed his weapon and waited. He expected nothing less from Abyssus and lacked empathy for the siblings, who seemed discourteous of others. The sight of them pleading stirred the Taint. He enjoyed their plight for a moment before beginning to question his morals and the voice inside that yearned for more chaos. Once he silenced it, he dug in his pack for the confection Fortuna had provided, and tapped Abyssus on the arm.

Abyssus glared at him. "What?"

Hero smiled as best he could manage. "There's no need to dirty your hands. Take this. I got it for you in Tir Na Nog." He took Abyssus by the hand and gave him the confection.

Abyssus puzzled, forgetting his anger to study the intricate treat. "What's this? It's cute." He released his grip on Luna, and she fell to the ground, grasping her throat as she choked back a few breaths.

Syo immediately rushed to her aid. He drew her head to his chest and ran his hand over her head with calming strokes.

Hero now gave a genuine smile, pleased that he fought the Taint's desire for mayhem and violence. "No need to thank me."

Syo's face flushed. "Thank you? You almost killed my sister! What's wrong with you?"

"How ungrateful."

"What the hell is wrong with all of you?"

"You're the strange one, if you ask me."

Abyssus paused his admiration of the confection and shifted his eyes towards Syo, causing the young man to shiver. "We went to Elysium and faced Queen Una before pilfering from the weak. Perhaps if your family wasn't so driven to murder the competition, we wouldn't need to stoop as low as you. Better to skin a snake than condemn an empire to its venom."

Firmus gently pushed the confection closer to Abyssus's face. "We're losing time. We got what we came for, so there's no use in debating now."

A part of Hero found great enjoyment and amusement in Syo's defeated expression, but the other part, which wanted to fight the Taint, asked himself how he ought to rebel against these ideas. "We should bring them along."

Abyssus froze mid-bite. "Huh?"

"They're your opponents," Firmus said, crossing his arms. His aura remained in balance, indicating that he had no qualms with the idea.

Hero spoke more so to the Taint than the others. "Because it's fair."

Firmus rubbed his brow. "They still have one sheet. They'll be in the running, Hero. Are you sure?"

Hero agreed and offered his hand to Syo. "Hmm."

Syo stared at the extended hand, wrinkling a brow. He slapped it away and assisted Luna to her feet, shielding her with one arm. "Don't think we're friends just because you pitied us."

"Pity? I feel nothing of the sort." After making the comment, Hero rested a hand over his heart. Indeed. He held no remorse or pity for the twins. Only his desire to rebel against the Taint and retain some 'moral' standing made him perform these actions.

Abyssus frowned as he inspected Hero and then sighed. "If it's what you want, then I have no complaints."

"Let's be on our way to Nex then," Firmus said, patting Abyssus's head.

Syo and Luna tagged along, keeping a close eye on their attacker as he carefully dissected and consumed his confections.

Hero watched them in return as the Taint's voice admonished him. *'You've made a mistake. What'll you do if they decide to turn on you again? You know how these things go, don't you? It won't be you. No. Someone else will get hurt.'*

Each person kept thoughts and comments to themselves, none quite trusting the others as they made their way north through the Eastern Woods.

At the border of Nex, Abyssus and Hero passed their extra garments to Firmus and helped bundle him up while the Twins bundled up in green scarves and ponchos. With Hero in the group, they traveled through the community without the hassle of the storms, an advantage for the Twins albeit for no reason other than Hero's struggle against the Taint.

Everyone received their stamps from Niteo. He grasped their sheets with his head lowered and slapped on his stamp while glancing between each page and his son. His eyes flicked up and down and he jerked back his hand as Hero reached for his sheet.

Hero smiled at him and lingered in front of the desk. "Thank you."

"Go now," Niteo said, shooing him, and then glanced to check if Hero had been angered. "Fortis, please escort them out."

Fortis heeded the request and apologized after he had accompanied them into the hallway. "I must stay here. Please, make yourselves comfortable and stay as long as you'd like."

The group stood in the hallway until Hero finally said something. "This is a good place to rest before we move on to the Capital. We can send for a carriage and leave together after everyone has taken a moment to unwind."

Luna wrapped her hands in her scarf. "Do you really think we're going to accept anything from our enemy? I hope you know our family can't be easily poisoned."

Hero tilted his head. "We're just candidates in the same tournament. The word candidate doesn't suggest we're enemies. I only attacked you to protect my friend. I apologize if that made you uneasy."

She pondered his words with a deep scowl. "You're weird, but you don't seem to be lying."

"Lying is an undesirable trait."

That's why I wish I'd never lied, but it's a decision I make. There's no one else to blame.

The Taint responded. *'It's a basic survival mechanism. Everyone does it.'*

Luna conceded. "We'll rest here."

Her brother remained on guard. "Luna, are you sure?"

"Yes. Relax. He's not interested in killing us. If he were, he would've killed us in the woods or in the middle of a storm. You must've noticed how easily we passed through this kingdom. I sure did."

Hero opened the door to the lounge and ushered them inside. Everyone, excluding him, sat down and removed their bags and heavy gear. Once they settled in, he folded his hands forward and twiddled his thumbs. "Can I get you anything?"

Luna set her scarf on her lap. "What about the servants? You're the Prince, aren't you?"

"They're frightened of me. They only come together for parties. I take care of myself when Fortis and Isis aren't here. It's always been this way."

She shook her head to snap free from her stupor. "I guess... something sweet. Syo will have something bitter. Anything warm is good at the moment."

Abyssus raised his hand. "Cake for me!"

Luna shot a look of disgust. "Praise be, you haven't had enough confections?"

Abyssus smiled back. "Do you want me to chew your head off instead?"

Hero left the room, wishing to avoid the unpleasantries. The palace was still, and even the kitchen appeared untouched since the last time he used it. He rarely met with any of the servants besides Lara. Even those interactions were far and few between as Niteo took her in as his daughter.

Niteo doted on her, most likely to hurt Hero for not complying with his wishes. He'd gone as far as moving her to the other side of the palace to ensure her safety.

Hero shrugged off the unnecessary thought and prepared the kettle. He then searched their frozen goods for sweets to serve Abyssus. They hadn't been visiting together as much, so he didn't have anything prepared, but he didn't mind making them. He filled the counter with bowls and ingredients, placing each object down in the order he needed it.

While he mixed the batter, Luna entered and leaned against the counter, curling her lip. "I thought I was surprised before. I'm even more surprised now. You bake?"

"I said I'm home by myself. Doesn't it make sense that I'd know how to cook? Abyssus likes sweets, so I learned to bake for him."

Her voice shrilled. "Wha—why?"

"Because he's my friend."

"What kind of joke is this? Are you fishing for pity?"

"Is that what it seems like?"

"Yeah. The Prince with no mom and a Rahma father... everyone dislikes him except for the person he pampers. Doesn't that sound like a pity story?"

Everyone? Not everyone.

"Oh," he said. "I'm fine though. I dislike my father anyway. I think his absence meant more to me when I was a child, but whether or not I pamper Abyssus is my choice. He's not forcing me to do anything. I stay inside the palace because I'm dangerous to others. Maybe it's not always fun, but that's what happens when you're a hazard. I enjoy studying, and I prefer not to be bothered, so it's a pain when my father comes home and orders me around. It feels like a stranger is invading my boundaries."

"You're so weird."

The Taint whispered, *'You're lying to yourself and to Luna. Truthfully, it hurts, doesn't it?'*

He poured the batter into a cake mold, set it into the oven he had lit and heated, then prepared the tealeaves and porcelain set on a platter. "Since you're here, take this upstairs and tell Abyssus I'm making his cake."

"Uh... okay." She walked to the door with the platter and turned back, appearing confused. "Hey, why aren't you rushing to get to the Capital? Don't you want to be High King?"

"There's no need to rush. It won't change the High King's decision. He's looking for the best suitor, and judges based on his opinion of our behavior."

"I don't know how to say this, but you seem listless. Are you okay?"

Hero laughed unconsciously. "You're worried?"

"No!" She blushed and stomped away.

His smile faded, and he stared at the oven. "It's a little hard though...."

6
FATHER

The final two contenders of the Astor Tournament appeared before the High King, each presenting their sheet of stamps for approval. Naturally, since only Hero and Luna received full marks, they tied for the position, but she passed her authority onto Syo due to his sensitivities about losing.

The two boys stood shoulder to shoulder and awaited the King's response in his private office, neither wanting to make a sound in the deathly silence.

The High King sat at his desk looking graven as usual. "Since it has come to this, we'll have no choice but to move this to the arena. I shall pass on the details to your parents by this evening. For now, you are dismissed. I look forward to naming one of you my successor."

The guards escorted them back to the Centre at the King's word, where they rejoined Abyssus and Luna. Each person paused, at a loss for words.

"It'd be a pain to leave now," Luna said. "Why don't we stick together for a while?"

Abyssus grunted as he stretched his arms. "If Hero wants to. I'm not really interested in playing with you."

"Playing? When have we ever played?"

He grinned with sinister pleasure. "Haven't we been playing from the start?"

Ah, there he goes again. Intimidating people. The Taint answered with endearment. *'It's charming, isn't it?'* Hero gasped, inaudibly, as he felt the smile on his face and shook his head. *It's not good.*

He pressed his hand lightly over Abyssus's face. "I'm staying to visit with my aunt. I'll leave in the morning. I don't mind if you tag along."

Luna twisted her mouth and crossed her arms with indignation. "I don't like how you made us sound like the extras, but I suppose we'll stay."

"We're going to buy food before we go to see Chi," Abyssus said.

Luna handed her brother a pouch. "Syo, go with them."

His expression was riddled with anxiety and concern for his sister, who conveyed contradictory composure. "What about you?"

"I'm not a baby. I'm going with Hero. Come back to me with food."

She went with Hero to see Chi at her cottage, but his aunt had not yet returned from her post, nor did he go searching for her.

He treated her cottage like his own home and went into the back room to find a book. This library always deeply fascinated him with its old folklore and tales of the Old World, Undal. He ran his fingers over the spines, content to find them clean.

Luna sat down on the cushion at the bay window. "You don't have a mate?"

"No."

"An interest?"

"I don't know."

"How do you not know?"

"I don't interact with many people, and maybe that's why I don't understand love."

He pulled a book down. On the cover, wrapped in a gold frame, the title read, *"Chrysalis."* He crouched down, his back against the bookcase, and flipped it open, trying to recall the details of the tale. Key words brought back the most distinctive part of the story, though he struggled to remember its relevance to him. *Did I used to know?* The Taint cooed. *'I can tell you, if you'd like.'*

Luna sank against the bookcase to peek at the novel. "What's that? Looks old."

"It is. I've only seen it once in this library. No one ever talks about it, but it's one of my favorites." A hint of sadness rose in him. "Yet, no matter how many times I read it, I struggle to remember the details."

"Sometimes talking about things can help you remember. Do your best to tell me."

He looked into Luna's snake eyes, taken aback by her kindness. His lips curled up to form a weak smile. "Perhaps we should have married, after all."

"It's not too late. We could finish this tournament right now... the two winners of the Astor Tournament... married. You and Syo wouldn't have to fight in the arena."

His resolve wavered as she touched his arm. The usual cold look in her gaze now pleaded with him to end their strife. He redirected his attention to the book. "I don't really care about ruling or the tournament. Most of the time, I don't even want to be alive, but the people around me have worked so hard for my sake. The only thing that keeps me going is my desire to know the truth about the Universe."

"I can help you. Syo and I are powerful. If he understands that our marriage is purely political then he won't argue."

The offer struck a point of intrigue. "You have the blood curse as well?"

Luna hesitated before nodding. "I do, but Syo's regenerative abilities are not like mine. I can teach you about our family. It might help deepen everyone's understanding of both the curse and the Taint. They say that Prince Abyssus is an unmatched savant. I'm sure that he'd be able to study both our cases and help us put an end to the stigma. When people are in need, they shouldn't be neglected... no matter the reason behind their condition."

Hero caught himself influenced by her again and stopped himself from being impulsive. "Let me think about it. There's a lot to consider."

She pressed her lips together, trying to conceal a broad smile. "Did you remember what the book was about?"

"Oh, um...." He scratched his temple with one finger. "It's about a man who awakens from a crystal chrysalis to find he's alone in the Universe. He travels the stars to learn about his existence. As he wanders, he learns that he is of one mind with all creation and that he must give meaning to existence, to have a purpose. He has to find a reason to be there."

Luna rested her cheek against her hand and sighed. "All the interesting books are about men. Is that like a commentary on theology? Sounds like it came from the Grandmaster's scriptures."

He perked up. "You've read them?"

She snarled. "Are you kidding? Don't tell me you're influenced by that council junk."

"Junk? The Grandmaster's scriptures? What are your beliefs, Miss Luna?"

Her eyes bulged. "Miss? You flatter me. Who says I have to believe in anything?"

"I just wondered if you did."

Her gaze wandered, pensively. "It's not that I don't believe in *anything*. I just think people are misguided in their faith. If the Grandmaster is so great, then why is our Universe such a mess? It's hard to revere someone when I think about it in that light."

He decided not to probe any further since she danced around the idea of her beliefs, and the Taint stirred inside him with hateful commentary. Conversations regarding faith and philosophy often triggered it in the worst ways.

In due time, everyone returned to the cottage.

Chi introduced herself to the Gishian Twins while Hero sat by the window, holding the book and staring out at the Centre.

He often wondered about his Bound. Would they ever meet?

In his daze, he missed Kyou pressing his face against the glass, and jerked back from the window in surprise. "*Baen ou ya!*"

'*You surprised me!*'

His mentor howled with laughter, throwing back his head of thick black hair, and opened his arms wide to Hero with his glimmering violet eyes. "You coming to greet me?"

Hero slipped away from the table and met Kyou outside, greeted by an arm around the shoulder.

"I won't go inside. I can already see Abyssus glaring at me." Kyou flashed his crooked grin at Abyssus and received a snarl in return.

Hero glanced back at the window. "I don't understand why he doesn't like you."

"Doesn't matter. He's a temperamental person. I'm not sure if he doesn't like *me*, or if he just doesn't like most people in general."

"Ah, that's probably it."

Kyou's breath caught the cold air and left a trail from his lips. "How have you been?"

"Fine."

"You don't seem fine. Want to talk about it?"

Hero often sighed around Kyou, who still caused a feeling of nostalgia and longing. He shrugged, hoping it would give off the impression he wasn't bothered.

Kyou's gaze noted every movement, and he tightened his grip around Hero's arm, jostling him gently. "Come with me."

On the few occasions that Kyou returned home, he'd stay in his room at the palace, sleep, and visit for a while before vanishing again. His ritual continued just like always. He led Hero to his room on the second floor and tossed his coat on a chair around a lounge.

Hero sat in an armchair and studied the unchanged room. "I wanted to see you."

"I'm sorry. Has it been difficult?"

"No."

"Lying again."

Hero pursed his lips to stop their trembling. "If you know, then why did you leave?"

"Maybe this is the real reason Abyssus dislikes me?" Kyou pulled another chair across the room and sat down in front of Hero, folding his hands. "I spent a lot of time training you. I know the difference between your honesty and your lies. You can't hide from me."

"Where do you go when you're gone? You promised me—"

"That I'd be here for you? I know. I'm here now. Don't I always come when you need me?"

Hero twiddled his thumbs on his lap, and the miasma stirred in response to his sadness. Each wave washed over him like an ominous cloud and forewarned of misfortune, anger, and chaos.

Kyou rested a hand on Hero's knee. "What's bothering you?"

Hero opened and closed his mouth, unable to form the words. They rested at the tip of his tongue, suffocating him as they brewed inside. He felt like a teakettle left on the stove for far too long, just waiting for someone to turn down the flame.

Kyou implored, "Be honest with me."

Hero shook his head in response. Every so often, he awoke to discover that there was no one to talk to. His father often asked Isis to tighten the seals on the palace to restrict anyone from entering.

A part of him still couldn't trust her, knowing full well that she was a member of the Council wishing to eradicate the Tainted.

During those times, Hero would remember being with Kyou, and wanted to see him, because Kyou could see through the lies.

Hero finally admitted to part of his discomfort. "Everyone thinks that I'm acting out for attention. I don't want to react. I don't want to be pitied."

"Is that what's bothering you? Everyone feels like shit sometimes. If you tell someone, they might even understand how you feel. Instead of burying your problems and worrying about how others view you, it's better to complain. That way they'll know for certain you're not looking for pity, and you'll know what they're thinking, too."

"Earlier, Luna thought I was being pitiful, and I said that I was fine, but afterward, I realized I was bothered. I think, maybe, I'm lonely after all."

Kyou ruffled Hero's hair and beamed. "That's something! I still remember the apathetic child I picked up in Nex. You've come a long way. Don't let anyone bring you down. I'm proud of you."

Proud? Hero's face stung with embarrassment and, gathering that he might be red, he pulled up his scarf to hide.

Kyou spoke again after a while. "How's the Taint?"

Hero's hand twitched as the voice in his head reacted. *'How sweet of him to worry about me.'*

Kyou rarely let anyone see him this serious but it came out naturally when the matter of the Taint arose. "It seems worse than before."

The Taint sulked. *'Am I a* him *or an* it? *What do you think, Leoht?'*

Hero shifted his eyes to one side and then to the other. "I don't know."

Kyou sat upright with a kind smile. "I know I'm not always here for you but believe me when I say I'm trying to find a way for you to find peace."

Hero could no longer hear the Taint speak. For a short time, he fully embraced the stew of emotions that welled inside. Usually, the Taint thrived on this emotion, good or bad. Only Kyou and Abyssus knew how to suppress it to allow Hero to breathe and be a normal, functioning person. He finally smiled back at Kyou, though it hurt. "I'm always waiting, Kyou."

Kyou embraced him, squeezing his head. "That's my boy!"

Hero accepted the embrace, taking in Kyou's aura and the calmness that swept over him whenever this person entered his life. He closed his eyes and let these emotions sink in.

Take me with you. Don't leave me in this place with him.

The spiral pattern on Hero's bedroom ceiling blurred and then cleared overhead. He tried remembering when he'd returned home, and why he awakened in Nex instead of the Capital.

What's going on? I was with Kyou.

A bell chimed in the hallway, and he threw off the covers to follow the sound. Dark water swept over the floor and down the stairway. His gaze trailed after the silhouette of a woman, who walked into the main hall. He sloshed through the flooded hallway and reached out to her wrist. "Hey."

She jolted her head towards him, and the bell chimed again. Her violet eyes appeared to glow against her pale skin and black hair. "Leoht."

He shook his head. "Is this a dream?"

The woman turned and crouched down. Only then did he realize his smallness compared to her. She held out her gloved hand with something closed in her palm. "You dropped this."

Hero watched as she opened her hand and revealed a tiny silver horse figurine. He picked it up, getting a sudden pang on the side of his head. A memory of the horse played in his mind. He had dropped it during a struggle.

The woman beamed. "You must take great care of things you treasure."

A click echoed through the room, and Hero turned, searching for the source. "What was that? Did you hear it?"

Dark water shot out of the hallway and, in a panic, he froze it.

The woman squeezed his hand.

He looked back at her but he found Abyssus there instead. "Aby—"

"It's okay," Abyssus said. "I promised to protect you." He raised his hand to the ice, causing it to crackle and break apart. It soon thawed completely and water rushed out, knocking Hero off his feet.

7
ODE TO YOU

A month after the start of the tournament, Hero waited in the preparation room at the arena, listening to the people's excited chatter. Shields and swords of various sizes lined the walls as a form of décor. He sat in a corner looking at them and leaning his head against the wall as he tormented himself about his options. He'd trained for so long and knew he possessed the power to destroy Syo. A blood curse might aid the Twins in survival, but only with certain parts still intact.

The Tainted jested. *"The removal of one's head would lay waste to anyone... or to rest, I suppose."*

Hero fretted over thoughts of Luna's proposal. Whenever someone came close, the Taint attached itself to them and made a mess of things; although, after spending time with the Gishians, he ventured to consider them friends. Even with the Taint picking relentlessly at him, they managed a steady flow of healthy interaction. He wondered if this was because their condition gave them a better understanding of his. Still, the Taint grew strong every day and it had its own agenda. If he thought he could control it, he would just accept her offer.

What's worse? Defeating them now or later? Imagine the Queen I'd make of her.

Abyssus knocked on the door and gestured for Firmus to stay outside of the room. "Mind if I join you?"

Hero tried adjusting himself to look more alive rather than like he'd already been defeated. No matter what he chose, he lost something.

Abyssus closed the door and sat beside Hero on the bench. "What's gnawing at you? You're like a half-eaten sweater."

"Should I just marry Luna? I don't want to fight them."

"It really depends. If you stand with the Rebellion's plan, then doing so would change your agreement with Fortuna. You've made little contact with the Spinner, though. If this is what you wish, I won't fight you. I can find alternative methods, if need be." Abyssus smirked. "Akira might fuss but that's nothing I can't handle."

"You're good to me, Abyssus. I don't know what I want. All I know is what I *don't* want."

Abyssus threw out his hands to each side. "Why not flee to Tir Na Nog right now?"

"What? I'd start a war."

"Not if they don't find you. You're trapped in the palace anyway. Might as well hide away with people you actually like. I'm sure there's nothing Kyou wouldn't do for you. I could say the same, really."

"That's preposterous. The Plague would decimate their people."

"Now you're just making excuses. What is the nature of the Taint, really? Miasma can be suppressed, and wounds can be mended."

"He seems to have a mind of his own."

"*He?*" Abyssus leaned forward and rested his hand on Hero's shoulder. "You're in control of your actions and your mind, Hero. I'm here if something is wrong. You don't have to try and cope with your stresses by yourself, and it's not weak for you to be depressed or upset about your predicament. The more we understand about the Taint, the more we can erase people's fear of it."

Firmus opened the door but spoke from the hall. "They're calling for Hero."

Hero stood, hoping to escape from the conversation as quickly as possible.

Abyssus also stood. "Hero, make your own decision about what's right. We can find a way out of this."

Hero stepped out of the room and walked the hall to the arena gates. He wanted to listen to Abyssus but the Taint distracted him. *'Do you want to be trapped forever? What would they do if you fled to Tir Na Nog? The Council would search for you. Isis would find you. She always does. Better to kill one or two people than condemn everyone you love.'*

He clenched his eyes shut. *I don't want to hurt them. They've been good friends.*

The Taint manifested itself as a copy of him and spoke at his side. "It's okay. I'll do it for you."

The arena gate opened, and Hero crossed the terrain to meet Syo halfway. Above them, a crowd cheered, and the High King and Queen calmed them to give a speech.

Khnum spoke to the people. "Welcome all, to the Astor Tournament finale. Today, I shall crown one of these two princes as my successor. May the better leader prevail!"

The crowd responded with a cacophonous din.

Syo sighed as he faced his friend. "This is it, huh? We can still settle this, Hero. I know I was opposed to marriage before, but this is different. You're important to Luna and me."

Khnum opened out his hands to his audience. "Let the match begin!"

Hero and Syo drew their blades.

"I want that too," Hero said.

Syo smiled with palpable relief. "We can stop this then. You're with us?"

Hero smiled back. "Yes, of course."

Syo waved his hand to draw the High King's attention. "He won't be able to hear us from down here. Let's go together." As he moved closer, Hero advanced and thrust his sword through Syo's heart. He pressed the blade deep until the grip pressed firmly against Syo's chest.

Syo pressed against Hero's hand as blood coursed down the sword, and then collapsed on top of Hero.

Hero held his friend's warm corpse, stained with his blood as everyone watched. The audience chatted among themselves. For them, it probably seemed anticlimactic, but for a few on the benches, like Luna, it brought confusion. They were too far to hear the conversation between Hero and Syo or to understand what had happened.

Hero brought his hand to the back of Syo's head and held him. "It's over now. You don't have to fight anymore."

A large tear fell from the bridge of Syo's nose as he shook. "How could you?"

Hero's fugue state broke. When he came to, the aftermath of their fight lay out in the open, but he knew not how they'd arrived at this conclusion. The odor of blood and the sight of his friend's corpse made everything hazy. Knots formed in his stomach as he took in the gruesome scene.

The Taint consoled him. '*He did it for you and Luna. He sacrificed himself. What a selfless boy.*'

The sound of Khnum's announcements and the din of the crowd went far away. Everything in Hero's world turned gray with spots of red—blood and miasma.

Tears streamed from his eyes as his fingers turned black with the Taint. "Why?"

'*It was meant to be this way.*'

Hero lurched upright, making a strangled sound as he fought to breathe. He sweated profusely and quivered. The dream had ended.

Fate sat on a chair by the foot of the bed and opened her eyes. She raised her brows as if to show subtle surprise, though her expression remained calm.

He gripped his head. "It's a lie."

She folded her hands. "What's a lie?"

"That's not what happened!"

"Why are you yelling? I'm not accusing you of anything, nor am I upset by it."

Her calmness only irritated him more. "Because it's a lie."

"You said yourself that you killed him. This shouldn't be a surprise."

He smacked the covers. "That's not what I meant!"

She glanced at his hand and then into his eyes again. "What *did* you mean then?"

He pressed a hand against his chest as he tried reasoning with her. "I blamed myself. They were so good to me. I should have just married her. It never should have happened."

"Okay. Why didn't you?"

He fumbled for words. His cheeks flushed as he repeated the question to himself. "Something would have gone wrong."

"Like what?"

"I don't know. Something. Something always does. The Stain—"

"Why do you personify the Stain... or the Taint, whatever you want to call it?"

Hero chewed the skin off his lip. "I don't like to talk about it."

She spoke calmly, without any change of tone, expression, or any gesticulation, and sank into her chair with complete relaxation. "Abyssus always knew how to help you because you trusted in him. I need the same kind of trust. Otherwise, I can't help you."

He fought for words.

"To repeat Abyssus's question.... *What is the nature of the Taint?*"

"Whenever I feel something, good or bad, he's there. I get this overwhelming pressure to make bad choices and do terrible things. It becomes enjoyable for me to watch others struggle."

Fate sat up and forward on her chair. "Miasma is spiritual blood. Like regular blood, it holds no ability to compel people to do things. Miasma, by itself, can't force you to make immoral decisions. If anything, it's there to show that you have a deep wound, a fracture." She reached out and pressed a hand over his heart. "That fracture is the result of this other person... this other you. The Taint is only a sign of your illness, not a cause."

"What are you trying to say? That I'm doing these things myself? I would never wish ill upon others."

She withdrew her hand and waved it to one side, balling it up as if collecting something. "Let's say that the fracture brought out two different sides. One of them is the original you...." She waved her other hand and balled that one up too. "...and the other one is the new you. Maybe one of them was created to protect the other one. What's his name?"

He ground his teeth. "I don't know."

She tapped her chin. "Maybe we should give him one."

He clicked his tongue at her. '*Some nerve.*'

She smiled despite his outward disapproval. "My goal is to uncover the reason behind this fracture and help put those two pieces back together. In order to do this, you must be able to accept that the bad things happening in your life are of your own doing."

"Miasma might be blood but it carries disease to others."

Fate nodded. "This is true. However, it's not the cause of *your* ailment, just a result. You can control it by learning to cope with your wounds. That is, if we can uncover the cause of those wounds. What's the significance of the silver horse?"

Hero felt a pang in his chest and the miasma inside him writhed. "I don't know."

"Then we'll just have to draw it out, won't we?"

His lip twitched.

Fate lit the candle on her bed stand again and let the aroma waft through the room. "Deeper now." She took his hand and dragged him toward the hallway.

The six doors appeared on the other side rather than the usual palace hall.

He examined the blue door, which creaked open on his right side. This one had a silver embellishment of a violin.

Fate led him again, this time to that blue door. The hallway behind them broke away behind their feet as they leapt through the new doorway and into another memory.

Snowflakes drifted from outside the bay window of the music room, where Hero sat listening to a violinist playing in the community. She had been visiting and earning her pay on the streets even during the cold weather, so he liked to sit and listen while he studied.

Isis read a book on the lounge sofa before a cup of steaming tea. She noticed his consistent interest in the woman outside and rested her book on her lap. "You like music?"

"I like it, but father says it's a waste of time."

"Did you look at the book I brought you?"

"I memorized all the notes."

She turned her attention towards the door for a moment and then smiled at him. "Would you like to play now? Your father won't be home until this evening."

Hero examined the white piano across the room, which had been left untouched since his father banned music studies several months prior. When his mother was alive, she played every day, though he didn't remember the sound. He enjoyed the challenge of writing music, and how much emotion it conveyed, even without words.

Isis swapped her book for her teacup. "Weren't you working on a piece?"

"Yes. It's called A Wistful Melody."

"Interesting." She teased. "Will you also write A Blissful Melody?"

"I don't think so." He brushed a hand over his study book and quirked back one side of his mouth in discontent. "I'm not sure I'll continue at all."

"Why's that?"

"My father said he wants to sell the piano."

Her brow knotted and the teacup clattered to the small dish in her hand. "What? That piano belonged to Elaine. I'm getting tired of that man. Wait here. I'll be back shortly." She placed down her cup and disappeared in a sweep of her coat.

Hero crossed the room and touched the edge of the piano. He always thought that if he weren't a prince, he'd want to be a musician or an astronomer, but these feelings displeased his father more than anything.

Music... or space... I like them both.

Niteo considered these activities unfit for royalty. By his standards, if Hero were properly trained, he'd never wish for more than the Capital Throne.

At times, Isis agreed with him, though her reasons differed entirely. She had told Hero that if he became High King, he could punish everyone who imprisoned him, including his father.

Hero wasn't sure that he wanted to punish anyone. If he could earn the freedom to follow his own path, he'd be happy enough. He sat down on the bench, tucked his hands under his legs, and reviewed his notes.

The Taint pestered him. *'She's right, you know. Some people don't know their place. A Rahma imprisoning an Ancient? You're much more than that, Leoht. Ah, what a sickening world.'*

"You're wrong," Hero said, drawing his shoulders in.

Isis returned, accompanied by the violinist from the community, and she offered the girl tea as they sat down in the lounge.

Hero gawked at the violinist from the piano bench, stiff as a post. He so rarely met with people from the outside that it stunned him Isis had even thought to invite the violinist inside. As it was, he hardly had the opportunity to meet with Abyssus, and *he* was the Second Prince of Nex.

Isis did as she pleased out of spite. As a Council follower and an Ancient queen, Niteo couldn't have stopped her anyway. "If it is of any interest, I'd like to offer you a job here at the palace when the King is away. You would be kept safe from the cold and treated as a guest."

The young woman watched Hero from her seat on the sofa opposite of Isis, her light hair pale as flax despite the fact that she was just a Rahma girl. "What kind of job?"

"The Prince is interested in studying music. He has grown fond of listening to you play, but the King refuses to permit his studies as a musician."

The girl's hands trembled at the mention of crossing the king.

Isis narrowed her eyes briefly as she examined the frightened musician, then offered a bright smile and a soothing voice to quell her concerns. "I am the Queen of Askedel, a loyal Council member, and I am responsible for the well-being of our young prince. The King will not hear of this, and if he does, I will take full responsibility, you have my word."

"What would you have me do? I'm a violinist, but I see a piano here. Does he have an interest in learning violin?"

Isis slid a teacup over the table and passed over a dish of caramel. It was her favorite sweet, and one she made often. She had offered it to Hero on numerous occasions, so he recognized it as her most successful bargaining tool.

The scent baffled him too much ever to try it, but their guest accepted both offerings.

Isis questioned Hero with a smile. "What do you think?" Sometimes she went out of her way to perform random acts of kindness. This always surprised him, as no one wanted to be near him, let alone express generosity toward him.

Hero glanced at his incomplete notes. Violin would be a good addition to his piece. If he worked hard enough, he could be king *and* a musician. He might even compose a symphony. The thought brought a smile to his face. "I want to learn. Please teach me."

The Rahma Girl emitted an air of contentment. "I'm so glad my music could reach you from here. My name is Priscilla. I live in Elysium with my younger brother."

Isis looked at the girl with genuine surprise. "You came all the way from Elysium to play music here?"

Priscilla blushed. "I heard there are a lot of nobles here in Nitor. I don't make enough money in Elysium. Our parents passed away a long time ago due to miasma poisoning, so it's my job to care for my brother now." The young woman virtually glided through the room in her blue gown and sat down on the bench. "How old are you?"

"Ten," he answered.

"My brother is ten, though it's not really the same."

"No." Isis held her pleasant tone.

"He doesn't have an interest in music, so I'm happy to share with someone else. We'll need to get you a violin."

"I can get him one," Isis said, calmly sipping her tea.

Priscilla clapped her hands together. "Great! When should we start his lessons?"

"How about tomorrow? I'd like you to come with me to buy a violin. We can discuss your pay on the way. I'll more than double whatever you make on the street."

It flustered Hero to know that Isis did this of her own accord and with her own money.

Priscilla shot up from the bench and bowed, causing the soft ringlet curls in her hair to spill over her shoulder. "Thank you for your generosity."

Isis patted the air. "No need to thank me. You'll be paid for your work, no? Thank only your talent for bringing you here on this cold day." She straightened the skirt of her gown as she stood and collected her coat. "Follow me. Hero, finish your studies before your father returns home. I shall bring Priscilla and your violin back tomorrow."

He nodded at her and waved back at Priscilla after noticing her kind gesture. Although the Royals kept his condition secret from the community, some people had caught on to the fact that those who entered the palace rarely came out.

Priscilla's visit made him anxious.

On occasion, the King brought in new servants, and they would bustle around tending to duties until they learned the truth of serving in the palace. Everyone who lived in there knew of the danger Hero posed to them, because they had seen many others perish before their eyes.

He sat down at the window again and focused on his studies, but shouts from downstairs soon distracted him—not uncommon when it came to a visit from Abyssus. His friend typically appeared without warning—not too often, just often enough for Hero to grow attached to him.

Hero rushed down to the main hall and broke up the argument between Abyssus and Lara. "Why do you two always fight? Stop it."

The Taint chuckled. *'They're fighting over us. It's just a display of affection. You should praise it, not abhor it.'*

Lara fixed her uniform and tossed a braid over her shoulder. No one ever knew why she had such a high tolerance for miasma. It certainly influenced her temperament, yet never affected her health.

"Oh, hey, Hero," Abyssus said, sucking on a colorful, swirling candy as big as his head. He usually appeared messy despite his expensive clothing. That day, his shirt stuck out on one side of his shorts, and even his wavy hair stuck up in every direction. Strangely, he still seemed put together, as though this messiness was completely intentional. He pushed his candy towards Hero's face. "Want some?"

"Uh...." Before he could say no, Abyssus put the end of it in Hero's mouth and grinned.

Should I take this gesture of sharing spit as an act of kindness?

Lara exploded. "That's so rude! Don't just shove things at his face! You just had that in your mouth!" She ripped the candy from Abyssus' hand and chucked it to the floor. It shattered into hundreds of colorful pieces and shot across the marble.

For a moment, Hero and Abyssus stared open-mouthed at the mess, and then Abyssus cocked back his arm, thrust his fist, and struck Lara's nose.

Her eyes filled with tears as she grasped her face.

Hero held his breath. *Oh... my father is going to kill me when he finds out about this.*

The Taint erupted with laughter. *'Well deserved!'*

Firmus's voice boomed as he stormed into the hall. "Abyssus!"

Startled, Hero hid behind his friend. He felt nervous around Firmus and didn't know how to talk to him. They rarely met unless Abyssus was involved.

Firmus leaned down and pressed a hand on Lara's shoulder. "Are you all right? What happened?"

She wept and jutted a finger at her aggressor. "He hit me!"

Firmus cast a look of dread at Abyssus. "Why?"

Hero peeked out from Abyssus's side, concealing a grin with his friend's arm. "She broke his candy."

When her hand moved from her face, a stream of blood poured down her lips. "Why are you defending him?"

"But it's true," Hero insisted.

She sobbed. "He hit me even though I'm a girl!"

Abyssus turned up his nose and snubbed her. "It'd be sexist *not* to hit you."

Firmus's brow twitched. "Abyssus, apologize to her."

Abyssus stomped a foot. "No!"

Lara wiped her face with her apron. "What a jerk."

Abyssus waved his arms angrily. "*I'm* a jerk? *You* started it!"

Firmus bellowed and his voice echoed through the wide hall. "Abyssus, enough! Go and play with Hero while I take care of Lara."

Lara whined, "Why does *he* get to play with Hero? He should be in trouble!"

Firmus sighed as he turned Lara towards the servant's quarters and led her away. "Let's get you cleaned up."

Abyssus dragged Hero into the study and slammed the door. He sat while Abyssus paced around, shouting and stomping, which he always did when mad. "Firmus is such a do-gooder! One punch won't kill her, and what's wrong with sharing? Augh!"

Hero disliked germs and disorder, so he understood Lara's reasoning, but he cherished Abyssus, so he took well to the gesture despite his surprise. "It's fine. Although I usually dislike germs, yours are probably okay."

Abyssus stopped pacing and sat down next to Hero in the armchair. "Hey, is Isis here?"

"No, why?"

"I don't think she likes me." He sank back onto the chair.

Hero, knowing himself well enough, tucked his hands under his legs. If he didn't focus, he would accidentally touch Abyssus's face or hand in an effort to be closer to him. "I don't see why she wouldn't."

"Maybe she's jealous!"

Hero smiled instead of laughing, since he still didn't fully understand what Abyssus meant. "Of what?"

"Because you like me more than her! Am I right?" Abyssus stuck a foot under his leg, occupying so much space on the chair that Hero had to sit in a ball.

"Hmm...." Hero swayed from side to side, teasing Abyssus with his delayed answer.

"Hey, you actually have to think about it?"

The feelings that brewed sometimes shook Hero to the core. "Is there anyone I like more?"

Abyssus started to nudge Hero's head and stopped mid-action.

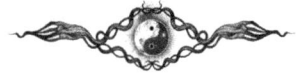

The shelves in the library flickered, and though the young Abyssus remained against Hero's side, an older, much taller Abyssus stood in front of the chair, staring down.

"*Ein agat*," he said.

'It's a map.'

Hero rubbed his eyes and shook his head for clarity.

A map?

A woman clutched his shoulder from behind. "There you are!"

He brushed off her hand. "*Farun ya?*"

'Who are you?'

"Try and remember. I've been looking for you."

Both versions of Abyssus dissipated into particles of light.

The woman plucked Hero from the chair and placed him on the floor. Her gaze seemed intense and judging, so he avoided it as much as she could. "You're dreaming. We're in your Dreamscape right now. This is the second door."

It struck him. He finally remembered her identity. "Mistress. The Spinner! No, Fate."

She gripped him by the chin and forcibly met his gaze. "Get it together. What did Abyssus say to you?"

Hero tilted his head as much as he could in her grip. "He said, *it's a map*. I don't know what he meant. What's going on? How did he—"

"I don't have time to explain. It's easy to get lost in the Dreamscape. Don't wander. If you keep this up, we'll never get out of here." She reached out and scooped him up in her arms. Her suddenness surprised him so much he stiffened as she strode forward and kicked open the door.

"Do you know how long I searched for you before you remembered me?" She passed through the main hall and kicked open the entrance with her heeled boots. This led to a large pool of water so clear that it reflected the stars above like a mirror.

Hero clung tightly to her shoulders so he wouldn't fall. "What's that? What are you talking about?"

"I need you to focus. We have to get through all these doors to put you back together." She placed him on his feet, held his hand, and pulled him along as they jumped feet first into the pool of space.

8
THE DREAMSCAPE

Fate and Hero sank into the pool of space, creating trails of smoke instead of bubbles in their descent. As their feet touched the bottom of the sea of darkness, she pulled him closer by the hand. "We only have so much time before the effect of the candles wears off, so we should at least travel to the next door safely. You're not finished with this memory yet."

A new hallway stretched out, reflecting light from the cosmos above. Stars radiated dim light across their path as they trudged through the water towards a white haze in the distance.

Hero had forgotten the struggle of being physically ten. "How are any of these memories going to help? Right now, it just seems like we're visiting the worst points of my life."

She gripped his arm. "They clearly mean something, or we wouldn't see them. It's my job to read between the lines so we can break the Council's seals. The memories themselves might not seem relevant but, if they result in us breaking the seal, we can hopefully uncover the reason behind your fracture and this taint."

"Tell me again, how did you learn this?"

"Akira has a friend who's an expert at traveling and manipulating the Dreamscape. He explained that our ability is different than Farseeing. We're more like spirit guides."

"I can only hope we resolve all of this before it's too late," he said, thinking of all the people who had been lost. If there existed a reason for this other him, he wished to uncover it and make himself whole again... before anyone else suffered at his hands.

Fate pulled him along from ahead to help him wade more quickly through the water. When they reached the haze, her expression relaxed. "All right, let's find out what happened with the violinist. This should lead you farther ahead of your last memory."

He nodded.

Hero entered the music room next to the moonlit window, where Priscilla stood in her coat, gazing outside. Lights from the community shone distantly off the snow, much like the stars grew hazy and small in the night sky.

The moment came rushing back at him.

Priscilla had noticed how his father had treated him and interrogated him to find out how long he'd been subjected to such negligence. That night, she asked if Hero wanted to return to Elysium with her and escape his life at the palace.

She tossed her hair from her coat and spoke low. "Make sure you wear a dark cloak when you leave. We won't have much time to get you out. After the entrance closes, come to my side. The moon isn't out tonight, so we'll be able to sneak you by the guards if you stick close. Leave from the side yard. I'll wait for a moment before I approach the gates."

Hero passed over her violin and exited the music room first to collect his cloak from the chair at his desk. He snatched it and threw it over his head and shoulders.

Every time Priscilla left, she ran into Lara in the main hall, which gave him time to slip through the celebration hall and in through the sparring hall next to Lara's room without detection.

He ran down the back steps and crept by in a lowered position, while Lara cheerily greeted Priscilla and asked about her music. The back door rested at the end of the sparring hall, and so did Isis, waiting attentively.

He slid to a stop in front of her. "Isis...."

She readjusted from her leaning position against the door and stood upright. "Where are you going?"

"The study," he said, glancing at the tapestry of the Moon Drips.

"In your cloak?" The clacking of her heels echoed as she walked. She bent down to meet his gaze with a lustrous smile. "Remember, Hero, I know when you're lying... because I can feel your mind racing." She poked his chest.

He said nothing; Isis knew him too well for him to try another lie.

She exhaled and stepped away from the door, allowing him passage. "Be warned. When you leave the palace, you will no longer have the seals to mask your aura. If you aren't careful, that girl and her brother might turn on you. They still don't know about your condition."

He grasped the bands around his fingers. "I brought the other suppressants. It should be enough."

"I hope for your sake that's true. I will not stop you. Some things in life must be experienced."

He left the palace with his eyes fixed on her, and lingered in the side courtyard while Priscilla finished her discussion with Lara.

When the entrance doors closed, Priscilla drew him close to her side and walked straight past the guards as she always did.

One of the men reached out and grabbed her arm. "Wait."

The arm she had wrapped around Hero grew rigid and her hand clutched his side as she faced the palace guard. "Yes?"

"Miss, it's very dark out tonight. It isn't safe to pass through the woods. I'd urge you to stay in Nex for a while longer."

A kind smile lit her face. "Thank you for your concern. The Western Woods are surprisingly bright at night. You should pass through some time. It can be quite magical."

"Are you sure?"

She waved at him. "I'm positive. Besides, I can't leave my brother home alone. He'll wonder what happened to me."

"I know the feeling. Please be safe on your journey." The guard released her arm.

Priscilla continued ahead with her natural pace. The lights in the community reflected from the vapor in the air, which glowed extremely bright around the buildings and the snow. She avoided this and headed towards the wooded area, growing some distance from Hero the quicker she walked.

She clutched his wrist when they entered the trees and lit a torch by cracking it against a boulder. "Come quickly. We must skirt the Eastern Woods before we can cross into the Western

Woods. The guard was right—it can be quite dangerous on nights like this. My brother will begin to worry if we don't get back soon, and I don't want him outside when that woman is lurking around. Stay very close. When we cross the border of Elysium, we must make haste for home. The Queen goes hunting at night, but don't worry, she won't cross into the light of the Eastern Woods."

They treaded the narrow path between the Western and Eastern Woods where the long elegant trees of Elysium met the gnarled vines blocking safe passage into Rosetau. Golden orbs of anima rose from the vines, faintly glowing before disappearing into the night air. Strange sounds carried on the breeze, giving the Eastern Woods an ever-more ominous feel.

Hero eyed the tangle of vines and ran his hand through the glowing orbs. "Don't you wonder what happened in there?"

"Shh, you need to be very quiet through here. We don't want to alert the Queen."

Hero staggered along behind her for what seemed like forever, struggling to keep up with her long strides. He fixated on the way her torch danced in the darkness and observed the handle, recalling that Abyssus had worked with a team of Capital officials to invent it. It contained fuel in the grip and, when triggered, usually with some amount of force, it could burn all night. To defuse it, one could apply the cap and retrigger the torch until it ran out of oil.

Hero had once overheard an official talking to Abyssus like an adult as they'd attempted to bribe him for a blueprint. They couldn't afford his services, though, as he needed a lot of money to buy his sister's freedom.

The memory of his friend reminded him that once he left Nex, they'd be apart. A wave of guilt and anxiety struck as Priscilla lifted him over a log and pulled him away from the dark branches of the Eastern Woods.

I should have helped him. What am I doing? How could I leave Abyssus without saying anything?

The Taint agreed. *'Really. That boy does everything for you. Leoht, you surprise me. I didn't think you were the type to abandon your friends.'* He laughed. *'We are of one mind, after all.'*

He jerked free from Priscilla's grip. "No!"

She stopped and turned back, reaching for his hand. "Hero, what's wrong? We must hurry."

He continued looking back towards Nex as they drew farther and farther away from home. The weight of anxiety in his chest asphyxiated him as his thoughts filled with doubt. It only eroded as he noticed the sky full of stars. Viewing them put him at ease again. If he hadn't known better, Elysium would have seemed a pleasant place to travel. There were so many trees it was almost impossible to see the buildings, and their structures intertwined with the woods.

Priscilla lived in a small home on the farthest edge of the community. A lantern lit the doorway, where a small figure waited. They walked up the stone path to the entrance.

Immediately upon Priscilla's return, her brother barked, "It's so late, I thought that the fiends had definitely gotten ahold of you!"

She patted her brother's head of champagne-colored hair. "I'm sorry, but lower your voice. We have a guest."

He clammed up and set a pair of big blue eyes on Hero. "Is that...."

She removed her scarf, looking uncharacteristically graven as she returned to her brother a second time. "Listen to me, you can't tell anyone that he's here. This is Prince Hero of Nitor. He has run away from home and come to live with us for now. You must be polite."

Her brother covered his mouth and ran in place. "You're a real prince?"

Hero nodded.

"That's so cool!"

Priscilla took off her coat and picked up the books and trinkets strewn around their small family room. "If it was cool, he wouldn't have to run away from home."

The architecture fascinated Hero despite its diminutive size. The stairway wound around the tree trunk from which it was built. The windows were long and shielded with lattice. Even the furniture was built into the home itself.

Priscilla's brother beamed. "Oh, right. I'm Myles. Can I call you by name?"

Hero's focus trailed from their home to Myles. He stood silently, waiting for the introduction to process in his head. "Ah, yes. Sorry."

Myles seemed to Hero a normal child—loud, pouty, and full of questions. "Why are you sorry? You're weird."

Priscilla chided him. "Don't call him weird. He's an Ancient and our elder. You should learn to be respectful."

Myles cocked his head to the side and skeptically eyed Hero.

"For now, why don't you two go to Myles's room. You can stay there with him until we figure out a more comfortable living arrangement."

Myles gripped Hero's arm. "Why? It'll be fun if we share!"

Priscilla seemed tired. "We don't know what he's comfortable with yet."

"Come on. Come up and see my room!" Myles dashed off, pulling Hero upstairs by the arm.

Hero caught his balance by grasping the railing, which formed from the branches of the tree and extended up the staircase in swirling patterns and designs.

"Hero!" Priscilla leaned against the rail, gazing up as Hero watched her over the curved banister. With a smile, she said. "I hope you're happier here than in Nex. It might be hard at first, but we'll figure everything out."

Hero broke free from Myles to walk down and pass her a pouch.

"What's this?"

"It's all the money I had saved. I know it's hard for you to raise Myles, so if you have me here, it'll be even more difficult. Now, you don't have a job at the palace either. It's not a lot, but you can have it."

Priscilla peeked inside and rubbed his head with a smile. "Don't worry. We'll get along fine. Maybe we'll even raise enough money to move away from here. Wouldn't that be nice? No more worrying about the Queen or your father's guards. Now, hurry along with Myles to bed. Don't worry about a thing. That's a job for adults."

"Thank you, Priscilla."

As soon as Hero was within reach again, Myles dragged him off to the room.

The design there was interesting too. It had a loft and many built-in shelves full of books that Hero had never read. Though they seemed a touch simple for his taste, he rarely got his hands on fiction.

Myles waved his arms. "Welcome to my room! If you want, you can sleep in the loft!"

"May I read the books in here?"

"You like books? What do you play at the palace?"

"Play? I don't play a lot, only with my friend, Abyssus. Chess or cards...."

"That's boring! You know, I sometimes pretend I'm a prince, but I've never met one."

Hero scanned the bookshelves for something of interest. "What about the Prince here?"

"Prince Syo? He doesn't talk to anyone but his sister. Don't tell anyone I said so, but he's kind of scary."

"You're not afraid of me?"

Myles tossed his hands on his hips and tried on Hero's cloak. "Nope!"

While Myles played, Hero chose a book from the shelf called *Sands of Time*, a story based on Ancient folklore. In the loft, he sat down on colored cushions and opened it.

Myles sat near him and watched. "You read fast."

Hero said nothing, so Myles shortly fell asleep. The quiet room was so foreign, and its scent, crisp. After all that had happened, Hero held onto his guilt of leaving without notifying Abyssus or bringing him along.

Why does it bother me so much? It feels wrong to be without him.

He muttered. "Abyssus...."

"Do you have a crush on my brother or something?" A woman lay with her face propped-up against her hand in the window's light.

Hero suffered a silent wave of terror and rolled away from her, perching on his hands and knees against the railing of the loft. "*Farun ya?*"

'Who are you?'

She said, somewhat irritably. "Are you going to ask me that every time? I'm your wife."

He whispered back, "I'm ten!"

The woman rolled her eyes and groaned as she rocked her body into a sitting position. "Honestly, how deeply are your memories buried that you can't remember your wife? You're starting to trail off again. Snap out of it. You know who I am."

"A liar."

"I'm going to smack you. I'm your wife. We were married in the Capital after you turned eighteen. We've had intimate relations. We made a pact. Why is it getting harder to snap you out of this?"

Hero slid forward and checked her face in the moonlight, squinting. "We're married?"

"I keep telling you that. You're not ten. You're eighteen."

"You're pretty." He clapped as he got a good glimpse of her. "Oh, Abyssus! Now I remember. You're Cruentus Fate."

"I'm getting really mad." She flicked him between the eyes.

Hero grabbed his head. "Ow...."

"What am I going to do with you?" Her face grew tense as she mumbled to herself. "I have a duty to protect you. I can't let you fade away in here."

The stars zipped across the sky and night turned to day. This cycle repeated many times, causing the light to flash through the window.

Hero pressed his hands against the glass and watched. "What's happening?"

"The Dreamscape is changing. If you interact with them any more than this, I might not be able to wake you up."

When time stopped, daylight shone through the window. The sound of coughing arose from the first floor. Hero crept down the steps of the loft to Myles and reached out a hand to identify the source of his ailment.

Fate pulled him back and shook her head. "The Dreamscape is trying to evolve. All you can do is watch."

Myles lay in bed and coughed violently until his nose began to bleed.

Priscilla rushed to his side and gently pressed a wet handkerchief to his forehead.

Hero stood agape unable to help. He remembered apologizing at the time.

Priscilla turned her head with tears in her eyes. "It's not your fault... we've walked across that tree our whole lives."

It was at that moment that Hero remembered walking behind Myles on their way home. He remembered the way the miasma floated up from his body in tiny particles of red dust. The sound of the fallen tree they'd used as a bridge, suddenly cracking, rang in his ears and mixed with the shrill scream that Myles made when he hit the icy waters below.

Priscilla swallowed hard. "I would have lost him that day if you hadn't pulled him from the river."

Myles coughed harder and harder, his face turning red.

Hero watched on as his lips turned blue and he gasped for air.

Priscilla's cries and Myles gasps proved too much for Hero to bear, so he covered his ears in a tragic attempt to numb the pain.

Fate held Hero close and pulled his hands down from his head. "Do you remember what happened?"

Hero dropped his hand to his side. "The miasma."

The memory of Myles dissipated into fragments of light, and the door to the room swung open. The memory in the front room showed the time Hero spent with Myles and Priscilla, when things were still going well.

Priscilla had praised Hero's improvement with his violin lessons. She had more time to teach him when they lived together.

That memory scattered as well. Priscilla's corpse lay in the dim light, where Hero found her after her suicide. He never knew if the miasma simply drove her to madness or if she despaired so deeply over Myles's death that she wanted to die.

Myles and Priscilla had accepted Hero as family before they knew that he was tainted. They shared their food and belongings and brought him into their home—and he loved them.

He loved that Priscilla cared so deeply and earnestly.

He loved Myles for his normalcy.

That's why he lost them.

The entrance shot open and the gusts of the winter wind whistled by. Hero turned his palms up and watched the black stains grow. "I didn't mean to."

The Taint consoled him. *'All things that come to pass are meant to happen.'*

Fate gave him a slight pat on the back. "Go home."

The storms blew so hard outside, he could barely see on his way back through the woods. He spent hours paving his way back to Nex.

As he approached, Isis stood at the border, waiting patiently in a heavy coat. She didn't ask questions. She just opened her coat, drew him close to her side, and said, "Welcome home."

Hero didn't say anything to her about what had happened. He just gripped the skirt of her gown and sobbed into the fabric.

As the dream dissipated, Fate stood in Isis's place, staring at the stars now surrounding them. "It's okay. It's over."

Hero wiped his face with his sleeve. "Sorry."

She crouched down and brought her arms around him. "You don't have to cry anymore. It's time to wake up."

Hero awakened in the study and wiped a stream of tears from his eyes, the memory of Myles and Priscilla seared into his mind. These memories had always been present, but now they burned like fresh wounds.

Fate rose from the table, collected the candles, and opened the curtains. Without a word, she rushed around and put the objects away.

He watched curiously. "What's wrong?"

"We were in there for two days. I need to hurry and leave for my meeting in the Capital."

"Two... two days?" He sat up on the foot of the bed, watching as Fate exited the room.

She returned swiftly and kissed his head. "I'm sorry to be sudden. I did learn something from your Dreamscape, so don't worry." She passed by once more, tossing on her coat. "I promise to find an answer to this madness. Even though you don't understand now, I'll protect you."

She's behaving differently than usual.

The Taint corrected him. *'You mean suspiciously.'*

Fortis meandered in and stood by the table with his hands tucked back. "Your wife is on to something."

Hero's gaze still followed her even though she was long gone. "She's different somehow."

"Maybe she doesn't want you to notice."

"I can't imagine why," Hero said, standing from his chair.

Fortis realigned the strands of hair sweeping across Hero's forehead. "She has grown a lot. I'm sure she's just trying to protect you."

From what?

The clock in the front hall chimed as they stepped out of the room. It was already cold and the morning had only just begun. It was going to be a long day, indeed.

A WISTFUL MELODY

Hero spent the first day after Fate's departure reviewing paperwork from the Capital about her restoration plans. This included a description of her intentions to break down the border between the two communities in Nex and expand the palace.

On the second day, he lay in the main hall, staring at the ceiling for hours, until Fortis broke his focus.

The tall Ignis stood over Hero and watched him. "I never thought I'd see you on the floor. What are you doing?"

"I've laid a blanket down, of course. I know exactly what I'm going to do here."

"Where?"

"There," Hero said, pointing at the ceiling. "Come with me. We're going to destroy the roof and create a sun window, or in my preference, an astral viewing window."

"A what?"

"You'll see. Where did that old man stash the sledgehammer?"

"I'm starting to see why he stashed it in the first place." Fortis clenched his fists and feigned a punch, then added, "and why use a sledgehammer when you've got Ignis force?"

Hero pulled Fortis outside by the wrists. "That's good enough."

They set up a ladder in the side courtyard, and climbed onto the flat platform along the exterior of the palace until they arrived at the right spot.

Hero inspected the target area on the roof tiles while waving his hand around to measure the distance, as he envisioned the window he wished to create. "This seems right."

"I hope you're right."

"I'm mostly never wrong," he said, averting his gaze in dismay of this declaration.

Fortis squinted and pursued his lips the way he might have if he had tasted something sour. "I sense some contradiction in your words."

"It's probably fine," Hero insisted, waving his hand in a flippant display.

"You're making me nervous. Stop using words that make you sound uncertain."

Hero grinned, hoping to reinforce an air of confidence.

Fortis cried out. "What's with that face? Fate is going to kill me if I make a mess of the palace!"

"Just blame it on me. She'll forgive us... probably." He had permission to destroy and rebuild anything he liked, so he wasn't particularly concerned, but Fortis's reactions amused him anyway. "Let's just have fun with it. Sometimes things don't go well the first time, but if you keep at it, you'll eventually find a way to succeed."

"You're strangely optimistic."

"Because of Fate." If nothing else, Hero believed in Fate's unparalleled tenacity towards his survival. She seemed hell-bent on breaking the seals without his demise, which often made him curious about her motives. *If she's really awake, then why is she so obstinate about stirring my memories? I'm forgetting something.*

The Taint murmured. *'I know something you don't... but I won't tell you, not until you give me what I want.'*

Hero frowned.

Fortis charged his elemental energy into his hands and struck the roof with such force, the palace rumbled.

Hero glanced down at the panicked guards, wondering if he should have warned them. Now it seemed too late, and they usually insulted him anyway. He moved some of the debris with his boot and dusted off the space he needed to map out the frame of the window. For a long time, his bond with Fortis vaguely resembled that of a stepmother and her adopted child, though Hero had refuted it during childhood.

Fortis stretched his arm and peered down into the main hall. "Hey, I think we cracked the marble."

"Yeah, don't worry. I'm tearing that up too."

"You're trying to usurp the Calamity."

Hero ignored the issue of the marble and the snarky comment. "While I was away, I had the chance to speak with King Askelon about the Spinner. He says the Spinner can't be infected by miasma because of the amount of anima she radiates." He knelt and flipped a piece of the rubble in his hand. "In a way, she's completely immune to my ailment."

Fortis plunked down on the broken tiles and exhaled into the cold air. "Then you make the perfect match."

Hero placed down the rubble with a clack and raised his hands, open-palmed, to both sides of his face. "Can you see them?"

"You're referring to the stains?"

Hero lowered his hands again and stared. "I hear that some people can control it. I don't know why, but everything I touch crumbles. Why did I turn out like this?"

Fortis hung his hands over his knees as he looked down into the main hall. His usual blithe expression disappeared, leaving behind someone thoughtful and empathetic. "I wish I could tell you, Hero. You've been like this for as long as I can remember... but I'm sure someone out there knows why you're spiritually fractured, and I'm sure Fate is trying to understand it as we speak." He stood and dusted off his pants. "Even supposing that you and Fate weren't intended Bound, that doesn't change how you feel in this present moment. You two must be connected in some way, or else your condition would likely worsen."

This eased Hero's nerves substantially. "You really think so?"

"I do. I believe that no matter what the truth is, it'll eventually come out."

Now, with his worries quelled, Hero focused on his work. He climbed down the ladder, smiling. "We need metal for a frame. Would you go on an errand for me?"

Fortis leaned over the edge of the rooftop and shouted. "For our king? Naturally."

Hero clapped the dust from his hands and reentered the main hall to sweep up some of the debris.

While he was cleaning, Isis stepped through the front doors and lowered a pale green scarf from her head. "What in the world happened here? Did a meteor strike the palace?"

He raised his head. "I'm the meteor."

"What are you trying to accomplish?"

"Renovation."

Isis cast a perplexed look around the destroyed roof, and finally shed her surprise. "Where's the Queen?"

"Fate? She's at a meeting with Lady Heqet."

"What for?"

Hero shrugged. "I didn't ask."

"You're the King of Nitor. You should be much more vigilant about these things. There's still a murderer on the loose, you know."

"If you'd recall, they'd decided that Sally was responsible for the murders."

One corner of her mouth curled up. "But you're smarter than that, aren't you? You don't really believe it was her any more than I do."

Hero disliked that she saw through him. "But I don't know who it is, either, so I mustn't be *that* smart."

She waved a finger. "The truth always finds its way into the light."

"Frankly, I've lost interest in solving the murders. It has become a hindrance and a concern for my family's well-being. How can I worry about a murderer when my miasma is doing just as much harm? I'm tired of people trying to protect me. For once, I want to protect the people I care about. I just wish I knew how."

Isis sounded unsure about his decision. "So, you've decided to stay in the palace to avoid hurting others? What good will *that* do, if it spreads through the air, like it does with that devil of a man they call Akira?"

"I intend to renovate the palace with crystal. That way, the miasma will be suppressed as long as I'm inside."

Her eye twitched. "*Crystal?* The seal broke?"

"Only the second. Why? You're not going to tell anyone, are you?"

Isis displayed a small frown. "Of course not. Who do you think I am? You know that you're very precious to me. My goal is to protect you, not have you erased for a crime you didn't commit."

The weight lifted from his shoulders, and he cracked a smile. "Thanks."

"I never liked this place anyway," she said, scrutinizing the hall. "I'm looking forward to seeing the renovations."

The time of their quarreling had long since passed. Some time ago, he had still been prickly about it, but understood that if Isis wished only to serve the Council in these matters, she'd never have allowed him to break the rules as he did.

She pulled the ends of her scarf to cover her shoulders, then checked her surroundings before walking closer and gesturing for Hero to follow her into the study. Once they entered, she sealed the room with a barrier.

He grew tense, cornered in the room and unsure of the intent behind her actions.

Her blue eyes canvassed his face. "Is it true that the second seal has broken?"

"Yes... Why?"

"How and why did this happen?"

"I don't know. I've been having dreams...." Hero trailed off at the thought of his Dreamscape.

Isis pried. "Dreams?"

"More specifically, I had a dream that I was cooped up in some room with a puzzle box. I couldn't figure out how to open it... but eventually, I realized, I needed light and darkness. In my dream, I could fuse them. When the box opened, space overflowed from inside and covered everything it touched. It was beautiful... and magical."

"Is that all?"

"Yes... but my Dreamscape has the same cosmos inside. There's an entire ocean of stars. I wonder what it could mean."

Isis's expression shrank. "Hero, I know that your memory is hazy, but if the third seal breaks, you will die. You're traveling the Dreamscape? With Fati?"

"Her name is Fate," Hero said, tilting his head to one side.

Isis furrowed her brow. "They are one and the same. You must know this."

He knew.

"Why are you doing this?"

"To better understand myself."

The Taint snickered. *'Yes, let's understand each other, Leoht.'*

"It isn't worth the gamble. It isn't worth your life."

"I understand." Hero glanced at the broom in his grip. "By the way, did you come here for something? You seemed to be in search of Fate."

Isis pulled her scarf closer again. "I came to see you... but this situation with the seals breaking has concerned me. I'll be checking in again soon."

Hero scratched his head. He shouldn't have mentioned the crystal, but it had already been over a turn since the second seal broke. It seemed so long to him that he assumed it must be common knowledge.

If Isis hadn't been so occupied with her queenly duties, she would have noticed straight away.

"It's nice to see you're doing well," she said. "I'll head out again. Feel free to call upon me whenever you like."

He continued sweeping after her departure, until he remembered the brief appearance of the older Abyssus in the Dreamscape. On the day Abyssus died, he had said the same thing. As he lay in Hero's arms, pouring out blood, he mouthed, *"Ein agat,"* but Hero had been too stunned by the attack to pay it any mind.

Now that he had thought of it, he dropped the broom and ran upstairs. It was probable that Abyssus left some kind of map within his journals.

Hero dug through his room around the desk, in the dresser, and all around his bed. He also checked both studies thoroughly, and even the King's Suite, where he and Fate were supposed to be staying, but he couldn't find them and returned to sweeping.

Where are they? What did she do with them? I should have asked before she left.

Hero found little point in continuing his search until Fate returned, so he lounged about and waited for Fortis.

When Fortis finally returned with the supplies, they focused on creating a metal frame for the new skylight.

The little tasks helped Hero rediscover what his life was like before meeting Fate. He tampered with the domed frame on the floor in the main hall. The project gave him time to think over his behavior and reconsider his current situation. He couldn't leave Fate to deal with all the work on her own. He thought he should at least attempt to solve the murders.

"Fortis, can you send a message to Fate?"

Fortis raised his gaze. "Yes, of course. What would you like me to send?"

"*Ein agat. Ulr en gual?*"

'*It's a map. Where's the writing?*'

"I'll get it to her right away," he vowed. He rose from his knee and exited the hall.

Hero's memories held the answers to their problems. As much as he wanted to avoid digging any deeper, he accepted that, for the sake of the Empire, he not only needed to dig, but a lot faster.

He carried the metal frame to the roof in pieces and attached it after executing the proper cleaning and buffering. A few feet from the window, he raised his hands and conjured the crystal glass in a laborious, yet rewarding, process. His element formed patterns and swirls above the main hall.

Thoughts of the future ahead filled his mind throughout the day. He worked in a trance, all the while carrying the realization of what might happen in the upcoming months.

The Taint prodded at him, excited by the prospect of freedom. Breaking the seals also meant dealing with him.

But Fate said that he isn't the Taint. He's a part of me.

In the evening, as night fell and stars filled the sky, Hero sat down in the main hall and watched through the window.

Since childhood, he'd loved to study space and compose music. However, his father had never allowed him to explore those fields. With Niteo gone, he now had the freedom to do as he pleased. Only fear of the Taint held him down, and he lacked the confidence to face it.

He stood and trekked up the stairs to the music room, where the gleaming white piano lay in wait. The palace had grown so quiet, with everyone that had filled the halls either having died or fled.

His music notes for A Wistful Melody rested on the piano, untouched since the night Fate saw him working several turns prior. The sheets contained his heartfelt thoughts and emotions, what little had remained after the Council placed the seals.

Music helped him connect to the Taint's knowledge and memories without facing this other part of himself. It allowed them to communicate without meeting.

He sat down on the piano bench and reviewed his music. Something about the song constantly nagged at him. Rather than play piano, he set down the notes on a stand and removed his violin from a case beneath the little table.

The memories of Priscilla repeated in his mind, now fresh and painful as they were during his youth. He had struggled to play the music after her death, but eventually resumed his studies of music in piano and violin. Music played too important a role in his growth and expression.

The tune for A Wistful Melody had been in many of his dreams. Whenever he heard a piece of it, he recorded it to memory, and then to his sheets of music. It had grown much since he first began. In truth, it told the story of Leoht Miina. He first began to experience these spells of memories after the first seal had been broken—it was the only reason he knew it had happened.

When he played the song, he grew more attuned to these memories, but when he stopped, they quickly faded. He knew one thing for certain: as long as he played the music, he could reach back to his roots.

He wanted to know why the stain existed... and when he heard the melody, he knew. The nostalgia swept through him like a gentle breeze. Each note of the soft tune lured out another piece of his past.

He collected his violin from its stand and raised the bow. After a deep breath, he closed his eyes, bathed in the coolness of the surrounding light, and commenced his tune. A vision of an ethereal world formed around him. Pastel-colored clouds hung above a maelstrom that spiraled into pools of stars. No matter how long he stared, he saw naught but a distant twinkle and the occasional Phantom. Something called to him from below. He only wished he knew what.

A man sat at his side, patting his head with a large, comforting hand.

He saw this memory clearer than before but it told him nothing about the stain—at least, nothing that Hero understood.

He uncovered a new, unscripted part of the melody. The strings strained as the man spoke with composure. When his voice reached Hero's ears, the string on his violin screeched, snapped, and cut his finger. Blood dripped down the bow as the trance dispelled.

Although the spell had broken, his heart ached tremendously.

His legs gave in and he dropped to his knee with his violin over one arm. He now knew the next part of the movement and needed to record it to the pages above.

I'm getting closer.

A shadow slithered at the bottom of the door, indicating that someone passed through the light in the hall. Hero placed his violin back in its case and left the music room to follow. When this shadow of a person moved through the hall to the back stairs and stopped in the celebration hall, Hero crept into the room behind it, watching from a distance.

Without turning, it muttered, "Everything I know, you know. We are one and the same. Why do you reject me so?"

Hero stopped advancing. "All you want to do is preserve yourself. You don't care what happens to others."

"Then neither do you. You lie to yourself to make yourself feel like a good person, but lying is bad too, Leoht. The sooner you accept these truths, the sooner we can awaken. Everything that I am, you already are. Everyone can see it except you... because you're blind to life, just like me."

"I am not, nor will I ever be, like you."

"We'll see," the shadow said, and spun on his heels. He moved fast towards Hero.

Hero retreated, his movements unsteady. He checked his feet, realizing that he stood in knee-deep water as dark as the night. Shadowy hands stretched out and grabbed onto him, dragging him under.

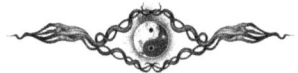

Hero jolted awake, his face pressed against the music room floor. His head rushed and made the room spin. It required some concentration to re-center himself before he could sit up again. He pressed a hand against his temple. "Now, how do I make you accept me?"

10
Our Tune

Fate returned after almost a week and ran into Hero in the main hall during renovations. She stopped and allowed her foot to hang over the wet floors for a moment. "What... did you redo the floors? It looks like space."

He'd replaced the white stone with black quartz and crystal, which he'd finished polishing only recently. "Is that a bad thing?"

"No, but how did you do it? Did this cost a lot? Wait...." She tossed her head back and circled the floor, viewing the sun window. "Praise Grim, a skylight? What else did you do?"

Hero averted his gaze. "Not much."

Fate lifted the front of her gown and tiptoed across the freshly mopped floor. "How have you been? Did you have time to think?"

"Committee meetings are never long. Did you intentionally leave home for an entire week?"

She stroked his cheek with a cunning smile. "I could have been gone longer, you know, but you're right. I did decide to stay in the Capital with Chi. I thought you might need time to think. We've made a lot of big decisions lately."

"We were separated for two turns. You weren't satisfied?"

"Of course, I've missed you. We have a lot of work to do, and I wanted you to have enough time to sort out your future plans. I had time when I was with Akira. Being around him helped me understand what I wanted to do with this life."

"Expand the Ussan?"

Fate snatched the mop from his hands and placed it against the wall by the front doors. "It's much more than that. It's an unachieved dream. No... worse yet, a dream that was achieved and stolen."

Hero locked his jaw to stop himself from commenting. Clearly, they both knew the truth about the fate of the Crystal Empire, but more dire things remained unresolved. He wanted to unveil all that Fate knew about the state of the Universe and how it fell out of balance. It seemed they both found it necessary to keep secrets.

She continued her thought. "It doesn't matter. What's important is that we stay clear-headed and focused. Now, will you take me to see the renovations?"

He guided her past the stairway to the glass corridor. String lights illuminated the room, bringing out a shimmer from circular pieces of crystal he hung from the ceiling. "Don't look yet."

Fate covered her eyes as he assisted her inside the room. "Yes, okay, I'm not looking."

He shut the door. "You can look. Just be careful not to wander."

She viewed the room, her eyes widening marginally as a gasp left her lips. For a long time, she stood silently observing. "It's beautiful." She tapped a crystal that hung from a string of lights. The strand swung and clinked with another assemblage, creating a wave of chiming throughout the room.

"It reminds me of a place I used to dream about," Hero said.

Fate's expression showed a deep sadness. "It reminds me of the Void." She lowered her gaze to the reflection of the lights against the dark floor. It appeared as though they stood on water in the illuminations. "Hero...."

Hero re-centered his attention on her, questioning her change in demeanor since their journey into the Dreamscape.

She shook her head. "There may come a day when you doubt me. I just want you to know that everything I've done has been for you."

He concentrated on her as she smiled softly. "Why would I doubt you?"

"I don't always succeed in my efforts, but I'm determined to make things right." She returned her gaze to the reflection of the lights on the floor.

Ironically, her answer struck a chord of doubt within him. He considered it silly to feel as he did, but he'd been increasingly suspicious of everyone around him. As far as he knew, they could all be Council associates. He just wasn't paranoid enough to fret about it. His eyes shifted to one side. If they tricked him, he'd just kill them, or die trying.

Fate looked at him with concern in her eyes. "The miasma has festered because of my travels. I must do something soon...." Although she said it aloud, she seemed to be talking to herself.

Hero crossed his arms, shielding himself. "I sent a message to you a week ago. Did you ever receive it?"

"The one about the journals, right? I replied. You never received it?"

He thought back over the course of the week. "Who did you send it with?"

"Fortis."

His body relaxed again as he thought of an explanation. "I hate to say it, but Fortis can be irresponsible when someone catches his eye. He might have passed it to another guard so he could philander."

"That sounds sadly accurate. Fortunately, I wrote something inconspicuous. You said there's a map? Does it have something to do with what happened in the Dreamscape?"

"Yes. I think my memories are jumbled. I get the feeling Abyssus told me that when he died but it's difficult to remember it clearly." He pressed a finger to his chin. "He always said that the best way to hide a secret was to hide it within another secret. The journal's content was one secret, so why not hide another? I believe it's also the map he mentioned."

Fate's expression lit up. "That reminds me. I read the journals very carefully while you were away. When you have time, I think we should review some of what I learned."

"How about now?"

"What about your renovations?"

He brushed back the hair over her ear where her crystal earring dangled, glistening in the light from the surrounding decorations. "It's not going anywhere. The palace has a better chance of survival than the people caught in this storm."

Her fingers intertwined with his, and she stared straight into his eyes. "Don't you die on me. I'll do everything in my power to keep you alive. Do you understand?"

Her obstinacy brought back another memory of the Spinner, who vowed to do anything for this same goal. Certainly, she'd meant it, and that's what killed her.

Fate hesitated. "Our pact is our promise, but my duty to protect you is much older. I can't afford to fail again."

Hero frowned, having finally confirmed that she had remembered something. "What does that mean?"

"Please, just trust me. I won't lead you astray."

He fretted about her ambiguous behavior. There was no telling whether he would really die from all this prying. Then again, if they managed to put together these fractured pieces of his consciousness, he could finally advance towards his goals.

Fate went on mumbling to herself again. "If only I could reach it... I think I would be able to bring *you* back, as well."

He had kept information from her too, at times, so he had no room to judge. Despite everything that had happened, and his doubts, his trust of her remained strong. He'd probably follow her blindly. "I'll wait. Tell me what you can, and I'll trust you."

Her expression relaxed once he expressed his trust. "Then come with me. I'll show you."

They left behind the glowing room and entered the downstairs study. Fate dug behind several rows of books around the room and retrieved the journals.

She laid them on the floor in a row, then sat on her knees and flipped through the pages. "You hid *The Story of Night and Day* like this, so I thought it might be easier for you to find them. I've been worried about other people getting their hands on them."

Hero knelt and turned one of the books. In the dark room, the pages glowed blue and unveiled their secrets. "What did you learn from them?"

She set her hand on the first book, *Solaris*. "This one tells about the Ancient folklores from the *Book of Ages* and the *Book of Beginnings*, the ones that I dream about. According to the passages, the Old World Ancients believed these tales told about the world before the Mortal Realms. They believed they were real." Her hand moved to the second book. "This one, which *Syo* gave me, is about the three realms—The Beyond, The Rift, and The Void. For whatever reason, it doesn't include much about the Mortal Realms, and claims that they are so separate from the other three that they must be considered as such. Furthermore, it taught me how the Lords of Light and Shadow are merely poor reflections of the truth that one was."

He ran his hand over the cover. "What do you mean?"

She turned her violet eyes to him with a deep, all-knowing look. "They were not part of the Mortal Realm, so they aren't exactly people. Folklore seems to desperately want to change that but, they, like everything before the Mortal Realm, were ethereal beings."

"The Folklore?"

"Yes! Have you ever noticed that the characters in the Ancient folklore correlate with the Lords of Light and Shadow? Some of them are harder to identify, but I assure you it's true." She pressed a hand to her chin. "Though, it does concern me that those I can identify are slightly less than those I can count in the folklore."

Hero felt as though she'd just stricken him upside the head.

She continued her excited rambling. "Not just that.... The most important thing I've gathered is the roles of the Lords."

His mouth twitched.

She took up the book in her hands, holding it close to her chest as a Council member would the Grandmaster's scriptures. "The temples claim there are presently eight of them—Fate, Chaos, Life, Death, Wrath, Order, Harmony, and Justice—and that finding them is the key to restoring Euphoria's balance."

Her newfound knowledge fascinated him. According to him, she ought to know about the Lords already. It left him to question what she meant to do by acting ignorant about it. He feigned the same ignorance. "I don't know anything about this. Where did you learn about it?"

She opened *Ulnaire*, the journal about Undal, and flipped the pages to the middle. "I had to connect some of the dots myself and go digging in the Dreamscape. Sometimes, Akira will let out interesting bits of information too. He has a friend...." She trailed off, looking as though she had been stricken.

Hero tapped her shoulder. "Fate?"

She said nothing.

He tapped her shoulder again. "Fate...."

She pulled her head up quickly. "Akira has this friend who knows a lot of facts about history. Well, actually, he kind of knows a lot about everything. His name is Jackyl. He's a Reaper, kind of rude and vain, and he eats way too much, but I think you'd enjoy him because he's very similar to Abyssus."

"I'm not sure there is anyone quite like Abyssus."

She pressed her lips together but kept the comment to herself. He squinted. "He helped you?"

"Yes. I asked him a lot of questions while he was around. You'd like him very much."

Hero collected the journal and shifted closer to her with it propped up against his legs. "Do you know a Reaper in a cat mask?"

She froze and seemed to dig back into her memory. "A cat mask? You must mean Besil."

"I don't know him personally. He never gave me his name, only advice."

"About?"

"My condition. He essentially warned me that I'd be in danger if I wasn't careful with my element, but I've already thought it over. I'd rather help and uncover the truth than continue living in fear of it. I've realized there's no point in living a half-fulfilled life. I can't let you do everything for me."

She gently brushed his cheek. "I believe in you. You can be quite capable if you put your mind to a task."

He appreciated her trust, even though he lacked faith in himself. "We always get off track. What were you saying about the Lords of Light and Shadow?"

"Ah yes. This is just my observation, but I overheard Tori calling Akira 'Lord' before. When I spoke to him in the past, I was able to uncover that he has been to the Edge of Time. As far as I can tell, his abilities surpass that of anyone we know, and we don't know what he really looks like. Actually, we don't really know anything about him at all. Do you think he could be one of the Lords of Light and Shadow?"

"I honestly wouldn't know. You said they were created to maintain balance?"

"I believe so. It has been recorded that, in the past, Oracles and Spirit-Walkers had the ability to seek them out."

Hero shut the journal and shifted the others around, cover to cover, on the floor. "I'm not even sure how you connected this information about the Lords to the folklore in the first place."

"Akira. I've watched him for a while. He can be very transparent."

"Is he? I don't understand him at all." His skin prickled with jealousy.

"It always seemed as though he was reaching out to me for help, as if he couldn't, but he wanted to." She relinquished the journal in her grip as he realigned the four journals.

"He never seemed that sensitive to me, but we don't get along."

"I think his animosity towards you comes from the fact that his condition has spiraled out of control. He struggles so much to remain stable, and you dawdle around unscathed."

Hero rarely lost composure, but the comparison unsettled him. His lips set in a grim line. "I don't *dawdle around unscathed*. You should know that better than *anyone*. Just because I choose not to dwell on my problems, doesn't mean I'm not having a hard time."

Fate remained calm. "It's good to hear you say it."

He expelled the frustration in a breath. "Don't stir up my emotions like that."

"That wasn't my intention. I'm just saying, I think it seems that way to Akira. If you hide behind a frivolous demeanor, people will believe you really feel that way. It's like *Benevolence of Queen*. She put on the façade of a kind person, so everyone believed it. Right now, a lot of people dislike you because you seem to skip around unscathed by your own wake of chaos."

Hero kneaded the heel of his hand against his forehead. "We need to focus on the map." He pointed at the aligned covers, and presented the map glistening inside the borders of the gold lining.

"If this matches up to Mu, then there's a star by the Crystal Cove." She pressed her index finger against the marked place.

"I can't imagine what might be there, but we should go and see tomorrow."

She smiled with the utmost excitement. "You're coming?"

"If I found it, I should at least go, no?"

"Wonderful! Now, show me the rest of the renovations."

Fate wanted to see all of the changes to the palace — the hanging lights in the main hall, the constellations painted across the ceiling in the upstairs study and King's Suite, and the lights intertwined with the labyrinth hedges — and at each place, she stayed for a long time simply studying.

The changes to the King's Suite were especially important to Hero, since his father had previously stayed in the room. He wanted to erase any reminders of Niteo from the palace.

They viewed the small lights in the yard from the bay window, and she sang softly into the bitter wind. It seemed probable that the Spinner's voice alone could compel the storms of chaos, as Hero, who may have been the storm itself, marveled over her inexplicable beauty.

He admired her momentarily, then viewed the lights outside. "It's hard to explain, but I've always had this urge to study what I find beautiful. I've always wanted to understand how something could be so dreadfully captivating."

"To what are you referring?"

He beamed. "You, of course."

Fate pulled the window shut and clasped the lock. "I've been thinking this since I returned, but I believe it's time to cleanse some of that miasma."

His heart pounded in his throat as her arms draped around his shoulders.

Threads of hair swept down her face from the tilt of her head when she gazed down at him. Her aura radiated throughout the room, bringing a warmth to her skin as she kissed him softly.

A surge of heat rushed from his fingertips to his face, stinging his eyes.

She pulled back once, lost in another deep thought. "Whatever it takes... I promise I'll save you." After finishing her thought, she made promptly for the bed, dragging him along by the arm.

For Hero, the world seemed to be spinning in reverse. He felt the mattress under his back sooner than he realized what was happening. Panic struck first, until some distant thought reminded him of Askelon's remark.

Fate couldn't, and wouldn't, get infected with miasma poisoning. Her eyes studied him with intensity as she gently ran her hand down his chest. "I can feel your thoughts."

His voice sounded smaller than he expected. "*Feel* them?"

"You don't need to worry." She smiled, emitting a strange darkness. Fate had never been particularly strong, especially since Hero trained since childhood, but at present, she pinned him down with one hand.

He gazed up at her, sensing that the woman he married and the woman before him may not exactly be 'one and the same,' as everyone suggested. A part of her aura held familiarity, just not the same as before. "Fati...."

Fate narrowed one eye, scrutinizing him. She kept quiet and studied him as though searching for a sign that he remembered her. Then the intensity faded from her expression. "Leoht... or should I call you that?"

Hero's spine tingled. The way she used the name unsettled him. He challenged her. "Whatever Leoht is, I am as well. Fractured or not, there's only one, true Leoht Miina. We share a common goal."

Fate leaned down, pressed the hair back from her face, and kissed him deeply, releasing anima that he rapidly absorbed.

Finally, the familiarity returned as her aura soaked into Hero with surprising power.

"Given that you're the one radiating all the miasma, I don't think you'll take fondly to my treatment." Anima surged through her hand as she traced his skin.

The sensation brought forth a fervent pulsation all over his body. The miasma stirred uncomfortably within him, like something alive. Hero struggled against her, unable to free himself.

Fate responded as though she could hear its dispute. "Be still. I'll be damned if I let him fall any further."

A sharp pain shot through Hero's limbs. The seals on his fingers disintegrated as he reached out, gripping Fate by her gown. He drew closer, until their lips almost touched. A monster raged inside, one that had been dormant for some time. It gripped him tightly, filling his world with darkness. "You can't destroy me, Miina Feir. Leoht and I are of one mind." He smirked. "...and I know something you've been *dying* to hear, but I won't tell you until you put me back together again."

Fate's expression went blank. The shock soon faded, and she leaned her head against his. With surprising might, she forced his head back down against the mattress. "Rascal. You've grown strong enough to resist me." A coy smile swept across her lips. "It's almost cute."

He used all his strength to try and throw her off but failed. In his fractured state, he lacked the power to resist her.

"Relax. I only want what's best for you," she said. "I don't find it fun to subdue someone who's resisting, so let's cooperate a little, okay?" Her anima swelled, creating a faint red glow in the darkness. This monster was greater and stronger than his own. She intertwined her hand with his, gripping him so tightly that he became locked in her embrace.

The miasma ebbed as she drew her mouth to his neck.

His strength diminished at the touch of her lips. All his negative feelings subsided as the warm anima coursed through him. His body relaxed and he accepted that, despite her intimidation, she meant no harm.

Her gentle hand trailed down his neck. "I'll put you back together again. Trust me. First, we must ease the effects of the miasma." As soon as she felt his resistance stop, she released his hands. "You're fighting so hard for survival that you no longer know who or what you're fighting."

He took her face into his hands. "I won't fight *you* anymore."

Her gaze softened and she ran her lips over his again, releasing more anima.

His body trembled as he drank it in and relented to her will.

11
A Little Unorthodox

The morning broke quiet and peaceful, except for the madness occurring in Hero's mind. He awakened before Fate and rested his head against his arm to watch her sleep. The Taint rested quietly thanks to her anima, but he knew that it was only a matter of time before both he and Fate lost the dissension against this other side of him. When the Taint decided that he didn't like something, he always found a way to remove it from his path.

He slipped out from under the covers and dressed in some of his older, worn clothing and boots, which seemed the best option given their plan to follow the map. The sun had just begun to rise over the community buildings, and the chef hadn't yet entered the kitchen.

After Abyssus's passing, Hero stopped cooking or baking since he had no further purpose for it. He only now considered it strange that he had spent so much time taking care of Abyssus, but spent little time taking care of his wife. *But what will she like?*

He recalled, she ate light breakfasts, merely fruit and tea, or toast and honey butter on special days. Cooking came easily but setting it up on the table took a lot longer. He shifted around the vase of crystal flowers that had been placed for decoration, and the plates and glasses, with such diligence he didn't notice her come downstairs.

Fate entered with an air of weightlessness. "Good morning."

Hero fumbled the silverware onto the table. "Hello. Morning."

She stared hard for a moment, then smiled. "What's wrong? Still not used to the nightlife?"

He blushed. "No. No! It is not that."

She swayed from side to side to see the table. "Are you hiding something?"

"I am not hiding anything. You just surprised me." He faced the table again, rapping his fingers on the back of one of the polished wooden chairs.

"Breakfast? Did you make it?"

"I just... I had never made anything for you. You've done well as the new Queen... and you know...."

"Hmm?" She clasped her hands together and looked over the table in delight. "How can I know if you don't tell me?"

He exhaled until the pressure left his lungs. "To be honest, I've been stressed about what married life is supposed to be like. Everything feels the same, but you're not exactly what I expected... not that I expected anything."

She pressed back a chuckle with her fingertips. "Stop overthinking. Nothing needs to change but our role as the King and Queen of this kingdom. Just be the same Hero as usual, and I'll be happy enough."

"I always thought that when you devote yourself to someone, you should express it in as many ways as possible. That's why I tried something new."

She brushed her finger across his face from one cheek to the other. "Well, you're not wrong." She pulled out both chairs, plunked down, and gestured towards the empty seat next to her. "Let's talk a little."

"About?" He slunk down to his place.

"You've gotten sheepish lately. Is there something on your mind?"

He shook his head. "Nothing out of the ordinary."

She picked up her utensils and ate with poise. "You don't feel better after last night?"

"What? I mean, I do... but...."

She prattled on. "Fretting won't change our situation. There's no way for us to tell what'll happen, or even when. I just want you to live a little before anything worse happens. At least if we run into trouble, we have each other. Have some faith in what we can do or become together."

Hero thought about the Taint and 'his' personality, unsure why anyone would wish to bring out someone so self-absorbed and cold. "You want to make us whole again... but what if you don't like who I become?"

Fate winced briefly but quickly replaced it with a practiced smile. "Society will always criticize us for what, or whom, we decide is worth living for. They say that we must be independent in order to be healthy in the soul and mind, but I don't think it's wrong to live because of someone else, as long as you search for your own purpose and drive. When a fire burns low, you must give it fuel to restart. People are like this too. Without a direction, we become lost. You still have a spark. It's fine if I must encourage it to grow. You too will blaze brightly."

His chest ached. At times, she spoke utterly beautiful words, a trait that made him breathless. "I used to think that time was an illusion and that love was science. Now, I think that only one of those things is true."

She stared at her food, then suddenly ate as though she'd forgotten how. "I think a lot of scientists want to overanalyze and dissect everything, just as those with strong faith wish to find faith in everything. Then there are those who wish to find the method and root of all creation—they're the few who restore the Balance in all things."

"That might be true," he admitted.

After they finished their meal, they cleaned up and boarded a carriage to the Capital.

The carriage clomped along through the forest, carting Hero and Fate, who stared out the windows in silence. Their journeys normally started quietly, like the calm before the storm. The days after their marriage seemed steadier to the untrained eye and more chaotic internally—at least for Hero it appeared as such.

He stretched out his legs across the seats, pinning Fate between his feet with a smirk. "Trapped."

"Not feeling very regal, are we?" she said, patting his shoe. She never seemed to care much about his behavior beyond her amusement. "It's funny how one so quick to respond falls silent when observed outwardly. Look, the bridge of your nose is red again."

He blew the hair from his forehead and sank down on the cushion, until the soles of his shoes pressed firmly against the back of her seat.

Her gentle smile softened the admonishment. "Don't sulk. It's unseemly of the King, though I adore you and every one of your strange quirks... it's unbecoming for you to act immaturely, so I would ask you to behave as a gentleman should."

He removed his feet from her chair and sat up, trying his best to swallow his pride at the failed attempt in frivolity.

She turned her head but still eyed him. "Only in public. I personally find you quite charming and have no objections to how you choose to behave in closed quarters."

She certainly knew how to calm the storms in his heart. The most subtle comments took the edge off him in a flash.

"Since there's still time before we arrive, would you like to share some of your past with me?"

"Now?" He checked for listeners, though he knew no one could hear.

"If not now, then when?"

He grew more uncomfortable the deeper they delved into his Dreamscape. The fact that she asked him for permission made it more difficult for him to refuse, though the Taint would do so without hesitation. He feared that this other personality would come back with a vengeance after Fate's suppressing him.

She gently prodded. "Would you open up to me in the Dreamscape?"

Hero tapped a finger against the velvet seat. He noticed his hands shaking and clenched a fist to conceal it. Something deep down inside trembled with something deeper than fear.

"Just rest. I'm close enough. I can find you. Now that we've been rummaging through your memories, it should be accessible." She pushed his legs down and tossed herself onto the seat next to him, shimmying closer as the carriage hobbled and creaked towards its destination. "This is better."

He burrowed his face into the knit of his scarf. After some hesitation, his fingers wove into the spaces between hers.

She leaned her head against his shoulder, saying nothing, not even to tease him.

His breathing slowed as the trees continued whizzed by the window, and they settled into their shared warmth. Like this, he could rest.

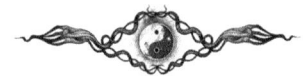

In the Dreamscape, a river streamed across a sky made from colorful shards of glass. Hero tilted his head at the sight and lowered his view to the clear blue water swaying against his ankles. Winding trees sprang up from the water and covered the landscape like grotesquely gnarled hands, their leaves made of open books instead of leaves.

Fate climbed over the strange, looping branch formations. "I found you! It looks like there's an entire world forming here now."

"Is that normal?" The trees grew up through the water from some unseen place deep below, casting a red haze that emitted an unpleasant scent. When he neared the haze, he covered his face and felt the crushing pressure its presence caused.

Fate stabilized her breathing after climbing her way out of the tangle of branches. "Everyone has a different type of Dreamscape. I've always wanted to see Akira's."

"Dangerous," Hero said, finding this obvious.

"I'm sure if I entered, even for a moment, I'd suddenly understand everything about him."

He studied her expression, which only displayed curiosity. "Then do you understand everything about me?"

She regarded the Dreamscape with outward befuddlement. "It's curious, but I think you're more of a conundrum than he is. No matter how many times I try to understand you, I can't. It's like there are all these little locks, and I have to pick each and every one to fully comprehend you." She lifted her hand towards the surrounding world. "I have no idea where this came from or what it means."

He shrugged at her. His vision of reality, or whatever it was, offered no discernable correlation to any part of his life. He guessed it had to do with how he viewed the world outside the palace, after being kept inside like a prisoner. *Maybe the Taint knows something that I don't.* For once, it seemed a shame that this other voice said nothing.

A click resounded, and Fate pointed. "Look, a door."

They crossed through the branches, laboriously crouching or climbing until they reached the white door embellished with the crest of a book.

At the door, Hero turned to examine the world again at a distance. Pages wafted down from the trees to the water, dissolving as they touched its surface. He examined them as they fell, spotting the music notes of A Wistful Melody. Instinct took hold of him as his life's work drifted towards its demise. He raced out to the water and grasped for the pages that still hung in the open air. Despite his efforts, a wind blew them out of his fingertips. Once they touched the water, the ink bled, and the page broke away.

Fate trudged towards him, careful not to splash, and waited behind him. She rested her hand against his arm. "Perhaps... this world isn't all it seems. It's unorthodox, just like you, but it still means something." She crouched down and scooped up some of the sopping pages.

Printed notes fell from the pages in his hands, into the water below, and billowed into a thick, expanding black ink, which in turn created a vast star-filled sea. As he leaned over to take a closer look, gravity fled and the water shot up around them. The pages scattered, drifting upward and away from him as sea enveloped his evolving world.

Fate reached out to Hero as the current swept her into the air, her eyes locked on the white door as it grew farther away. "We have to hurry. The Dreamscape is transforming."

The hourglass floated out from Hero's shirt, twinkling in the reflective light from the surrounding stars, and the silver horse figurine drifted up from below.

Hero reached out to it as Fate yanked him by the arm. The tiny, silver object brushed against his fingertips, then spun away from his grasp.

Something called to him. As he grazed the horse, he felt a sense of familiarity and clarity, but it left as soon as Fate pulled him away.

She gripped the white door by its frame and climbed in through the opening. "Hold on. Here we go."

The Dreamscape twisted and flashed with colorful lights.

Hero flinched and fell onto something soft, then opened his eyes in his bedroom. This time, he recalled traveling through the doorway, and that, even though he appeared to be four or five turns here, he was in fact an adult.

A collection of books lay around his body, all over the bed, some open and others stacked. Unsure of how long he might retain his memory, he ignored the books and crawled off the bed.

Simple tasks turned arduous in such a tiny body. Even opening the door seemed cumbersome. At that age, the palace had been especially quiet.

Fortis still hadn't moved in, and Niteo left as often as possible to find amusement and safety away from the palace. Few servants interacted with Hero because of the accounts of the disappearances.

That had left him alone and uncertain about how he should live his life. His father always said that to study meant to be smart, and only smart people had a place in the world.

Hero always found this ironic, since his father was not exceptionally wise, just privileged.

On mornings such as this, Hero would set a stool down against the kitchen counter and climb atop in search of fruit or bread. Unfortunately, his father didn't listen or care enough to notice whether the servants paid attention to a child so small.

Hero had a bad history of injuring other royal and noble children, but no one had cared to hear why it happened in the first place. Thinking back on it, the Stain had misbehaved even before he realized it existed.

During childhood, he thought his only worth in life was to Niteo, so all he did was study and train to succeed the throne.

Niteo would often say, "You were meant for bigger things," and then he'd disappear for days at a time, leaving behind only piles of books from which he expected Hero to study.

Oftentimes, Hero couldn't yet read the content inside, and, consequently, he carried around a large dictionary, and memorized the words the way a person of faith memorized the pages of their scriptures. He'd recite information as his father wished, but grew up unaware of proper social structures.

The memory from that time went about the same as every day, with continuous confusion and endless studies about things his father said were important, like economics, politics, and the variables that made them up.

For some reason, Niteo had returned that afternoon and spoke with Isis in the main hall. Murmurs passed back and forth between them as Hero exited the study, dictionary in his arms, and greeted his father.

He recalled being uncertain and embarrassed about his joy whenever he saw Niteo. Any emotional response seemed to Niteo a simple distraction from more important business.

Isis glanced at Hero without moving her head and waited for Niteo to respond. This is when she first became aware of Hero on a personal level, as she had never really interacted with him before then.

Niteo waved Hero off and continued talking without pause. "...as you know, since Elaine passed away, they've begun questioning my right to rule. They've already mentioned Hero succeeding the throne when he is of age. It's only a matter of time."

Since Hero still had enough of his present consciousness, he fully understood what his father meant back then.

If I had been older, I would have known precisely why he loathed me so much. I was merely a bargaining tool to protect his position as King. My clan name was just a way for him to maintain a high status. Our hatred was mutual, Niteo, but I suppose that, in the end, mine was much stronger.

He had tugged his father's coat that afternoon and opened his dictionary to ask for help. After a swift slap on the hand and a look of disgust from Niteo, Hero withdrew and redirected his attention to Isis, who appeared quite stricken herself.

By her reaction alone, one would've thought that she had been slapped instead of Hero. Her facial expression displayed overt rage within moments of the admonishment.

Hero might've realized by then that his father hated him because he tugged on Isis's dress next and opened the dictionary again. "Help, please."

She gave Niteo a questioning glance and crouched down, possibly out of curiosity or obligation. "How may I help you?"

Hero pointed to a word. He still hadn't undergone training, and the book, large as it was, weighed heavily in his small hands. "This word... can you say it? I'm not sure if I pronounce it right."

Isis held the dictionary on both sides. "*Concomitant*... but what do you need this word for?"

He repeated the word to himself, then answered. "It was in the book I read."

"What were you reading?"

"It's about economy."

"How old are you?"

He held up four fingers. "I'm old to *ba'ai*."

Isis collected the dictionary from his hands and flipped through the tabbed pages carefully. "What does diaphanous mean?"

"It's a word for fabric that's translucent."

"What's translucent?"

Hero stifled a laugh.

She did the same, as if his reaction amused her. "What's funny?"

"You don't know?"

"Of course, I know. I'm asking if *you* know."

"It's something partially see-through, that allows light to pass through it."

The dictionary released a loud thud as she closed and raised it, placing her hands on her hips. "To the Rahma, you might seem older, but to me and all the other Ancients, you're just a child. Even if you're smart, you don't need to read out of a dictionary."

"Why?"

"What you really mean is 'why not'."

Niteo rubbed his brow. "Lady Isis, you don't need to fuss over him. He does fine on his own. The life he has lived in this world has been greater than most."

"Perhaps it's because you're Rahma that you don't understand, but your son is just a child. I'll give you the benefit of the doubt here, but, as you can see, his size is telling of his age. How do you expect him to survive on his own if you haven't taught him how?"

"I read," Hero said. "I can learn everything from reading."

"Not everything. You can't learn to interact with a book. You can learn the basic structure of conversation, but you'll never be able to apply it properly to real life. When you speak with others, they'll notice something isn't right." She lowered again and returned the dictionary. "How would you like me to teach you? I won't always be around, but I'll try to assist you as much as possible."

"You're wasting your time," Niteo said.

"I am fully capable of making my own decisions, as you well know. Let's not forget that I am much older than Hero, which makes you just as much a child to me as Hero, so do not trifle with me." With a hand pressed against Hero's back, she stepped towards the study. "Come now, there's much to learn."

12
AMISS, MISS

The Dreamscape melted away, reforming once more as Isis and Hero stepped through the doorway to the study. She, and everything else in the room, turned to smoke, and a clear blue sheen expanded across the walls, materializing into his room. It waved like a pool of water, surged, and hit Hero with such tremendous force that he thought he might be rendered unconscious.

He blinked and found a book in his hands, something about *Rota Fortunae* from the *Book of Ages*. He once again lay on his bed surrounded by books, this time organized in tall stacks on the side of his bed.

Someone rapped a fist against the door and entered before he could respond, and because people usually didn't bother him, he sat up on his elbows, startled.

Isis leaned against the doorway, shining a coy smile while she fixed the silk scarf draped around her arms. "*Saha, boue nam.*"

'Hello, imp.'

"*Nam pa. Ca'ou?*"

'I'm not bad. Am I?'

"*Nui.*" Her stride emanated the grace and confidence of a Queen. She ran a hand through his hair as she passed by and took a seat on the edge of the bed. "I heard you met your Bound."

Her words created a resonance.

A bell chimed faintly beyond the door, and then Hero returned to the memory. He knew precisely of the conversation about to ensue. At the time of the memory, he was sixteen and Abyssus still lived.

"What you mean is, I met the woman who *might* be my mate," he corrected her, and pursed his lips to conceal a smile.

She bounced back with a snarky shake of her head. "Well, is she?"

"I think so." The last time he had met with Fate, she knew he was Tainted. If she saw with the Annulus Eye, she was supposed to be the Spinner—his bound.

"You seem pleased."

Hero shrugged. "I guess."

"You aren't? That's peculiar."

"I feel like I'm playing to the Rebellion's hand. All I want is to please Abyssus."

"I think your loyalties are misplaced, dear."

He often wondered what it meant to be so close to someone on the Council's side.

To the present day, Isis still wished he would switch his loyalties to her, but never considered it a priority or a cause of divide in their relationship.

"Maybe you're right," he said after a while.

"I'm sorry. I must have made you uncomfortable again. That wasn't my intention."

"No... sorry. It's just... I feel like I owe you a lot, since you taught me so much during my childhood, but, to the Council, I'm just a plague they wish to eradicate."

"I have a lot of power with the Council. I can stop that, but only if you prove your loyalty. I won't push you or tell you what to do. If ever you wish, you may come with me." She had promised that if he left the Rebellion, she would help him leave the palace and earn his place within the Council.

Hero ran his fingers along the edges of the book cover. "I don't know... I swore my loyalty to Abyssus. Right now, even if I think I might be Bound to the Lady Fate, I don't know her well. If not for Abyssus, I'm not sure where I would be right now. When I'm with him, I feel at peace."

"Abyssus... you've grown very close to him. Even closer than before. I thought you might grow apart, but that doesn't seem to be the case."

He murmured while rubbing his face with the sleeve of his sweater. "He's... *special*. I don't know how to say it."

"Special? Interesting. What will you do about your mate if you're so attached to her brother?"

"I'm not sure what you mean."

"She might be jealous. Will you still cling to him when she's near?"

"But I don't even *know* her."

"That's something to consider. It seems to me like your affections have been placed in the wrong person, or maybe I'm misunderstanding. Maybe you're Bound to him?"

Hero had felt threatened by the comment. No matter how flippantly she said it, the suggestion bothered him because he still couldn't sort out his feelings on the matter. "Isis, it seems like you're the one who's jealous."

Isis turned to black smoke as Fate swung open the bedroom door. The vision had been dispelled, and Fate stepped in quickly. "Found you!"

Hero faced her, relieved that he escaped interrogation for a second time. "Can you tell what's going on if you can't find me?"

"It echoes and appears in images in the halls." Fate crossed her arms, swaying slightly from side to side as she thought. "Which brings me to say, you've been quite cozy with Isis for some time. Why didn't you tell me sooner?"

Hero climbed off the bed without the book. "I'm not sure. I guess it didn't seem important, since she hasn't been around." He avoided her gaze, feeling trapped.

"It didn't seem important that you're close to a Council follower? The Queen of Askadel, no less?" Her head jerked to the side slightly, like a cog stuck in a mechanism.

"You're angry."

"No, I'm not. I'm concerned."

"Isis has been beckoning me to the Council's side for as long as I can remember... and honestly, I've considered it a few times."

"Why not go?"

"I didn't want to leave Abyssus."

Fate crossed her arms with a slight squint, keeping a fixed tone and expression as she contemplated. "There are three more doors. I think I might understand what's going on, but I don't have any proof. If we don't find any, we're going to have a bigger problem." She turned and strode down a long, white corridor to a black door.

"You won't tell me?"

"I can't. I understand why no one could say anything. Of course, I could still be wrong, but if I tell you, the seal might break. It's still too dangerous. We need to cross through the other three doors." She reached the door and tugged on the handle. "Weird. It won't open."

"Let's go back. We'll reach the Capital soon, if we haven't already. Something will trigger it eventually."

"Soon, I hope." Despite her calm appearance, her aura radiated a crushing sensation of wrath and malice. A red, glowing light hovered over her shoulders.

Miasma? No, it's different. Her aura is red?

She pressed her hands against his shoulders and leaned her head against his. "*Muora, Leoht.*"

'Wake up, Leoht.'

Fate sat in the carriage wide awake and staring at something distant, something that wasn't really in front of her. Even when Hero gently rocked her shoulder, she remained fixed and staring into nothingness.

He wondered if she lingered in the Dreamscape.

In time, her trance broke and she moved herself, shifting on her seat.

The trip neared its end and Fate still felt dark and withdrawn.

Her cold hand swept the hair back from his forehead, and she forced a weak smile. "I won't let this be the same as last time. I'll protect you."

He resisted any urge within him to react. At the moment, he held the Spinner's favor and wished to keep it for as long as possible. It struck him as surprising that she exuded such a menacing aura. Now, he questioned if this somehow was a response to an older offense.

"They will pay for their crimes," she said, clenching her jaw.

As much as it relieved him to arrive at the Capital and cleanse himself of Fate's overwhelming malice and rage, he also found it a shame to waste a perfect moment of observation. When they arrived at the Centre, he continued to ruminate on his conversation with Fate, so he failed to greet his aunt.

Fate stepped down from the carriage still seeming distant and bowed to Chi, her body rigid as if held up by a post, and then she waited in silence.

Chi upheld her usual aloof air and grinned. "What brings you here?"

"We need to find something that might have been hidden in the ocean," Hero answered, glancing at his wife for response. "And we might need your assistance. I'm not sure yet."

Chi replied with understandable reluctance. "The ocean? There is crystal in the water. You should not be digging around for buried treasure. I have warned you before about the dangers of the crystal, not that you listen."

"Well... it has to do with Abyssus. He left a map. We don't know what he marked, but I'm sure it's something important. Better we find it than someone else, no?"

"Why do I always feel like I am being tricked by you? How is this any different than the last time?"

Fate's eyes moved towards him. "Because you are. He has always been impish. I will answer any questions you have on the matter directly, if you wish, but we must retrieve whatever my brother left behind."

Chi scrutinized Fate's expression and relented. "So, where is this mark?"

Hero faced the location marked on the map, hit by a bitter gust from the ocean as he gazed towards the stone wall. "It's by the Crystal Cove."

"The most dangerous place to swim."

He still hadn't told Chi about his childhood adventures to the cove. If he had done so, she'd have whacked him right then and there. "It won't hurt to conduct a short investigation. I'm a crystal elemental, so I'll go down."

"Do not overuse your ability. Nothing good has ever come out of a crystal elemental showing off their skill. You clearly learned nothing from being sealed."

"I'm not showing off." He sighed at her as they strolled in the direction of the beach.

"I am just worried," she said. "We still do not know a lot about the Council's seals. I cannot stand to lose you after what happened to Elaine."

He trod through town and onto the cliffside, then down the

steps. It reminded him of a time when Chi listened to him and not vice versa. "Yes, I know. I appreciate your concern, but I'm still going down to search."

"Of course, you are an imp after all."

"He must," Fate said. "It's his sworn duty."

Chi examined Fate's face closely and parted her lips as if she wanted to say something, a common trait of the Fox Clan, though they rarely spoke such thoughts aloud.

Fate continued her thought. "We can discuss that later. First, we find out what has been buried."

Hero ran down the stairs to the shore and removed his shoes. "*Egh, jiat.*"

'Ugh, dirty.'

She quipped. "*Jiat ein jya rul yan?*"

'Dirtier than you?'

His cheeks flushed. "*Nei, kui'lla!*"

Chi's eyes widened, her shoulders shuddered, and she cackled. "My, my, you two get along nicely. Should I be expecting an heir?"

"Most certainly," Fate said.

Hero jumped inside the water as quickly as possible to escape the awkward conversation. He swam much deeper than ever before, scanning the glowing crystal that jutted up through the sand.

Going down was one thing, but as the surface grew farther and farther away, he started to wonder about how long he could stay underwater. He scanned the openings of the crystal, and he reached out a nervous hand to check for a barrier.

Nothing.

He resurfaced for a moment, tossing the wet hair from his face.

From the shore, Fate shouted, "I thought I lost you for a moment."

"No, I'm okay!"

She gestured up, and a tall wave swept him under the water, dragging him down deeper and deeper, until he was almost impaled on a cluster of crystal.

The water had caught him in its grasp, jolting the air from his lungs. As he stared up at the surface, the sea rippled around him. A distant static filled his ears and darkness flooded his vision, leaving only the light on the surface of the water. Something pulled at his arms and legs from below. The dark substance writhed through the water like tresses of hair. He struggled against the force, unable to break free.

It dragged him down into the darkness, wrapping around his entire body.

Hero reached his hand out towards the light as the darkness crawled up his arm and covered his fingertips.

He opened his eyes sharply and sat up, covered in sand and completely dry.

Chi knelt by his side and hugged him. "Oh, praise be. Are you all right?"

"What happened? I thought I drowned for a moment."

She ran her hands down his arms. "What? You never got in the water. The moment you touched the sand, you collapsed."

Hero shifted his eyes, unsure of what to think. He remembered having a conversation with Chi and Fate before diving into the sea.

Then, what was that?

Fate climbed onto the shore, swinging her whole body as she launched a chest from the ocean into the cliffside. As the chest crashed into the rock, it broke open, spilling its contents onto the sand. She flipped the hair from her face and wrung out the water. "Is this what we're looking for?"

Hero and Chi stared, slack-jawed at her display of brute force as they approached the broken chest. They leaned over it, inspecting each of the sandy objects that were now strewn around their feet—a red journal, a fox mask with crystal beads, a lock of hair, a snake brooch, a ring, and various other things.

When Hero saw the journal, he felt shaken, but it could've been a side effect from his visions. His head was still fuzzy. He let a moment pass before trying to grab it.

Fate stopped his hand gently. "I've got it."

It continued to hold his attention, the thick red leather breathing and urging him to pry open its innermost thoughts.

Chi got down on her knees and helped Fate collect the objects from the destroyed chest. The way they huddled around it, quickly scooping up each object, prevented him from assisting, as they blocked much of the available space with their shoulders.

Hero felt the world around him rippling and breathing, the air moving like a sheet of plastic or a silk blanket. He pressed a hand against his hand, wincing. *What's this feeling? Something is happening.* The silver horse weighed in his pocket and in his mind as a reminder that someone in the Universe still knew the truth about him. The feeling of curiosity turned to one of annoyance. *Someone is fucking with me.*

Fate paused while picking up objects to dwell on something. She raised her head to look at Hero, contemplated briefly, and returned to scooping up the remaining pieces.

Chi sighed with a troubled expression. "Should we give these to Sclera?"

Fate nodded and stared at the red journal. "Except this one... this belongs to Jackyl."

Jackyl? That person who reminds her of Abyssus?

Chi brushed the sand from her armor and carried some of the artifacts up the stairway. She lingered behind with Hero for a time, since Fate had rushed ahead.

He ruminated. "Why did Abyssus know about these things? And what's Sclera?"

Chi moved a little faster up the steps. "Just a group that likes antiques."

He squinted at his aunt as he followed her to the cottage. Once again, he found himself thinking of a time when his word drove the actions of the entire group. The fact that they tried to keep him in the dark made him distrustful towards them, as he already knew much of what they intended to hide. However, it perturbed him that he knew nothing about this new group, Sclera. *Where did they come from? Another branch of Bedad's organization?* Mu always frustrated him. This specific pocket of time never worked out for anyone—not himself nor Bedad. He wished to find a loophole, a way to surpass this constant issue of time.

Back at the cottage, Fate and Chi muttered frantically among themselves while Hero watched from the doorway. He always got the impression that Fate wasn't fully or truly on his side but, rather, that he served some purpose in her dance with someone else. Basically, he only meant as much as his purpose. Otherwise, she would choose anyone who fit the bill. It made him ill to realize that no one in his life felt anything for him.

Isis served her faith.

The Mistress Fati served her vengeance.

Chi served her clan and her deceased king.

Even Kyou served his empire.

Hero clicked his tongue at them and hastened to the backroom to peel through the books. No one around him understood why he'd bonded to Abyssus, because they didn't see their own actions as unloving. He remembered the silver horse in his pocket and pulled it out before sinking against the built-in shelves of Chi's library. Faint light from the window cast an outline along the horse's pointed hooves. The rough, grooved metal fit perfectly into his hand and conveyed subtle warmth, an indicator of the craftsmanship that took place—a gift full of love. He hummed to himself while running his thumb over the silver.

After a time, Fate found him in the darkness and carried in one of Chi's crystal lights. "What are you doing over here in the corner?"

"Thinking," he said, stashing away the figurine.

"About?"

"A lot."

The lamp clunked against the wood when she set it on the floor. "Hmm... this is how you used to speak when we first met. Are you upset about something? The miasma is festering around you. You know how you start to think when it gets to your head." She held one of his hands between her own two and blew warm air onto it. "I know that I might seem secretive or distant, but I'm just trying to protect you."

He disliked when people said this, and only grunted in response.

She exhaled slowly through her nose. "You're fretting too much. I'm not going to pretend that any of this is easy for either of us. There's still this nagging fear that something might happen to you, but I will do everything in my power to protect you."

He analyzed her face for a long time and ran his fingers over each facet. There had been a time that he longed to reach out and touch her but couldn't. As much as he wanted to crush her like a frail insect, he also wished for her genuine affection. He pushed back the negative thoughts stirred by the miasma and concentrated on something that sounded more loving and sensitive. "Am I doing enough for you?"

"Why are you worrying about that?"

"I was away for a long time and, when I came back, I started to feel useless."

Fate grasped him by the arms, and then his hands, which she played with the way adults sometimes did with infants. It could have been a sheer expression of her adoration. "When you put your mind to something, and do your best to help, it makes all the difference in the world. We help each other in different ways at different times. Sometimes, one of us will take the lead, but that doesn't change our worth as individuals. What you're contributing now is fine. If you want to do more, then do it because you feel like it, not because you think your worth is less than mine or anyone else's."

He laughed faintly. As always, she had a way with words. "You're right. Sorry."

"You don't need to apologize. I went through this as well, and I don't even have the miasma to influence me. I don't belittle your efforts in the slightest."

Hero rubbed his neck. "My condition is a burden, so I wouldn't want anyone to slow down for me. Since I see it that way, it seems I'm adding more problems than I'm contributing solutions."

Fate caressed his face with tender and loving care. "I can hear what you're saying but hear me too. If you're making efforts to maintain balance in these difficult times, then you're allotting the time I need to resolve other issues. I'll be here for you to lean on, but I won't ask you to share the responsibility if you don't want to. Keep going as you are. If you let me in, then I can help you uncover the truth. We can get through this together. Whatever you do, don't forget that taking responsibility for your condition is still contributing to our goals. That's all I ask of you. Don't forget how much you've helped, or that we all know how your condition can create rifts in your knowledge or ability to assist in certain ways. Just do what you can, and trust me."

He yielded to her request with his usual silent nod.

She smiled back at him. "Let's rest. Chi is presenting the box to a member of Sclera. She told me you don't know anything about them yet, so I'll tell you what I know." She left her place by the shelves, pulling him along by the hand.

"Fate...."

They paused in the hallway outside the guest bedroom, where soft, white light from the Centre shone in through the windows. Her red aura traced the darkness around her in shimmering streaks.

Hero shook his head and pulled her into his arms. "*Minua.*"
'It's nothing.'

He understood that he didn't always need to express himself with words. Surely, she understood what he felt, even if he kept his thoughts tucked deep down inside.

Her arms came around his back, and she nestled her face against his chest. "*Irln so.*"
'I understand.'

She reassured him that it would be okay, and that she held nothing against him for what the miasma had done to her or anyone else.

But we have to stop it.

13

LEIHS OT EGAS

Hero and Fate enjoyed the remainder of the evening in the Capital as a reminder of what they were fighting for. Late that night, after a long, sentimental chat with Chi and an explanation about the Organization, they settled into the guest room.

Fate propped her head against her hand and lay reviewing her plans for the upcoming months. "I've been thinking about this for a while, but now that I'm Queen, I've decided to hold a trial against Mortis. I need to knock down as many of the suspects as possible, and I can sense that he's only going to become a bigger problem along the way, if we don't do something now. There are enough witnesses to testify against him. The real problem is the perpetrator of the murders. I still have no idea where we'll gather evidence against this person."

"I'm uneasy," Hero said, removing his scarf and setting it down on the side table by the lamp.

"I've also started to move forward with some of the Restoration Plans for Nex. Right now, we're stuck because of Neco. Until he keels over, we won't have full authorization to proceed, but Akira had warned me not to remove him from power."

"That's strange. If that's the case, it might mean it'll create an opening for someone else, but that also seems to suggest that whoever rises to power might be the perpetrator."

"I feel that way as well. I know it doesn't make sense, but I trust Akira. If he says not to do it, then I won't. Chances are, even if we identified the perpetrator at this point, we're not ready to handle that person. Maybe, if we break the seals, we'll find an answer or evidence."

"I hope so." Hero pondered the possible results of breaking the seals, certain that Fate had not prepared herself for what would follow.

"Anyway, let's get some rest. There's a lot to think about."

He labored to sleep for what seemed like ages because he was concerned about the seals and the murders. His efforts to protect others had failed all but once, and yet, everyone on the Rebellion's side had put their faith in him.

At some point, his mind succumbed to the stress and exhaustion, and he fell asleep thinking of the first day he accepted Kyou's offer to join their cause.

Hero's eyes fluttered open and he drank in the Dreamscape with his back against a wall in a white hallway, beside a black door that contained an engraving of a crow. He was alone, but he passed through the door anyway.

The memory began with a ticking. The sound clicked loudly with a perfect rhythm in his ears. He'd snapped his head up and took in new surroundings, finding that he stood at his balcony, where he watched the still yard and the unnaturally green lawn that stretched out below him. He recalled the events that led to him standing on the balcony railing. Every day for a week, he sat below the chandelier, waiting for his father to return. He had turned seven that day and received a letter from the guard that said:

Don't wait for me.

Niteo merely used Hero as a pawn to maintain his position amongst the Ancient Royals. Of course, since Hero was a child, he had no choice but to follow his father's authority. However, it didn't upset him any longer. His emotional connection with the world had been lost long ago, leaving him with a love for facts and logic rather than affection. At least, such was the case during his childhood.

His detachment often proved useful to him but concerned Fortis and Isis. The two kept a close eye on him, worried he might turn to mischievous behaviors to fill the strange void.

Niteo kept the backdoors chained and arranged for the exits to be guarded at all times. He even cemented some of the furniture to the floor, preventing Hero any method of escaping. Only Niteo could take him outside, and he alone decided when and why Hero could leave.

The lure of the outdoors called to Hero every morning, but on the morning of his seventh birthday, this desire overflowed. He had climbed atop the balcony railing and stared down, deliberating between a monotonous life and an expeditious death.

All people died eventually. At least if he ceased to exist, he'd have some opportunity to live another, more fulfilling life as someone else. He swung a foot over the edge of the balcony, then caught sight of Isis staring at him from the yard.

Her ice-blue eyes widened as she stepped back to see him more clearly.

"Isis," he said, swinging his foot again.

A small voice cried out, "Don't jump!"

He tilted his head at a girl at the left corner of the yard, Cruentus Fate. They hadn't met, but he remembered following her at her birthday party and seeing something he shouldn't have.

Her emergence in the yard stunned him, since he knew that she had been sold to the brothel. It shocked him even more to hear her plead as she did.

Isis called out as well, her voice strained, yet not quite a shout. "Hero, what are you doing? Get down from there!"

"Down?" He leaned forward to look into the yard, teetering slightly to frighten Isis. Her horrified expression amused him.

She pointed a forefinger. "Don't you dare jump!"

"Why not? You won't catch me?"

A pair of arms wrapped around his torso and snatched him from the balcony. "Gotcha!" Fortis placed Hero back on his feet, and then closed and guarded the balcony doors. "You weren't really going to jump, were you?"

Hero glanced over the balcony. If he waited for a moment longer, Isis would likely arrive and he could escape interrogation.

As expected, she rushed in and knelt beside him to begin her inspection. "Are you all right? What were you doing up there?"

Hero smiled. "Playing."

Isis and Fortis exchanged a glance of bewilderment. Neither adult could seem to decide if he meant to be sarcastic, or simply failed to deceive them.

Only Hero could have said whether the manipulation worked, and it had, indeed, incited the very reaction he sought—confusion. After all, he never played... at least not in the way people liked. His games were much deadlier. Only on the brink of death could he ever find enjoyment. The thought of pain excited him.

Fortis set a hand on Hero's head and attempted to meet his gaze. "Luckily, I came to tell you that your father has returned. You should see him while he's still here."

Hero finally lifted his head. "He's back?"

"That's right."

Isis rose from the floor, smiling with palpable relief. "Let's go and see him."

Hero accepted their offer with a nod and trailed after them into the main hall. He found Isis particularly amusing, since she always rushed to his aid whenever he tried to do something drastic. At times, he found this intrusive to his experimentation with mortality, but most of the time, he just liked watching her reaction.

If anyone asked Hero about his relationship with Isis, he would say they were not personable. It would cause problems if someone knew he had befriended a member of the Council. He knew she had Ancient blood, like him—rumors said she came from Askadel, but she didn't look Aska, the Ancients with vibrant green eyes and flaming red hair.

When Isis and Fortis approached the dining table, they greeted the High King, Khnum, and his son, Prince Kyou, who had visited to meet with Niteo upon his request.

Hero inspected the pair, noting the way the High King postured himself like a bird before it's mate, full of ego and frills. His son, however, held more interest for him. The young man fascinated him in the way he lit up the dreary room with the brightness of his aura.

Only after Khnum and his son had paused the conversation did Niteo turn to find the source of the disruption.

Fortis cleared his throat. "Sire, your son is here to see you."

Niteo bellowed in an unusually welcoming fashion. "Oh, good! Hero, please greet Lord Khnum and his son, Prince Kyou."

Hero shifted his eyes back and forth over his father's face and followed the order. "Good morning."

The High King waited as though sensing Hero wanted to say more. If so, he had been correct.

Hero wanted the freedom to see Abyssus. His father generally abhorred when he made requests, so he expected rejection, but wished to try anyway. "Father, I—"

Niteo lifted a hand to stop him, and grumbled, *"Not now, Hero."*

Hero realized he might not have another chance to speak to Niteo, so he tried again. "Father."

Niteo glared at him, provoking a rather unexpected response from his guard.

Fortis had witnessed Niteo's irresponsible behavior on countless occasions and had admitted how much he detested the way the King treated his son. In a most devious manner, Fortis addressed Niteo's most valuable bond, the High King. "My apologies, Highness. It is Hero's birthday and he wishes to speak with his father for a moment."

Khnum studied Hero like an appraiser questioning the worth of a jewel. "Of course, that is only natural."

Hero sighed inaudibly. "Father, may I see Abyssus again? Even if I can't go outside—"

Niteo waved him off towards the stairway. "We have rules, Hero. Don't slight me. I really must speak with Lord Khnum."

Prince Kyou glanced between Hero and Niteo.

It seemed the conversation might die out, but Hero made another attempt to win his case. He gingerly tapped Niteo's arm. "Just once, may I—"

"Hero, I will not tell you again. You are not to meddle with Abyssus. The children in Macellarius have grown tactless! Spending time with the likes of those children will only hold you back from your true potential as a future king."

Hero frowned at the remark. It sounded like an insult to Abyssus, who showed much more promise than a mere Rahma like Niteo. "What if I don't want to be king?"

"What?" Niteo certainly never dreamed of Hero asking such a thing before the High King. He wanted nothing more than to appeal to the Capital Royals and earn his place beside them.

Hero declared, "If being king means I can't see Abyssus, then I don't want to be king."

Niteo's expression darkened. "Hero, I am your father. You will listen to my orders. Go to your room. I will discuss these matters with you privately."

Hero's eyes wandered, then returned to his father. "By definition, you are my father, but parenting requires a more nurturing hand."

Niteo reached back and struck Hero across the brow, unintentionally cutting him with his ring, and knocking him against Fortis. "There is your nurturing hand."

Fortis's eyes flashed as he noticed the stream of blood trickling down the side of Hero's face. Flames erupted from his body and created a scorching white light. He ripped Niteo from his chair.

Isis lunged forward and gripped Fortis by the wrist, extinguishing his flames. "Fortis, let him go." Lowering her voice, she reminded him, *"The High King is here."*

Khnum folded his hands and observed with a grave expression, letting out a low hum as he judged without remark.

"It was a simple accident," Niteo defended. As much as he might have wanted to punish Fortis for his behavior, he couldn't challenge an Ancient, and certainly not an elemental of Fortis's status.

The High King never chastised Niteo for his parenting and, as usual, sat back to let the fight develop. Anyone might have guessed he visited to study something.

Fortis shook Niteo again like a ragdoll. "An accident? How about trapping him in the palace while you ran around Mu, drinking and playing! Was that an accident?"

"Fortis, your accusations are uncalled for." Niteo patted the air in a struggle to calm the witnesses around him. "Hero pushed the matter too far. It won't happen again, right?" He looked at Hero last to prompt an answer.

Hero slowly rejoined the discussion, touching his injury and inspecting the blood on his hand. His Taint writhed around inside of him, hissing and spitting.

Isis helped him stand upright, and knelt at his side to clean the wound with a handkerchief. "Let's get you cleaned up, okay? I'll take care of you."

Hero's head rushed with too many thoughts. Initially, he'd felt too despondent to react, but thinking about how Niteo treated him made his anger fester. No Ancient in all Euphoria would permit a mere Rahma to strike them. He determined that Niteo must be punished, if not for disrespecting a higher breed, then certainly for child abuse. More importantly, the man served absolutely no good purpose to the world or to Hero if he continued living.

Fortis still hadn't concluded his argument. He shouted back at Niteo, ridiculing his inappropriate behavior, and struck him so hard that Niteo flew off his feet into the middle of the hall.

The corners of Hero's lips twitched, and his cheeks flushed. His gaze rose to the chandelier dangling over Niteo and, at once, he knew what he wanted to do.

Isis pulled Fortis back by the arm. "Enough! The miasma is driving you mad!"

Hero trusted his elemental abilities even without proper training. If he wanted, he could stand perfectly still and conjure it by his will alone.

A quiet crackle surfaced from the ceiling. At any moment, the chandelier would crash to the ground and crush his father. The longer it dangled, the greater Hero's anticipation. It tickled his fingertips, exciting him and the miasma more.

The instant the cord snapped, Kyou vaulted over the dining table and dove straight for Niteo. Both men slid across the floor as the chandelier crashed to the floor, shattered, and sprayed crystal through the air. The vision of crystal shooting out elicited a distant memory but it was too fuzzy for Hero to call it back to mind.

Isis and Fortis jumped back instinctively, their mouths open and their eyes fixed to the hole in the ceiling.

Hero remembered the pure, red rage that flashed before him when Kyou glanced back, his relaxed expression and deep violet eyes full of disapproval.

If not for Kyou's actions, Hero would have been handed over to the Council for the murder of his parents, no doubt, but at the time, the miasma made it impossible to care about any repercussions that might follow.

He left the adults to the chaos while he took his escape to the music room, two steps at a time up the stairs. His head ached a little more with each clamoring movement and, yet, he still slammed the door to the music room just to make a final point. The miasma gnawed at him, stirring up aggravation as if tiny insects crawled under his skin. Whenever he found himself in this state, he took his place on the piano bench to distract himself and keep from lashing out in any way. He knew of no other way to quell the beast writhing inside. Besides, he had a mission to fulfill, a symphony of four complex tunes, and he barely knew one-third of the first movement.

Hero concentrated hard on the notes he had already inscribed and began the tune, struggling to draw up the newest part of his first movement. He did this for as long as he could before Kyou and Fortis entered.

Fortis sat down in the lounge area while Kyou plunked down on the bench, setting his fingers to the keys and strategically transforming the jarring algorithm to something softer and blither.

The second interruption disrupted Hero so much that his aura cracked the piano keys. Now Kyou interfered with his lifelong mission. His hair stood on end and the room darkened. "What do you want?"

Kyou wiped his hands on his dress pants and spoke with a smooth, calm voice. "I'm Iunu Kyou, the First Prince of Inoue. It's nice to meet you."

Hero narrowed his eyes.

That doesn't answer my question.

"You're talented, but you shouldn't take out your anger on the piano," Kyou said, folding his hands over his knee.

Hero blinked once to show he heard the suggestion.

Kyou didn't appear to mind the silence. "Want to talk about what happened?"

"What is there to discuss?"

"The chandelier."

Hero ventured off mentally, trying to elude Kyou's accusation. "Ah, that was scary, wasn't it?"

Kyou tipped his head with a smirk. "I know you're a clever kid." The man smiled in an all-knowing way that said, *"Do I look convinced? We both know what you've done."*

Hero inspected his new opponent carefully, down to the fiber of his coat. This would be a difficult and trying battle—not a hair seemed out of place, every fiber in order. "What do you want?"

Kyou shifted, placing a leg on each side of the bench, and faced Hero. "Your abilities as an elemental show great potential, but I must know… did you mean to drop the chandelier?"

Hero knew by Kyou's question that he need not answer. If Kyou had noticed that Hero's capabilities as an ice elemental caused the chandelier to fall, he also knew Hero did it intentionally.

Even trained Elementals often struggled to control themselves under emotional stimulus. If Hero had simply lost control of his element, it wouldn't have been so calculated. The ice would've spread in every direction, not simply to the cord of the chandelier.

Hero twisted his jaw in discontent. This new opponent troubled him.

"No response?" Kyou leaned forward, as closely as Hero allowed. "What if I told you there's another Caeles?"

Hero squinted hard. "My clan is lost."

Kyou grinned, brimming with pride. "That's what they say, but it's not true. Your family is rare, not lost. Ever heard the name Caeles Chi?"

Hero's glower intensified. He never trusted anyone or believed anything without proof.

"She's the Captain of the Elite Guard at the Capital," Kyou said.

"Never heard of her."

"Then, I will take you to her. It's time the two of you formally met."

He scrutinized Kyou with bafflement and doubt.

"I'll ask my father. I'm sure he'd love nothing more than to help strengthen the Caeles Family." The strange man stood and sauntered out of the room.

Silence set in as Hero pondered, but he eventually found his way to Fortis. "What he said…."

"Hmm?" Fortis rested against his hand, simply listening and watching the aftermath of Kyou's ploy.

"Is there really another Caeles?"

"Yes, she's a real person." He patted the cushion beside him until Hero sat down. "Chi's wonderful and a close friend of the High Queen. You wouldn't remember but Chi visited several times when you were an infant. She just adores you." He laughed, looking back on his fond memories.

"Fortis, you're old."

Fortis protested gently. "I'm not old, Hero. You're just very young."

"It's all a matter of perspective."

He smirked. "Oh, really? If that's so, then you are very short, and even if you object and say I'm tall, it's all a matter of perspective."

Hero scrunched his nose. "You have a point."

Kyou returned minutes later, gripping the doorframe. "You should be packing! Why are you still sitting there?"

Hero blinked hard. "I... he said I can go?"

"My father *is* the High King," Kyou said, looking around the room for the cause of confusion. "If he says you can go, then you're going."

"But, he *said* it, right? That's what you're telling me?"

"That's what I'm saying. You can go! Pack your things!"

Hero rushed to his room, grabbed a bag from his wardrobe, and collected some clothes. He had almost finished when he stopped to deliberate between two blue shirts.

Kyou came looking for him and leaned in the door, griping. "What's taking so long?"

"*Leihs* or *egas*," Hero said, thinking very deeply.

Kyou threw out his hands to each side. "Why does it matter which color you choose? What is the difference?"

"It affects my mood."

"By all that is, it's just a shirt!" Kyou lifted the shirt in Hero's right hand. "Just choose this one."

Egas. A vibrant color, like that of the flowers in the land below.

Hero stared hard, then grunted quietly to express his agreement. He used everything, down to the color of his shirts, as variables to determine Kyou's personality and intentions. The man interested him. Hero held Kyou in high favor despite the disruption in his plan to terminate Niteo. So far, he seemed to be a free thinker—completely independent from the Council and the Rebellion.

Kyou held up a pouch full of black bands designed like bracelets and rings. "I need you to put on some things before we leave. These are special suppressants that you must wear to suppress the miasma. If you do, your condition should improve slightly."

Hero took it and observed silently for a sign of deception. The idea of wearing something unknown from someone he barely knew concerned him for several reasons, but Kyou seemed well-intended, so Hero relented and slipped them on, curious as to where this new variable might lead him.

"All right then, let's be on our way."

The regal high prince walked ahead, occasionally checking to see if Hero followed. He carried the equanimity of a soldier and the charm of an entertainer, which, to Hero, reflected the very principles of an Iu. It made sense that they ruled in both Mu and Thule.

"Hurry! Come look!" Kyou waved him forward from the opening of the entrance and gazed up at the clearing skies.

Even after causing Nex to suffer from a wake of endless cold fronts, Hero never considered that the cause of the Capital's weather might be another Caeles like himself. Everyone knew his clan was lost, and yet no one had mentioned the existence of another relative. In that moment, he realized how easy everyone found it to lie or bury things, because this man, whom he only just met, spoke the truth so simply.

Hero was not so foolish that he'd believe everything Kyou said—not just yet. After all, the simplest way to gain one's trust was to tell them something true that others had not.

Kyou held out his hand to Hero again, urging him to come closer. "Clear today, huh? You must be happy."

Hero grasped Kyou's hand and nodded. The weather proved his happiness, even if he couldn't feel it. The High Prince resembled what he imagined a good father to be.

Kyou hesitated, glancing at the hand that had grasped his own.

Present Hero understood that his younger self misunderstood the purpose of Kyou's outstretched hand, but he had held Kyou's hand because he saw no other purpose that he should have extended it.

The Young Prince Hero held so few affections and emotions towards people and surroundings, he usually viewed things from a simplistic viewpoint, and this caused many misunderstandings. He believed that everything was in its place for a reason.

Kyou laughed outright and firmly clasped the boy's hand. "I can't wait to show you the Capital. I know Chi and I can teach you a lot in seven suns." They approached the carriage waiting along the stone path, and Kyou lifted Hero inside. "When you're with me, you're free to be whoever you want." Kyou climbed in next and the footman closed the door. When he and Kyou met eyes, the man's face turned red.

Kyou smirked.

Hero glanced between them, unaware of the suggestive meaning behind Kyou's actions. "What was that?"

"What was what?" Kyou leaned against his hand.

"Why did he turn red?"

Kyou laughed hard to himself and poked Hero between the eyes. "When you're older, you'll learn all kinds of things, so you have to nurture that studious nature of yours."

Present Hero knew, and the ignorance of his younger self embarrassed him. Kyou was always up to something raunchy, just like Fortis. They secretly held power and influence over others through seduction.

Yet the young Hero had known nothing, and asked in all his naivety, "There are things only adults know?"

"Yeah, that's right."

He looked up and around the carriage in thought. "I think that's called ageism, Kyou."

Kyou laughed even louder and harder than before. He inspected Hero with his peripheral vision and turned his head to the side. "So, what did you bring?"

Hero kicked his feet back and forth on the seat, bothered that the floor of the carriage lay just out of reach. "Books and clothes."

"Chi has a lot of books, if you're interested in reading."

The carriage began moving with a lurch, and Hero slid across the seat to look out the window. He hadn't said anything or expressed any excitement because he always feared his father would appear and drag him back inside the palace. "Education is important. No one will like me if I'm uneducated."

Kyou calmly analyzed him. "That is completely untrue."

Given that Hero didn't receive the same attention from his father, he felt unusually pressured. He questioned his logic, the very logic his father had instilled in him. "How so?"

Kyou raised his head, his expression one of calmness that soothed Hero. "I think you're somewhat studious by nature, but there's more to you as a person. You just haven't discovered it yet." His eyes narrowed onto something faraway in his memory. A lot of older Ancients did this. "You're still a child. You should be outside playing with other children. By any chance, are you friends with Abyssus?"

"Friends?" Hero bit his lip nervously. He had met Abyssus and analyzed him enough to dissect his personality but didn't know him on a personal level. Technically, the answer was no, though Hero recognized that he might have been expected to have introduced himself. He had not.

Kyou stretched out a hand and pinched Hero's cheek. "That's not a trick question. If you don't know, then say so, and don't chew up your lip like that."

Hero raised a hand to prevent his habit. He decided at that moment that if Kyou didn't like something, he wouldn't do it.

Kyou's forehead wrinkled and his teeth bared, forming a grimace. "Also, I don't know what your father has taught you, but my ways are not the *only* ways, nor are they necessarily the best. You don't need to listen to everything that everyone tells you."

Hero clenched his jaw. His father drilled so many rules into his head that he panicked when Kyou challenged them. "I don't understand."

"Your father is manipulative, Hero. When you're around him, you only need to do what keeps you out of harm's way." Kyou sighed with a look of empathy. "Now, I personally don't believe in discrimination, but you're an Ancient. You're much stronger and smarter than he is. If he's abusing you, then you need to establish your difference in power. Elaine would have beaten him to death with a spoon if she knew what he was up to."

"You knew my mother?"

"Did I know her?" Kyou chortled at the thought. "The whole Capital *knew* her. She wasn't exactly introverted... which reminds me, the woman I told you about, Chi, is Elaine's twin sister—your aunt."

Hero's eyes widened slightly. "What? Why didn't anyone tell me?"

"Because Niteo somehow convinced the Council that it would be bad for you two to meet. Chi is going to be so surprised when I take you to the Capital. I can't wait to see her face." Kyou reclined comfortably and kicked his legs up across the opposing seat.

Hero scrunched his nose at this. He was a proper and conservative child who never disgraced his father without severe repercussions. It seemed surprising that the First Prince of the Capital would behave this way.

Kyou chatted mindlessly. "Recently, she has been throwing fits about stealing you away from the palace, but my mother always manages to calm her temper."

Hero rested his head against the window of the carriage and extended his hand to the passing trees. He imagined what Chi might look like, and whether she would be excited to see him. Everything happened so quickly — the fight with his father and the sudden journey to the Capital. The rush of stimulus overwhelmed him to the point where he lacked response.

"Hero, I wanted to mention...." Kyou's words pulled Hero's attention back into the carriage. Their eyes met, conveying Kyou's sincerity and observation through a glimmer in his gaze. "I've heard from Fortis that you often feign smiles or tears. You don't need to bottle up your emotions. When you're angry, just let it out. If you feel sad, then cry, but don't pretend."

"But I don't *feel* anything. How will I convey my thoughts without portraying a normal reaction?"

"I'm trying to tell you it isn't normal to *pretend* you're feeling something. I can tell you get angry but... isn't there anything else?"

Hero's brow twitched as a sharp pain struck his eye. He tried his best to think of an answer, but....

"I see. As an elemental, you must learn to connect with your emotions, or you'll never be able to reach your full potential. I want you to see Chi's skill. I think you'll start to understand what you're capable of." Kyou concluded the discussion and sat quietly for the rest of the ride.

Present Hero couldn't imagine why his memories of Kyou were important. It seemed that without Fate there, he might have just gone off path and gotten lost in old memories.

Everything suddenly stopped just as it was — Kyou resting and the carriage no longer in motion, even the dust hovered in place — and a white, glowing shroud appeared on the opposite seat, forming into a fennec fox with one gold eye and one mint green eye.

Hero lifted his head and stared back it. "Are you —"

"This is one of your most precious memories," the fox interrupted him. "It may not be very telling of the murders, but it is quite telling of you."

"So, it's not of use?"

"To whom? Traveling through the six doors brings you closer to a spiritual awakening, but be wary, for sometimes what you *think* you want evokes more than you have bargained for."

Hero confessed, "If traveling through the six doors brings us closer to the truth, then I don't mind sacrificing something."

The fox's tail twitched. "Are you sure? You have no clue what is buried in here. Are you prepared to martyr yourself for the truth? I sense that you still harbor some doubt about the results of your journey."

"More so now than I had before...."

"I urge you to enjoy the sentiment of your memories now. A storm lies ahead. If you still wish to continue, you may step through the carriage door."

Hero raised from his seat and stood in front of the carriage door, hovering his hand over the knob. He turned back to the fox once, clenching his hand. "May I ask you something?"

The fox nodded back at him.

"Do you think I'll regret it?"

"What you may regret, or doubt, is your ability, but I believe that your intentions of protecting the Mistress and those you hold dear shall remain true."

"Then... I don't need to question these matters any further." He faced the door, grasped the knob, and stepped outside.

14
WHAT I HOLD DEAR

Hero recalled that the original trip passed quickly. They crossed through the woods and approached a large waterway separating the Capital from the rest of Mu, and wasted more time waiting for the gate to clear than during the rest of the journey. It surprised him that Inoue rested so close to his kingdom and yet felt so far away until that moment. When they finally arrived, he jumped out over Kyou and cast an eye over his surroundings.

A forest of glowing crystal trees towered just beyond a gateway at the edge of the Centre. Most of the buildings and pathways consisted of carefully placed stones. In the distance, hundreds of small houses stood roof-to-roof all the way down the slope of the highland with the palace placed on top like a cake decoration. Despite the allotted space, the community clustered together in a bustle of tightly knit homes, shops and carts. A ring of shops traced the Centre with strings of tiny white lights as a plethora of people moved about their daily business.

Kyou stepped down from the carriage and placed his hands on Hero's shoulders. He spoke with a sort of dramatic and deep voice that Hero found himself wishing to hear. "Welcome to Inoue, the Capital of the Empire."

Inoue Com's air smelled distinctly of salt, honey, and spices. The sound of the ocean waves swished through the Centre, and the entire place exuded a peculiar resonance of his lost clan. The slight sound of chimes mingled with the gentle breeze, creating a soothing lull. The chilled air and fine mist calmed Hero immensely. He breathed in the crisp scent and smiled at the sights before him. "It feels like home."

Kyou patted his back. "Right? I thought you would say that."

Several guards stood around the gate to the woods. Some meandered over to greet Kyou but gawked at Hero instead. "Praise be! Is that Elaine's son?"

Kyou shushed them. "I'm trying to surprise Chi! Don't ruin it!"

One of the soldiers whispered frantically, "I thought he couldn't leave the palace!"

"My father was there. We happened to witness some of Niteo's *unsightly* behavior."

The soldier snarled. "Ugh, that again? Not sure if I should call it lucky or unfortunate." He beamed at Hero in acceptance. "Welcome to Inoue Com, kid! Go greet your aunt before she storms out here and skins us alive."

"Hide behind me," Kyou said, pushing Hero back in excitement.

They toddled towards the right side of the Centre and into a cottage. As they made their entrance, a woman sprang out, startling Kyou. He shouted and his posterior end hit Hero's face, much to his disapproval and alarm.

The white-haired woman cackled riotously, her armor jingling as she slapped a hand against her stomach. "Oh, Kyou! You should have seen your face! I thought Cibul would enter, but this is even better!"

Kyou put a hand against his chest. "I brought you a surprise and this is how you repay me?"

"Surprise?"

He stepped aside and patted Hero's head. "This one."

The white-haired woman breathed in sharply, her mint eyes welling with tears. "Hero?"

The moment he saw her, the feeling of familiarity struck him again. This time, he grasped it better than when the chandelier had fallen and immediately recognized the woman. Reflecting on the moment, the present Hero now understood exactly why he got that feeling. At one time, he knew her and others solely by scent and sound. Thus, he found her scent of potions and spices incredibly familiar, as well as her resolute tone of voice.

Everything about her created a deep resonance of the past, the first trigger in his memories for a long time.

"Go ahead," Kyou said.

Hero bowed politely, reciting his usual greeting. "It's a pleasure to meet you. I am Prince Hero of Nitor." He remembered Kyou's suggestion to be natural and corrected himself. "Um... are you my aunt?"

Chi dropped to her knees and flung her arms around him. "I was about to kick in the doors at Nitor Palace just to see you." She took in his scent by burrowing her nose into his neck. "I have missed you so much."

Hero said nothing as he also took in her scent.

Kyou rallied. "I had to bring him here. Elaine would have killed Niteo if she saw what he did!"

Chi stroked Hero's head. "What did he do now? I will kill him myself!"

"Should I tell her?" Kyou and Hero locked their gaze. "Or do you want to do it?"

Chi sat back on her haunches, pressing her hand to Hero's cheek as she inspected him. "What? Why? What happened?" Her mint eyes appeared almost transparent, as though he could see straight into her soul, which shone with similar vibrancy as Kyou's.

Hero yearned to be around that effervescent presence. He wanted to trust in them. The life and purity they exhibited differed so vastly from his own corrupt aura that he both envied and admired them.

Chi caressed his face with warm hands. "Hero, I am your aunt. You can tell me anything."

"He struck me," Hero said, lowering his gaze to the floor. "It was the first time. He usually isn't around."

"What?" Her gaze turned cold, a reminder that behind her kindness, she still embodied the will of their clan.

Hero expected ice to form, but she had incredible control over her emotions and abilities.

Chi stood suddenly. "I am taking this news to Heqet."

Hero tilted back his head to see Kyou. "Who's Heqet?"

Chi's mouth dropped open as she interrogated Kyou. "He doesn't even know the name of our High Queen?"

Kyou appeared stoic for once. "My mother."

Hero had known about the High Queen, just not by her given name. Everyone considered it rude to call Royals by their name, unless their status was equal or higher than that of the person they addressed.

Chi took many slow, deep breaths to calm herself. "Hero, you are of Royal blood and the last heir of our clan—you are a part of the High Court and should be treated as such. Anyway, before that happens... welcome to Inoue Com."

Kyou sat down at the large table by the window, borrowed the spare mug, and helped himself to a milky drink in the silver kettle. "What shall we do first then, go sightseeing?"

Chi snatched the mug from his hands and offered it to Hero. "Try this. I think you will like it. You did when you were much smaller." She sat on the floor in front of him, watching him sniff the drink as she began smacking Kyou's side. *"Me'em ouin! Oliar kun yan?"*

'I'm happy! Have you eaten yet?'

"Vol pa," Hero answered, sipping from the mug. The taste of the drink paralleled the scent of the air in Inoue Com, sweet like honey and rich of spices.

Chi launched forward on her knees, just inches from Hero's face. "Did you just respond to me?"

"Yeah, why?"

She spoke in nearly a whisper. *"Irln so aen L.o.A?"*

'You understand the L.o.A?'

Hero tilted his head. "The what?"

Chi jumped up and left the room. When she returned, she opened a book and pointed to a small passage. *"Raos qui?"*

'Can you read this?'

Hero read the passage as requested, but only because she was his aunt. *"Sael ke leai rem nurul."*

She lunged at him with the book. "Which means?"

He jerked away from her. "The light of tomorrow shines brighter."

She shrieked at a hair-splitting volume. "I can't believe it, Kyou!"

Hero winced as he looked to Kyou for an explanation. "Did I do something weird?"

Kyou rubbed his chin. "You're speaking the Language of Ages."

"So?" Hero drank the interesting beverage to dodge questions. Even if they didn't say anything, he knew the language to be a remnant of the original Ancients, those who existed before the creation of the Mortal Realms—the First Thirteen. Only a few still spoke in this tongue.

Kyou rose from the table and gave Hero a final glance with his peripheral vision. "Chi, how about you show Hero one of your ice performances?"

Chi lowered the book. Silence for the Caeles could mean a lot of things. They didn't always need words to respond. She simply didn't disagree, which showed her acceptance.

Kyou pointed a thumb towards the door. "Hero, let's wait outside."

Hero placed the mug on the table and hurried after Kyou. "She seemed upset."

Kyou grabbed Hero's head, holding him close. "Don't worry about Chi. She has a lot of hope in her heart. She'll dust herself off."

Hero didn't fully understand what Kyou meant, he was just happy that he wasn't in trouble. He waited with Kyou outside the cottage for some time, wondering what to expect.

The cottage door opened, and Chi appeared wearing long white material that draped around her body, exposing her midriff and legs. She wore various pieces of jewelry on her ankles, wrists, and across her forehead.

Hero wondered aloud, "Why is she dressed like that?"

"It's the traditional dance robes from your clan," Kyou said.

A crowd gathered around as they noticed her attire.

She stood pin-straight and tossed back her head, inhaling slowly, but not yet exhaling. She extended her arms over her head and respired, releasing a stream of soft ice into the air. The delicate sleet whirled above, forming a circle as she spun on the balls of her feet, using her arms to control her element. Her movements were so practiced and graceful, that of a dancer performing a routine. One of her whirlwinds fashioned a small fox that bounded through the air to Hero's feet.

He knelt and curiously touched it, allowing the particles of the ice to rush through his fingers.

The Centre teemed with Chi's creations, the fox, birds, fish, rabbits, a team of mice and a flurry of butterflies, all moving as she willed. The birds and butterflies flew, while the fox chased the rabbits and mice, and the fish swam around them all, swirling through the air much to the crowd's delight.

Hero studied each creature, and finally fell back onto the fox, which stopped its pursuit and sat in front of him just observing him closely. *Why isn't it moving like the others?*

Chi stopped and raised her hands again. All the ice gathered above the crowd, then burst into smaller particles that glittered in the sunlight.

Hero watched in awe of her presentation. For once, he felt the wonders of the world expanding around him. He saw the potential for beauty in abilities he'd used maliciously.

Chi walked back and leaned down, beaming. "How was it?"

"How did you learn to do that?"

She sighed blissfully. "My cousins and I used to practice together and experiment with our abilities. Elaine too. The world was different when we were all together. I wish I could show you."

Hero touched her arm to comfort her. He didn't have to feel anything to see the pain in others. He understood well enough that he should comfort a person when they expressed sadness. "You're alone?"

"Alone, but not lonely," Chi reassured him, caressing the side of his face. "I have you, always." She held his hand and stared out at the crystal forest, as if calling to the trees with longing and questions.

Why 'always?' How would she know that?

Hero watched it with her, listening to its chimes and wondering precisely what created the sound. "What's that?"

"Oh." She took a shallow breath before answering. "That is the crystal forest, the Ussan."

"Why do you look so sad?"

Kyou stepped up to Hero's opposite side and put a hand on his head. "There was once a magnificent crystal empire. The Caeles lived there before the fall."

Hero looked back and forth between them. "What happened?"

"I couldn't say. The story is incomplete."

"Incomplete?" He frowned. The endless variables frustrated him. For every answer he received, many new questions surfaced.

Chi closed her eyes and breathed in and out again, though she labored against her pain. "We lost almost everyone in our clan in the fall of the empire. It was horrific for those few survivors. Even if we wanted to talk about it, it just hurt too much. The Crystal Empire fell with our rulers, but I cannot tell you how they died. No one left alive knows, because anyone from our clan who'd been close enough to see perished." Her voice grew unsteady, angry even. "And those who caused it hide in the shadows like cowards, unwilling to take the blame for their actions."

Hero observed the Ussan a final time. Like many Ancients, he felt its call and knew it held many secrets. He noticed the guards standing watch around the entrance of the forest. "Is the forest dangerous?"

"Extremely," she said. "The crystals grow when they touch any form of moisture. The nature of crystal is simply too dangerous to tamper with."

Hero twisted his head. "Even for the Caeles?"

Kyou flashed a cheesy grin. "That's what she says. You see, your aunt specializes in studies of the Ussan. She's an expert when it comes to remedies."

"That is precisely why I know it is dangerous—even for the Caeles."

Hero wanted to ask why the clan chose to live in such a dangerous place, but sensed that neither Chi nor Kyou intended to divulge such secrets to him.

She bowed her head down to meet Hero's gaze. "Would you like to eat?"

Hero agreed by emitting a small sound resembling a grunt.

Chi giggled softly. She wasn't his mother, but she exuded the same level of adoration he expected of one. "*Keiyan*, little Caeles."

Kyou shook Hero by the head. "What part of this is *cute*?"

"*Ya!* Stop that!" She slapped off his hands and plucked Hero from the ground.

Kyou backed away. "Okay, okay. What should we feed him?"

Chi swayed subtly from side to side with Hero in her arms. "Let us go back to the cottage. We can talk more there."

They returned as suggested, and she placed Hero down so she could prepare food at the furnace. As she spoke, Kyou and Hero sat at the large table by the window to listen. "Hero, if there is anything you would like to know, please feel free to ask me. I would love nothing more than to share my knowledge with you."

"Aunt Chi, who am I supposed to be?"

"What?" She turned with her wooden spoon in hand. "What do you mean by that?"

"It's just... Kyou said I did something bad... but I still don't see how I made a mistake."

She glanced inquisitively at Kyou. "What is he talking about?"

"Interesting topic," Kyou said, sipping a new mug full of the sweet tea. "Hero dropped a chandelier on Niteo this morning."

Chi stretched out her neck, reminding Hero much of a turtle trying to reach a piece of lettuce just barely out of reach. "Did it hit him?"

"Nope," he said with one firm swish of his head.

"Oh." Her body relaxed again. "So, what is the problem?"

"Basically, Hero doesn't *feel*," Kyou finally answered, waving a hand around his chest. "There's no output, and the input doesn't faze him."

Chi faced her nephew. "Hero, when you saw my performance, did you feel anything?"

Hero looked up at the ceiling as he envisioned the performance. He needed to put himself back in the moment to remember if he felt anything. "I thought your abilities were amazing."

"Thoughts and feelings are different things. Thoughts can influence our emotions, but they are not the same. Emotions play an enormous role for us. We are Elementals... if we do not measure our limits and understand our emotions, we cannot control our abilities."

Hero twisted his jaw. "I don't get it."

Chi smiled in response. "It is okay. You just do not have anything that you feel attached to yet. It is our job to provide you the proper care so that you can understand how to make healthy life decisions." She thrust the spoon against Kyou's chest and strolled towards the hallway. "Kyou, feed him. When you are done, you can go to the back and read my books. I will be out again soon."

Kyou and Hero exchanged a confused glance. Neither of them knew the reason for her departure, so Kyou stood and finished cooking the soup she had prepared.

Hero leaned forward with amazement. "You can cook?"

Kyou chuckled. "Of course."

"But you're a prince."

"All adults should know how to cook. You never know when you will find yourself without a chef."

Hero bobbed his head, accepting Kyou's logic.

While Kyou cooked, Hero gazed out the window, continuously surprised to see the Capital. He wanted to connect emotionally to Kyou and Chi, and it upset him that he lacked understanding.

Kyou ate with Hero, sharing that he wasn't sure why exactly Chi left and felt he should wait for her to communicate. They finished their meal and opened the back room to read until she returned.

The night fell before she finally entered, holding something behind her back with a smile that stretched from ear to ear.

Kyou sat up, pulling down the black scarf from his face. "Ah, she's alive."

Chi crouched down in front of Hero. "I have something to give you."

"You mean...." Hero paused, suffering from one of his mental hiccups. "...like a present?"

"Yes, of course! I intended to finish today, but then you came to visit, and I could not pull myself away." She lifted out a white stuffed fox the size of a cat. "Happy birthday to the youngest member of the clan."

Kyou stuck his hand into his coat, removed a wrapped package, and flippantly placed it next to Hero. "Happy birthday, kid, or maybe termite is more accurate? Small and menacing."

Chi cracked Kyou's arm to stop his heckling.

Hero swayed back, as if compelled by some invisible wave. Maybe it was emotion, or just plain shock, since he'd forgotten about his birthday after the incident with the chandelier. He grasped the stuffed fox, tilting his head at it. "What's its function?"

"Hmm?" Chi checked Kyou again, as though she wanted him to jump in and explain Hero's commentary. "*What*, you ask? Well, I suppose you can consider it a symbol of the Fox Clan and my affections for you. We are two out of three remaining Caeles in existence, so we must be proud of our lineage."

Hero's eyes widened slightly. "You made it?" He squinted hard at the fabric and made note of each material she used. "What's the Fox Clan?"

"The Fox Clan is a small group within the Caeles Family, a tiny branch made up of those who did not fit in with the wolf pack. I suppose you could say we are the misfits."

He stored the information away for later and moved back to his lingering question. "There's *another* Caeles?"

"Yes, my cousin. He is constantly traveling so we rarely get the chance to speak... but I will try and hunt him down for you some time."

Kyou leaned against his arm. "Just this morning, you thought you were the last Caeles in all existence. How does it feel to uncover the truth?"

Hero opened his mouth to speak and stopped partway. At the time, he had thought: *I don't feel anything. Am I supposed to feel something?*

Chi laughed in a forced manner. "It is okay, Hero. I know you have never received anything like this before. At least once, I wanted to give you something made with care."

"Thank you," he said, trying to be polite.

"Get some rest so we can take you on a tour tomorrow."

Kyou closed his book and blew out the candle, then grunted as he sat up. "Yep, time to rest then."

Hero collected the fox, and Kyou's present, and followed into the front room. They turned right into a hallway and walked straight into the guest bedroom. All the furniture in the cottage had been fashioned of wood. Even the colorful quilt on the bed appeared to have been hand-stitched, which made Hero wonder how much of the place Chi had put together by herself, if not everything.

Kyou crawled over the bed on his knees to draw back the sheer curtain. "Look, isn't it pretty?"

Hero gazed out the window from the bed. The sky glowed white as soft snowflakes fell to the Centre's stone pathway. Mist hung over the community, enhancing the illumination of the Ussan. "Six suns."

"Are you counting down?" Kyou knocked Hero over and pulled back the covers of the bed. "If you keep that up, you're going to get depressed, and that's a feeling you don't want to feel." He gestured for Hero to come closer with a small nod and a wave.

Hero responded to Kyou's beckoning, and they lay on their stomachs looking out the window at the forest.

"Want to tell me about your life at the palace?"

"What's to tell?"

"Feelings."

Hero perceived a deep resonance from the chilling chime of the forest outside. The longer he watched it, the louder it sang. He wanted to be as expressive as the forest. "Every day is the same. I wake up. I stare at the ceiling. The world feels still."

"Maybe it's not the world but something inside of you." Kyou pressed a hand over Hero's heart.

"How come you see me?"

"What?"

Kyou could charm anyone in the world. His eyes held infinite adoration for the people around him. His laugh sounded so deep and true that Hero admired him.

"Kyou, you're amazing." Hero embarrassed himself slightly, but he didn't hide. He decided to respect Kyou just as Kyou had respected him.

The older and admirable prince ruffled Hero's hair. "So are you, you just don't know it yet."

"How do I learn?"

"Everyone's different. Some of us find it in the world, our Bound, our parents, or even ourselves."

Hero tilted his head again. "Bound?"

Kyou stared agape for a moment and then wrapped his arms under his pillow and rested his face on it. "Bound are our missing halves, our soul's only true desire."

"You mean... like a soulmate?"

"Hmm... that's a Rahma term though." Kyou turned his head from side to side in deliberation. "Rahma like to dream of being Bound. That's why they talk about soulmates, but being Bound is a little different. When you find your mate, you can feel the entire world come to a stop. Everything that they are and everything that you are become one. Sometimes, without realizing it, you can feel your soul's journey through time with them."

The explanation carried deep emotion that even Hero sensed and yearned to understand. "Soul's journey?"

"When you're Bound to someone, it's infinite. No matter how long you live or how many times you die, you will always find each other, and your love will persevere." Kyou's violet eyes glowed brightly against the light from the Ussan. He stared out the window again, traveling someplace far away. He showed a completely new smile, full of sadness and longing. "When you meet your Bound, you can feel the stars align. If you've lived together, you can feel those worlds come together to form a singular moment in time. It's like you fall in love all over again, with every life you've ever lived together. They are your world. They take away your breath only to breathe it back into you, and there is nothing more comforting or fulfilling in existence."

Hero's heart hurt just watching Kyou speak. Through his observations, he gathered that being Bound meant as much pain as it did bliss. He contemplated it deeply and wondered how to properly view it.

"Hero, when you return home, I want you to think about how you would like to live the rest of your life. If you don't have an answer, then seek one." Kyou pulled up the covers to Hero's chin and prepared to sleep.

"Okay," Hero said.

"You promise?"

"I promise." He nestled into the blankets with the stuffed fox.

"By the way, are you going to open my present?"

"No," he said. "I want to open it when I return to Nitor. I want to save it for a day when I am all alone."

A sadness washed over Kyou's face and he patted Hero's head. "I see. I am glad you kept it then."

Present Hero felt some pleasure in remembering Kyou's gift. That was when he received *The Story of Night and Day*, and he had always cherished it.

Kyou yawned. "You might not find our gifts practical, but sometimes it's more important to give something meaningful. You've been deprived of care for too long, and if we don't show it to you now, you'll never understand."

Hero responded with his usual grunt-like sound. He heard Kyou even as the room started to blur around him.

"Goodnight, Hero. Happy birthday."

Kyou's strong, gentle hand ruffled Hero's hair again. It brought a deep comfort that Hero hadn't realized he sought.

This bond stirred something deep and forgotten, something he yearned to recover. He had succumbed to the darkness, sinking deeper and deeper inside its reaches. Perhaps he once felt something—if so, he wanted to feel it again. All his earliest memories faded one day, leaving behind an empty capsule. He felt like a shell. Maybe the shell once held something, but how would it regain its contents? Even if it did recover the lost pieces, would they be the same? He thought of a hermit crab; if the crab outgrew the shell, only another could move in. His brain grasped how sad this was, but his heart remained unfazed. Whomever he decided to be might not have been the same person he was previously. In a way, that caused him discomfort.

I wonder why I can't remember... who I wanted to be.

15
SOLACE

Emptiness always seemed boundless to me. No matter the depths I traveled, I never found an end. Perhaps that was my mistake — I too often sought an end to something when I should have been searching for the beginning.

"Hero, wake up." Kyou shook Hero's arm, forcing him awake.

The white light from the Ussan and the lights around the Centre glowed from the bottom of the closed curtain.

Kyou carried Hero from the room, set him down, and tried to stand him upright.

Hero stirred, slowly emerging from his deep slumber. By the time he opened his eyes, Kyou had dragged him into the front room. They trailed behind Chi as she rushed to the back, quietly closing the door.

Hero lowered himself by the bookshelves, listening to gain an understanding of the situation that had begun to unfold while he slept.

Chi whispered. "Niteo has sent word and wants Isis to take Hero back to Nitor. Bastards, sneaking through the night like trained assassins.... If I get my hands on that man...."

Kyou shook his head. "This is the Capital. By what right—"

"Council, most likely," Chi growled. "Isis is their eyes and ears in Mu. If that man complained enough, they would comply."

A knock resounded throughout the cottage, and she took Kyou and Hero by the hand. "Kyou, take Hero to the palace. I will do my best to deter them." She removed a piece of paper from her back pocket and placed it in Hero's hands. "Just in case, take this with you. This is the only memory I can share with you. Please take care of it." She kissed the top of his head and exited to answer the front door.

When she had gone, Kyou snuck Hero through the shadows. He gestured to keep low and checked the back windows. "They've surrounded us. If we can get to the palace, we can speak with my mother. I need you to stay close."

Hero crept behind Kyou towards a dark corner of the room, tucking the paper from Chi in the breast pocket of his shirt.

Kyou watched the street with furious concentration. "This is going to happen in the blink of an eye."

A soldier burst through the back door and grasped Hero by the arm. The stuffed fox he had tucked against his side flew across the floor and, though he thrashed, the guard who had grabbed him passed him onto another pair of soldiers while blocking Kyou with a spear.

Their scuffle ended quickly, as Kyou struck and dislodged the spear from the soldier's grip. All the while, the guards kept passing Hero amongst each other against his thrashing. He soon found himself by the gate, watching Chi and Kyou quarrel with the guards.

Chi landed a solid punch to one of the guards, knocking him to the ground. "That child is under the protection of the High King!"

Isis then stepped forth and silenced everyone with a wave of her hand. "I have a Council mandate to return Prince Hero to Nex. Cease your objections. The law will be upheld under penalty of treason."

Chi stomped across the Centre and lunged at Isis. "This is Capital ground! Do you think I'm stupid? You cannot bring your men here and do as you please! Release Hero and give him back to me!"

Isis stood her ground. "I'm afraid my servitude is to the Council, not to you. Unless the High King himself comes here and asks me to release the Prince, I will have to return him to his rightful place."

Kyou forced his way through the guards and stood beside Chi. "My father is the one who gave him permission to be here."

Isis signaled to her soldiers to put Hero in her carriage. "If I recall, I've heard that King Niteo didn't and, without the permission of both, you weren't allowed to bring him."

Kyou countered with a snap, "The High King's declaration supersedes the Rahma King."

"Your father gave you strict instructions to follow Council law. Do you intend to disobey him? I'd expect nothing less of the Wayward Prince."

Kyou's retorts fell silent. The dispute ended and the outcome was clear.

Hero stopped thrashing and glanced at the Ussan, the closest escape. Ice pierced through the surrounding soldiers, forcing them to release him. He hit the stone road, jumped to his feet, and darted off into the forest.

Kyou and Chi called out to him as the soldiers at the entrance sprang to grab him.

Hero shoved the armored men with a furious shout. Anima concentrated into his hands. A loud pop and the shrill cries of the guards echoed out before they darkened and burst into ash that slipped away on the icy breeze.

Kyou and Isis gasped.

Chi pleaded, "Hero stop!"

Hero stared down at his blackened palms and then ran aimlessly into the crystal trees. He sprinted, darting one direction then another, until the trees wound around him in a swirl of white light and a chatter of bells. The resonance hurt his ears. As hard as he tried to cover them and block it out, it rang so shrill that he shuddered, helpless to do anything except shield himself from the unrelenting sound. Soon, he collapsed in a flood of blinding white light.

Fate's voice trailed distantly, and a hand brushed against Hero's forehead. As he opened his eyes, a blurry, white illumination appeared before him. "Hero! Oh, praise be, can you hear me?"

He squinted, unable to see beyond the muddy flood of light. "Fate?"

Her figure doubled and created a fuzzy, indistinguishable blur. "Yes! It's me. Can you get up?" She helped him to his feet.

Hero's body ached when he sat up. Everything still blurred, the shapes around him having lost shape and clarity, including Fate. The light dissipated as soon as they exited the forest, which was obvious to him by the absence of the resonance and the diffusion of the light, but when something else moved and approached him, he could hardly tell it was a person, let alone his aunt.

Fate gripped his arms. "Hero, what were you doing in the forest?"

He shook his head at her, still squinting. "I... I was in the Dreamscape."

He recognized Chi's voice even though he couldn't see her. "Two of my men were found, disintegrated, outside of the Ussan, fortunately by Fate and not another. We will have to bury this, or you will be taken by the Council."

Disintegrated?

"Chi, his eyes...." Fate clung to his arm, offering him support.

"I see it too," Chi said. "For now, return him to the cottage. I will report to Heqet."

Fate put a hand against Hero's lower back and escorted him inside the cottage. The scent of Chi's herbs drifted through the air on their way through the front room. There was no use in Hero trying to see, so he allowed Fate to guide him from room to room.

One of her hands clutched his side and the other held his wrist to keep him steady. "We're in the guest room now," she said, carefully leading him to the bed. It creaked as they sat down.

Hero faced forward, keeping his hands between his legs for warmth. The Capital had never felt so cold. It was strange for him to even notice.

Fate rubbed his back. "What happened?"

"I found myself in the Dreamscape, but you weren't there. Behind the next door, there was a memory of when I joined the Rebellion. Back then, I was temporarily blinded by the Ussan, and I hadn't thought about it, but I think Akira might have tightened the seals to help me regain my sight. Now, I'm not so sure." He only felt shock, not sadness. No matter how hard he tried to see, he failed.

Fate caressed his face. "Your eyes look different."

"Different how?"

"It's like all the color has been washed out—they're silver and there's a white ring around your pupils."

He reflected on Undal. History had a way of repeating itself, so he'd expected all of this, but now that it finally happened to him, he worried.

"Can you see anything at all?"

There was no point in trying to look. "No."

Fate usually hid her feelings well, but her voice sounded tense. "It's that bad?"

"It would depend on what you consider bad." His eyes strained from the amount of light flooding into his vision. The effect on his vision made it appear as though he gazed through a prism.

"I'm sorry, Hero."

He thought back to the fox in the Dreamscape and recognized that it served as a sign that he was going to break the Third Seal. He rested his head back against the ground and swallowed hard. The third seal remained intact for now but, clearly, whatever stood between him and it breaking had been released. "When I was in the Dreamscape, I saw a fox. It warned me that I would have to sacrifice something in order to uncover the truth." According to the Rebellion, they traversed the Dreamscape to find evidence about the murders in Mu. However, Hero sought something more vital, something bigger than Mu and Thule combined.

Fate's hand brushed his hair back, grazing his ear. "If we could just find some evidence, then we'll be able to prove the perpetrator is guilty, but Hero, maybe this is about something else. Our purpose here is much greater. What if this has to do with your growth, and not the person who committed these crimes?"

He kept his thoughts about the bigger picture to himself, despite his theory that Fate wished for the same thing. "What if there isn't any evidence? Would there be a point?"

A man interjected. "There would be."

Fate took a deep breath and left the bedside. The whole mattress shifted when she moved, and Hero detected a faint adjustment of light.

She whispered from across the room, "What are you doing here?"

The man said, "Word travels fast in Niall. I'm sorry, but can you give us a moment?"

"Of course." Her footsteps left the area, and the door clicked shut.

The man dragged his feet as he walked and sat down where Fate had been. "Even if you can't see, I'm sure you can recognize me." His familiar voice brought a wave of relief over Hero.

Hero's heart raced when he felt the man's touch. He let the shock pass over before concentrating on the aura that radiated through the man's hand. It filled him with a heaviness and revealed a deep sorrow. He closed his eyes, soaking in the dark aura.

The man's spiritual energy was so strong, it created a shape in the nothingness.

Hero opened his eyes, taken aback. The darkness before him gradually took upon a more distinct shape. He swallowed a lump in his throat, unable to stop the tears filling his eyes.

"You know me," the man said, "but we're also strangers."

He probed. "Are we?" Something in his distant memories stirred like a creature from the Abyss.

The man let out a humored breath. "You tell me." His grip eased, and he pressed his hand flat against Hero's.

Hero sat for a moment and drew in the man's aura once more, basking in the memories that kept him feeling sane and whole. He spoke softly. "What do they call you now?"

"Jackyl."

Hero repeated, "Jackyl...."

Even though Jackyl had just loosened his grip, Hero once again held his hand tightly. He wanted to see Jackyl and study his appearance. If only he had come sooner.

Jackyl virtually mumbled when he talked. "I'm a Reaper from Niall... a Doll. I didn't come from this time, but I remember everything clearly."

"How? Is it a skill of Dolls?"

Jackyl struggled to find the proper words. "You could say that. Remembering is my skill. Even if Ancients and other Dolls have an awakening... my memory is better than most. That said, thanks to the Echoes, I'm able to remember everything about Abyssus... and everything that came before."

"Echoes... like reverberations from the past?"

"Right." Jackyl seemed content with the response.

Hero got the impression that Jackyl smiled, as the dark aura lightened slightly. Without thinking, he let his thoughts slip. "Were you the one who left the horse?"

"Yes."

The answer lifted all of Hero's concerns. He now knew that it wasn't a malevolent stranger but someone dear to him and directly tied to the artifact. "I'm glad."

Jackyl gripped Hero's hand, his touch resolute but not painful. "It's time to wake up. The Guardians are ready to move forward. Are you?"

The name reached a deep part of Hero's consciousness. He just couldn't recall what it meant. "Guardians? I don't know what you mean."

Jackyl's dropping energy indicated that he frowned. "You remember much but I suppose the Organization is too new."

"The Guardians are part of the third party? I've heard about them somewhat."

"Not really. We Guardians are the Protectors of Space and Time. It's an important job but not one you need to understand now. Once you awaken, you'll know. All you need to know right now is that I'm here for you."

Hero realized that he had begun to smile. No matter what form he came in, Jackyl brought Hero the utmost comfort. "Thank you."

"But... let's keep it a secret from Fate for now, okay?"

"Okay," he said, though he wondered if Jackyl meant it as a joke.

Jackyl embraced Hero and pressed a hand to the back of his head. "Just hold on a little longer."

16
A WHITE LIE

Life without vision grew routine after a while. As it turned out, Hero had spent so many long turns in Nitor Palace that he had managed to map out his environment in no time at all. Sometimes, he lost his footing, or walked into Fortis or Firmus. Counters, furniture, and corners became his greatest enemies.

From time to time, he accepted Fate's help, but *only* hers. When she left the palace, he dawdled around and retrained himself to associate with his surroundings.

Now blind and unable to spend countless days and nights reading, he decided to formally attend meetings to help Fate proceed with her restoration plans. She needed the time to collect evidence and prepare for her trial against Mortis.

Although the man had been at the back of everyone's mind, few wished to approach him because of his 'indestructible' constitution, and his standing as a Council member *and* the heir to the throne of Askadel. He bordered on untouchable, but Fate relentlessly pursued her options to corner the elusive Aska. It seemed that every time someone accused him of fleeing or presumed him dead, he reappeared to wreak havoc.

Hero said little about the matter, though something about Mortis left him unsettled, and he kept to his tasks as best he found able.

Within the following months, the Council took Mortis into custody for further questioning, after Fate rallied witnesses to testify. It was uncertain what progress they made, but many felt relief to at least have him temporarily in custody.

Despite her success, Fate acted strangely during the passing months. She disliked being touched, and sometimes flew off the handle unexpectedly. Her behavior proved highly out of character but she quickly regrouped after her outbursts.

Hero fretted that he may unintentionally be the cause, especially since he'd lost his vision. He had done his best to remain useful during these difficult times, even though she had done her best to explain that the strain she felt had little to do with him. It was difficult to reverse the thoughts Niteo had planted in his head and he wound up ill at ease.

In early spring, Hero spent a lot of time in the kitchen with the cook, Weimar, relearning his way around with blind eyes.

Weimar pulled something out of the oven.... *Rolls.*

Hero knew the sweet scent of the dough. He had always been observant, so he could still remember many things about the palace. Still, he figured he'd eventually forget. All things faded with time.

Weimar placed the tray on the counter with a soft scrape. "I've never asked before, and I'm not sure if it will bother you."

"If it does, I'll just say so."

The miasma poisoning didn't seem to frighten Weimar. Most of the time, he just kept Hero company while Fate was away studying the Ussan. "What is it like to be Tainted?"

The question reminded Hero that his energy emitted a dark aura like Jackyl's. The first time he'd passed a mirror after being blind, he shocked himself. "When I was young, people would tell me that I looked like a Child of Light."

"Child of light?"

Hero scratched his head, feeling foolish as he realized that a mere Rahma wouldn't know the history of the Ethereal Realm. "There's a place called the Beyond... the Realm of Light. Some people even referred to it as the Realm of Gods. They called it this because it held the Throne of the Universe, where the overseer and creator of all contemplated his dream of the worlds he conceived. Though many children lived in the Beyond, those touched by light, by the Grandmaster's spiritual strain, also radiated light in their aura and appearance."

The cook prepared his rolls as he listened. "These are the myths of the Ancients?"

"Myths...." Hero reached under his scarf and ran his fingers over the silver hourglass. He often wondered if his siding with Isis occurred because they shared a similar faith. When one called the tales of the Ancients and the scriptures mere myths, he found this equally as unsettling as the murders and Mortis's undying.

Weimar also touched the hourglass. "What's this?"

"A gift. Even though the person who gave it to me is a little crooked, I can't help but have a fondness for it."

"What does the symbol on the bottom mean?"

"Symbol?" Hero had observed his hourglass many times and couldn't remember there ever being a symbol engraved on it.

Weimar moved Hero's index finger to the bottom. "Here."

He traced the shape, confirming the presence of the symbol.

"Can you understand what it says?"

The symbol was so small.... "Do me a favor. Bring a pen and paper from my room and draw the symbol as big as you can."

"Of course, Highness."

Hero stepped down from the counter as Weimar left, continuing to run his finger along the symbol. He wondered if Akira had painted over the symbol before giving it to Hero.

Weimar interrupted his thoughts. He continuously checked the hourglass to copy the shape of the symbol. "Not sure if I did it justice, but I did try."

Hero raised out his hand. "Show me."

The cook took Hero's hand and brushed it over the shape of the symbol.

"Well done," Hero said, standing back. "I have some things to think about. I'll be excusing myself for now."

"Of course, Highness. I hope that I was able to be of assistance."

Hero's mouth twitched. "Absolutely."

For now, he had time to reflect on his discoveries. He crossed the main hall to the study and sat down on the large armchair that faced the fireplace. It had been his favorite spot to read; now it was his favorite spot to think. He touched the smooth leather and sank onto the cushion, relaxing. He then closed his eyes, and the symbol flashed clearly before him. It said, 'alone.' It seemed unlikely that *nuire* would be inscribed on the object, so it most likely read with the old dialect. *Bedad*.

The darkness pulled at him from some deep part of his consciousness. His rumination lured it out and forced him into a trance.

He awoke in his Dreamscape. Below, water reflected from unseen light, odd considering he was surrounded by darkness. Something stirred beneath the surface of the water. It rippled beneath his feet.

Static crackled in his ears.

He strained to listen. Within the sound, he perceived a woman's faint whisper. The static grew louder and shriller the longer he listened but he couldn't understand her words through the dense white noise.

The darkness improved his vision, a trait of the Annulus Eye, he recalled — an occurrence in those blighted by the Void.

Hero crouched down and pressed his hands against the icy water, peering inside with difficulty. Something stirred, the water rippled again, and the voice whispered from closer than before. *Inside the water?*

A hand gripped his wrist with crushing force and dragged him inside. Limbs of darkness wrapped around his arms and legs, pulling him deeper into the reaches of the emptiness below.

Although he saw only darkness, it somehow felt full. *Too full*.

Hero struggled to pull away, once again noticing the way the darkness swayed like strands of hair, and the static turned to a piercing scream as he reached the limits of his lungs. He wanted to cover his ears, but he could neither move nor breathe. The scream caused a vibration in the water and deep, harrowing sorrow that shook his soul to the core.

Let me out. Let me out!

Hero awakened with a jolt, the shrill scream louder than ever. He hunched over his knees and pressed his hands over his ears but couldn't stop the sound. It wasn't in his ears. It was in his mind.

He groaned as a stabbing pain stemmed through his body.

"Hero? Praise be...." Fate touched his back. Anima flowed through her hand and over his back, soothing his muscles and nerves. The warm energy not only alleviated his pain but stopped the scream. "Are you all right?"

Every muscle in his body seized, so he kept his head pressed to his knees.

"The stain...." Fate held his hands. "It's grown so much. What happened to you? What did you see?"

Hero shook his head and sat upright. Utterly drained, he leaned to the side of the chair, struggling to stay awake. "I don't know."

Fate brushed the hair out of his face. "Don't fall asleep. Talk to me."

He saw nothing but the stark white light again. "I can see in the darkness, Fati."

She kept quiet for an unusually long time. "What did you just call me?"

His consciousness waned.

"Hero?" Fate shook his arm. "Don't fall asleep. Stay with me. Hero!"

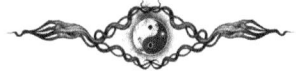

Hero stirred from a deep sleep, this time lying on something soft—his bed. He knew the scent of clean linen and the sensation of the smooth covers running across his fingers. He hadn't dreamt of anything this time and appreciated the silence after that horrifying scream.

Fate touched his hand tenderly. "How do you feel?"

"Better."

"Did you have any dreams?"

"Not this time."

"I'm relieved. What happened in the study?"

He tossed off the covers and sat beside her on the edge of the bed. "I don't know. I had a dream that I was in darkness. Someone was screaming. It was awful."

"Screaming...."

Hero's hands trembled. He clenched them shut then folded both forward to control what had become a full-body shudder. "Something is about to happen."

"I can only imagine what."

"That scream... it was a woman. My mother."

Fate must have jolted, because the bed shook. "How do you know?"

"Who could forget?" He cupped his hands over his ears and closed his eyes. The memory of the scream wanted to surface again... to remind him of his duty. *I'm remembering. It's coming back now.* The ticking of a clock echoed through the room. Each time it sounded, Hero delved a little deeper into his unconscious mind, reaching out for something buried inside. He had forgotten something important. A mission. Something silver shimmered as it fell to the floor. The silver horse had fallen from his pocket and rolled towards a woman who gazed at him with a somber look. *What have I forgotten?*

Fate broke the silence. "I know this is a bad time... but I had something important to tell you today." The moment she spoke, the memory faded away.

Hero tried to retrieve it and move back down into that hidden place. Blind as he may be, he saw vividly how each door seemed to slam shut on him and throw him back into the present. He opened his eyes again, realizing that he'd missed his opportunity. Once again, he felt nothing, not even anger, as he turned his attention to Fate.

"I wanted to think of a really interesting way to do this," she said. "Everyone had so many ideas. I've been exchanging a lot of letters with Heqet, and even Fortuna."

What is she talking about?

"I have something I want you to read."

"Read?" He tilted his head left and right, then crossed his arms.

"Yes. Ever since you lost your vision, you seem so heartbroken that you can't read. You don't say it, but I see the way you touch the books in the study. We spent some time putting together letters with textured print. It might take you a while, but I'd like you to read them. I'll sit with you, so come with me."

She pulled him along in the tenacious way she had always done when they first met.

He took the stairs carefully after her until they arrived in the dining hall, a place he knew by the aroma of bread. It reminded him of Abyssus and, now, of Jackyl. The memory that had been swept away nagged at him once more — another link in the chain.

Fate beckoned. "Sit."

Hero listened carefully to decipher where she had chosen to sit, and joined her. *How do I remember Jackyl?* He questioned the deviant personality hidden within and what it hid from him. Either he or the consciousness of Leoht Miina knew something that the other didn't. Hero suspected the voice of the stain knew more than he let on, as he always hid something.

Fate placed something next to Hero's hand — a stack of letters, he realized after nudging it gently.

"I put them in a specific order," she said. "The only one *I'd* like to read is the one that I wrote."

He picked up one of the envelopes and removed the note. The textured print of the letters shaped characters, so he found it easy to read. It did take longer, but he was grateful that he could read at all, and suspected that with time, the task would become easier.

Fate neither said nor did anything while she waited, at least nothing he could perceive.

> *Dearest Hero,*
> *Whether or not you remember, I've watched you grow since Elaine first announced her pregnancy. You've grown up to be a fine young man. I'm glad I can entrust you with our dearest daughter. I'm so proud of you and Fate for coming this far. I won't say too much, since I know my letter will come first, but I have hope and faith in you two and the future that lies ahead.*
> *Best wishes,*
> *Fortuna & Nigel*

Hero paused after the first letter and tried some of the tea Fate had prepared. He raised his brows as the sweet taste of honey and Quimora sap touched his tongue. The taste reminded him of Fati, who'd first made him the tea before teaching it to Chi.

Fate's voice always changed when she smiled, imbued with a subtle amusement that coursed her tone the way a spice altered the flavor of a consumable. "What tea is it, do you know?"

"It's the tea that Chi makes."

She hummed in agreement, as she tended to do with a nod. "It's the first tea we had together."

Hero couldn't think of anything intelligible to say without blurting the question that constantly filled his mind: *Are you Nuvem Fati?* He knew the answer but couldn't risk her noticing that he too had awakened—at least, not until he uncovered the last missing memory.

"Are you ready to continue reading?"

"Yeah, sorry. I was distracted by you."

"Then here's the next one." She passed another letter.

> *Congratulations Hero and Fate,*
> *I have a big mouth so I thought I should go last, but I've been told otherwise. I miss you, Hero, but I have some important business that I must attend to. I wish you the best in this new chapter of your life.*
> *I'm the proudest father,*
> *Kyou*

Hero tilted his head at the letter. "What is this consistent tone of felicitation? Am I missing something?"

Fate leaned against his shoulder. "That's the point, silly! Here, read this one next."

He snuck a sip of tea before taking the next letter. This one had an inscription on the outside with Chi's name.

> *I send this letter for myself and Heqet, who does not wish to exhaust you with her prattle. To be honest, we were both extremely worried about how you would grow up when you were young. It is a little hard to believe that I am writing this now. I am so proud and excited for you two and for myself. Heqet and I will wait for news like old women awaiting their grandchild.*

Hero squinted in the direction of the page. "Did I read that right? That's a strange joke."

"I know. They don't even look old," Fate said.

That's beside the point.

She patted the back of his head. "Two more letters. One of them is from me."

"I'm not quite awake. Let the caffeine set in first. My head is reeling."

"Hero, I'm an anxious woman! Let's finish the letters. Just trust me on this."

He relented, as pushing her patience never did a bit of good. It was impossible to win an argument against Fate.

"This letter is from Jax," she said, divining his thoughts. "He didn't write his name."

Hero took the letter at her request and sipped his tea with his free hand.

> *To my brother in arms, I hope you're doing well. I'm sorry I haven't been there to meet with you. Since I'm the second to last letter, I have permission to say something about these blessings, and I can't tell you how much I fought for this position. I never imagined this day would come. I know you'll have a lot of doubts in yourself, because of your condition and your eyesight, but know I have faith in you and Fate. You'll make wonderful parents. I can't wait to meet 'boue'!*

Hero inhaled sharply and tea shot up his nose. He grabbed his face to nullify the burning, though it didn't help. "*Kui.*"

'*Fuck.*'

"You're so graceless. *Ven?*" She continued to the next letter without waiting for a response. "Since you're already like this, I'll finish up. This is my letter.

> "*To Caeles Hero of Nitor, my best friend. I'm sorry for keeping this secret for so long. I thought about telling you earlier, but, after everything that happened, I decided to keep quiet and lay low. I wanted to surprise you, even though I've been nervous about your reaction. Our meeting was strange, and we didn't always get along, but I cherish*

you just as I'll cherish our child. I'm so proud to have reached this point, and I look forward to our future together. No matter what happens, I'll work hard to protect our family. I have faith in you and know you'll be a wonderful father."

Hero's mouth hung open. *Impossible. It's impossible for us to have a child. What the hell happened?* He hadn't considered that he and Fate would have a child. He hadn't realized it was physically possible for a Doll to conceive, but then he remembered that the High King requested for a High Queen capable of producing an heir. Even so, he feared what it meant for someone Tainted to have a child with a Doll. There had never been recordings of such a being.

"It'll be okay," Fate assured him, rubbing his back. "This is our child. I'm sure they'll be capable of withstanding the miasma. I mean, look at me. I'm still healthy enough to scold you for wearing your shoes to bed."

"Are you sure?"

"I'm certain. Remember, I have the Annulus Eye."

"I do remember, Fate. When is—"

"Not for some time. I believe the medic estimated late spring. Sorry I've been so irritable lately. I didn't want you to notice."

Hero shook his head. "I feel like a fool."

Fate laughed so hard and deep, her body shuddered. "You've been so sweet. We may not know what will happen, but I'd like to keep this a secret from everyone outside our family. We must protect our child."

"Wait, what about a name?"

"I thought we could go the traditional way and choose a name on their third birthday. What do you think?"

"So, we'll just use a title for now. *Boue* is the standard."

"Yes. I told Jax, so he said it in his letter."

"Okay, but has anyone discussed the potential results of a Doll and someone Tainted having a child? We have no idea what to expect. I've never heard of such a thing."

"I won't let you fret for a moment longer. We're going to get through this together, no matter what comes of it. Understand? You've feared your condition for too long. I won't let anything happen to our child. Trust me."

Fate had been saying 'trust me' over and over for many turns. Her tone never seemed quite pleading, just insistent, as though, at some point, she expected he would learn to trust her. Maybe *she* trusted him to come around eventually.

He had been hearing her promises for so long that the day had come when he started to release that choking fear of his condition. He might never escape its clutches. He might disintegrate their child with a single touch, just like the guards outside Ussan.

"I can't guarantee I won't panic," he said. "But I'll try to rely on you this time."

Her aura glowed bright red and swayed in smooth waves. It seemed to smile. "I'm so glad. I can't wait."

Tangled are the threads of Chaos. I'm still but a knot in the flow of life and existence. I can't be undone, only snipped from the fabric of the Universe, but Fate doesn't wish this for me. As the wheel turns and wrenches the threads, she extends her own will upon the storms of vengeance. Her song beseeches it to release its grip on me, but for what purpose? I only wish I knew.

17

THE LIGHT OF TIME

The day of arrival came in a flash. Hero paced around the main hall in a small circle while Kyou, Heqet, Chi, the Ignis Brothers, and Jackyl waited around for news.

"Maybe you need a drink," Jackyl said, touching Hero's shoulder.

"That's a terrible idea."

The entrance opened, and Hero paused his pacing to listen for who had arrived — soft footsteps, someone trained and regal. *Nigel.*

"Fortuna has sent her blessings, and this handkerchief with her tears of joy and envy." It was immediately clear to whom Nigel passed the sentiment.

Fortis groused. "Yuck! What's the matter with her? Why would anyone want that?"

"I thought you liked bodily fluids," Firmus said, laughing at his own joke.

He's like Fate that way, laughing at his own jokes.

Heqet shook Hero from his right side. "I'm so excited, I can't bear it! I'm going to be a grandmother!"

"Usually people are worried about sounding old," Kyou said.

Chi spoke calmly. "All of you settle down."

She says that, but isn't she most excited? Her aura is dancing.

The medic entered the hall, her shoes clacking with every step. "We have finished. I'm not sure if you want to know the gen—"

Hero began moving towards her and someone shoved him over into Kyou, who shouted back. "Hey! Get back here! How can you shove the father? Chi!"

I knew it.

Heqet raced out of the room after her. "What a cheat!"

So, I guess I won't be the first.

"I'll stop them at the door," Jackyl said, and his aura vanished from the room.

Hero had a strong sense towards darkness users and creatures of the Abyss. They appeared like vaguely shaped inkblots when expanding their element.

Jackyl actually had a shape, albeit unclear—it still resembled a person.

For some reason, Fate was more difficult to see than Jackyl. Her darkness always bled into Hero's vision in a way that reminded him of ink spilling across a white page.

"Come," Firmus implored, pushing Hero's back.

"I can't believe I was slighted by my aunt." Hero didn't know they'd reached the room until a baby cried. As he heard the sound, he retreated from the door.

Kyou and Firmus put their hands on his back. "Go on," they said.

A servant woman stepped in front of Hero. "Traditionally, no one is allowed to enter until after the mother is cleaned and comfortable."

Fate snapped. "Oh, quit it. Do you think our baby just came out of thin air? Let him in."

"Yes, Highness."

"Hero, come in and sit," she said, patting the mattress with a loud thump.

Hero crossed through the room and, once he felt the bed against the back of his legs, sat.

"Would you like to hold him?"

He placed his hands on his lap, avoiding. "Him?"

"Yes, *him*. Are you nervous?"

"I'm worried about touching him."

"It's okay," she reassured him, and gently reached out to readjust his arms. "Like this. Ready?"

He nodded, and she rested their son carefully in his arms.

"You two will be just fine," she said.

Hero hadn't expected to feel anything, considering he spent most of his life being devoid. People often said that mothers experienced an influx of complex emotions, but he discovered fathers did too.

Fate would normally laugh about his emotional confusion, but not this time. She laid her head against his shoulder and brought him closer. "How do you feel? You're trembling."

He hadn't realized it, but she was right. His fear incited the miasma. As a result, his emotional state, already complex, was further strained and heightened.

He traced his fingers along their son's face—his nose, his eyes, and his cheeks. Everything was so small. He swallowed hard as a tear slipped free.

"Oh my. I never would have guessed you were so gentle, when we met," Fate said, laughing softly and kissing his face with much greater force.

"I don't know what's wrong with me." The aura their son emitted moved through him, causing his feelings to fill him to the brim.

Kyou came up to his opposite side and hugged Hero's head. "We've done well, if you're this softhearted. When we met, you had absolutely nothing in your gaze. Now look at you! You're a father. Those seals have kept you locked up so tight. It's good for you to feel things."

It was overwhelming, suffocating, but not in a terrible way—more of a crushing sensation and anxiousness. Hero *had* been sealed up so tightly that he had no idea how to manage his emotions, especially not under the influence of the miasma. "What do you see, Fate?"

Fate stroked their son's head closely enough to brush against Hero's arm. "Hmm, his hair is silver—Wolf Clan silver—and his eyes are not quite violet but lavender. He has a pouty mouth like you, and my nose. Looks like he has your eye shape too, actually."

Hero managed to get along without his vision just fine but, at that moment, he regretted that he couldn't see. Just once, he wanted to see what their son looked like. "That's great."

"You're crying again," she said, wiping away his tears. "Are you okay?"

"Yeah, I'm fine." Amidst the joy and fear, a trace of sadness lingered. He accepted the pain and carried it forward with him. No use would come out of regret—not now.

Their son's aura shone blue and silver, a glimmering light that filled the room.

"I'm happy," Hero said after a while, and he meant it. "It doesn't make any sense, but I feel like this is the first time I'll be able to do something right."

"You do a lot of things right," Fate said, rubbing his back. "You've worked hard. Thank you for bringing our son into this world."

"Oh...." Her throat made a loud sound as she swallowed. "Let's work hard together. There's still a lot to do. The Queen never rests!"

Heqet said, "And that's the truth."

Fate continued. "Hero will have to take my place for a while. I'll run down the rest of the plans, and we can figure out how to move forward from here."

Kyou chuckled. "You never stop, do you?"

"Didn't you hear me? The Queen never rests."

"All right, everyone," Heqet said, clapping her hands. "We have a lot to do now that their son has been born. We must step up and assist."

Nigel said, "Highness, if I may ask, where is your aide?"

"You mean Akira." Heqet sighed in such a way that she almost sounded sad. "He has taken leave for health purposes."

"Hmm... that is a shame. It is rather quiet without him."

Heqet laughed raucously. "It is, isn't it? But now we have a new addition to the family, so I imagine things will become lively again. Let's guard the new heir to the best of our ability."

Hero touched their son's face again in adoration. He had never seen or touched a baby before and feared that he would make mistakes.

What kind of person will you grow up to be?

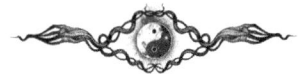

Time is my nemesis, a burden from which I can't break free. When you can't see the world, it can be difficult to measure the time that has passed. We measure this by change and growth in our surroundings or those we know. In a world of nothing, days can feel endless or brief.

On their son's third turn, they sat in the study upstairs.

Fate skimmed old books and relayed her thoughts aloud. "I've been pondering a lot about this naming experience, and I thought, what if we use 'for light' as the root of his name?"

"Light? Okay." This seemed intentional to Hero, given that *Leoht* meant light.

"It seemed right. Ever since he became a part of our lives, we've been happier."

"Then, in my clan's dialect, his name would be Leon. What if we use the suffix *-Ru?*"

"*Ru* for time?" She hesitated. "Wouldn't his name be the Light of Time?"

"Yeah, essentially."

Fate experienced one of her long silences, during which her aura shifted uneasily. "What made you think of it?"

"Some names are outdated in Ancient culture. Also, if we're basing his name on the story from *The Book of Ages*, then it reminds me of the hourglass — so... time."

"Leon-Ru," Fate repeated, with some hesitance. "I like it. Let's go tell him."

Their son had developed a knack for language at a young age and picked up the habit of reading to Hero in the study during the evening, so he waited there for his father.

They met again in the downstairs study, this time with Fate. "Today, we have chosen a name," she announced.

Their son responded in his small and monotone voice. "Whose name?"

"Your name!"

He answered again in his dry tone. "No, I don't have a name."

Fate still tried to convince him of his new name. "You do now."

"What name?"

"It's Leon-Ru," Hero said, folding his arms. "Leon for light and Ru for time. Leon-Ru means the Light of Time, since you have brought so much joy into our lives."

Leon-Ru's small hand grasped Hero's finger, and he repeated his new name in a mutter. He had grown attached to his father.

They spent many days indoors together, avoiding the notice of the people outdoors.

Hero spent the next few seasons working with Leon-ru, watching his son's aura grow into a vibrant white light as his abilities expanded.

Leon-ru crawled over to Hero's chair, his aura pulsing with excitement.

Suddenly, Hero glimpsed a pulse of blue. He scooped his son up, noting his icy fingertips. "Ice... oh, your momma is going to be so proud."

He missed Fate when she left on assignments. Normally, she conveyed all of Leon-Ru's actions. In these quiet times, he tried to imagine them.

Leon-Ru garbled and cooed in Hero's arms.

In a flash of red, Hero retracted from the fiery sting against his arms, accidentally dropping Leon-Ru. He quickly collected his wailing son despite his burning arms. "I'm sorry, oh sorry, Leon."

Leon-Ru cried and cried as the burning faded.

Hero held his son, overtly aware of his own pounding heartbeat. He rocked the small boy and tried to calm both himself and his small son.

When Fate returned, he told her of the incident, and they checked Hero's arms confirming that Leon-Ru had, in fact, used the element of fire.

They monitored their son for several seasons. Each time he manifested a new skill, their concern grew.

Eventually, Hero and Fate had decided to hide Leon-Ru from as many people as possible, in hopes of protecting him. They wished to give him time to learn about his abilities before introducing him to others. Both remembered the strain between the Council and the Rebellion. Now, they needed to worry about the Organization as well.

Fate took Hero's hand. "No one will expect anything out of the ordinary. He'll be with you."

Hero nodded and squeezed her hand. "Agreed. It'll give me time to work with him."

He stroked Leon-Ru's down-like hair, feeling both overwhelming love for his child and strangling fear of what may happen to him if others knew about his abilities.

Fate sounded exasperated for the first time in ages. "I'll manage the staff, plan contingencies...."

"It will be all right. People are already used to my reclusiveness. Don't forget that."

The tension in her voice eased. "Of course."

Over the next turn, Hero kept to the seclusion of the palace, something he never wished for his son, but their time together proved fruitful.

Leon-Ru grew into a toddler, one that possessed superior elemental capabilities beyond anything they'd ever witnessed. So far, he could manipulate almost any element, if he put his mind to it. Whether it be based from anima, darkness, or nature itself, Leon-Ru could bend and conjure it to his will.

With a being as remarkable and new as Leon-Ru, his parents fretted about how difficult his life might become. Above all else, they sought to protect him.

Every day, Hero practiced with him and tried to teach him about the world they lived in.

Fate spirit walked with him, wishing for him to gain full control of his abilities so he could protect himself and those he loved.

Together, they taught their son everything possible for the small boy to retain.

Leon-Ru spent most of his time trailing behind his father and learning about the world.

One afternoon, when Fate returned late from her meetings, Hero caught her in the foyer. "Momma, come and look."

Fate shuffled about the foyer and then hurried up the stairs. "Something new?"

Hero moved quickly towards their room, surprising even himself at how accustomed he'd become to his blindness. He entered the bedroom, witnessing a flash of green.

Fate entered behind him and gasped.

Hero clutched her arm. "What is it? I can tell that it's an illusion of some kind."

Fate laughed through her hands. "It's magnificent."

Hero waited impatiently for more description.

Fate fumbled for words. "Animals, all kinds, and they're dancing and jumping."

Hero leaned against the door with a smile. His heart ached, and he desperately wished he could see their son's creation.

Later that evening, Hero lay in bed thinking.

Fate climbed under the covers next to him. "I can feel you thinking. What are you fretting about?"

"Did you check him?"

She sighed and patted the blankets. "I did, as I do every day."

He waited.

She rested her head against his shoulder. "He shows no signs of the Taint or miasma poisoning. When will you accept that he's like me?"

He let his concern for Leon-Ru melt away, and lay back against his pillow.

Fate pushed the long strands of bangs away from his eyes. "Leon-Ru is strong, smart, and healthy. It's not you we need to protect him from. You're a good father."

Hero held up his hand. "He asked me why there were black bands on my arms and hands today."

Fate lay quiet for a long moment. "It's getting worse."

Each turn brought a new concern. The potency of the miasma had intensified since Hero had opened the previous door. After he lost his sight, they lost the ability to see inside the Dreamscape. The expansive world he had gazed upon had been reduced to mere fragments, broken and left to float in the empty sea of space. His miasma caused a mental fog, and sometimes, out of nowhere, he'd fall asleep. Each time this happened, he slept longer than the time before, something familiar and expected but, nevertheless, problematic.

Her voice quivered. "What will I do if you don't wake up?" She had set him to a schedule for meditation after deducing that, with practice, he might be able to rebuild his memories from what he *remembered* seeing.

Hero chewed his lip and questioned whether or not to confess. "I fell asleep the other day. Leon woke me. I think I scared him." He disliked causing his son this concern, so he worked harder to prove his strength. His abilities as an elemental helped immensely in cultivating the crystal, as Fate wished.

Fate draped her arm over him and released a warm blanket of anima. "You're still here with us and that's all that matters. I accept you and so does Leon-Ru. Rest. You need your strength to cultivate the crystal. How is that going?"

The fatigue rolled in and his body relaxed. His response slipped out before he drifted off to sleep. "Good. We're on track."

Hero worked hard on Fate's restoration plans for Macellarius. Together, they had spent the last few turns preparing to renovate many of the streets and houses. He even managed to recruit Weimar, who spoke with many of the local farmers and cattlemen to donate food when the time came.

Fate bustled about the kingdom gathering all available supplies and contributions for the destitute Macellarius. Her works were well known throughout Nex and many were aware throughout Mu. She made a ripple in the Royal conversations all the way to Thule.

The plan, however, screeched to a halt at the arrival of the High Queen's messenger, Aurelius, who announced that he came with a letter.

Fate opened the envelope, and yelled with such ferocity that Leon-Ru jerked. "This can't be."

Hero picked up their son and gently stroked his head. "What's wrong?"

Her red aura shot out into sharp peaks and fell through the air in defeat. "The Restoration Plans have stopped by the High King's order. Neco signed over the kingdom to another ruler."

"What the hell! Who?"

"Isis."

Leon-Ru patted Hero's cheeks. *"Ba'ai?"*

Hero's heart sank. He felt as though he had swallowed a stone. *"Ven so.* Aurelius, please take me back to the Capital with you. I'd like to discuss these matters with Heqet myself." He passed Leon-Ru into Fate's grasp and gathered his coat from the hanger by the front doors.

Her footsteps echoed behind him, and she tenderly pulled him back by the arm. "You're going now? It's already evening. You won't reach the Capital until very late."

"You've worked hard for this," he said, kissing her head. "Wait for me. I'll return as soon as I have news."

"Let me go with you."

"No, stay here. We need to keep Leon safe. I won't be able to protect him as well as you can."

"We can ask Fortis to watch over him. Don't go alone."

Her aura burned a bright red and fluttered erratically, unsettling him. Being Bound and having a child had brought them closer than ever, and her stress crushed him. As much as he wished to fulfill her request, history had a way of repeating itself. He knew enough about the past to refuse her.

Hero hugged her, hoping he concealed his distress well enough. "I must go alone. I need to speak with Isis."

She finally relented. "Be safe. Aurelius, please keep an eye on him. If there's any trouble, of any kind, just summon me. I have a terrible feeling about this."

"Consider it done," Aurelius replied with a hand over his heart.

Hero waited for Aurelius to exit and followed his aura to the carriage. As soon as they settled inside, he put his mind to work.

Isis attained the throne?

Something stirred inside of him, and he sensed a wave coming. He reasoned that he should be happier about her attaining the throne, since she'd raised him, yet he couldn't shake the feeling that something had gone terribly awry. It seemed impossible for her to rule both Askadel and Nex effectively — to even consider it bordered on irrational.

This doesn't feel right. What's going on in this Empire?

18
A Resolved Riddle

The Ussan sang and resonated louder than ever as the carriage crunched across the pavement and rolled to a stop. Hero pressed his hands over his ears and stepped down, pausing to wait for Aurelius.

Aurelius stopped and said, "Are you all right?"

"*Ven.* I just need to move away from the trees."

Since childhood, Hero had known that Aurelius, serious as he seemed, often took things to an extreme. Underneath his graven air and looming presence, he possessed a strangely soft center. When the silence arose, Hero realized it might've been better not to respond the way he had.

Two well-toned arms scooped him up from the ground.

"I can walk! I'm fine!"

"Queen Fate asked me to take care of you."

"This is not what she meant!"

"Are you su—"

"Put me down!" On his feet again, Hero strode briskly ahead, embarrassed. More than anything, the loathed when others coddled him, especially after he'd worked so hard to be independent. The humiliation dug at him as he climbed the steps to the palace. They hurried inside, until Heqet's aura burned bright and violet before him.

By the tone of her voice, he determined that whatever happened had taken her by surprise too. It hadn't been a part of her plan.

The violet light waved madly in the air where she stood. She took his arms and gasped. "Oh, praise be, you got my message. I'm terribly sorry. I had no idea that my husband had endorsed this ceremony. He always finds a way to undermine me. I can't believe I missed something this detrimental. Ever since Akira left, things have been a mess."

"It's not your fault. What can we do? I'd like to speak with Isis myself."

"She's having a meeting with my husband in the Conference Room. Hero, be careful. I don't know what's going on around here. I'm losing my head."

Hero touched her hands softly and beamed. "*Ven, Reinka. Morta'ei.*"

'Leave it to me.'

The High Queen needed a moment to collect herself. The war with the Council and her husband had worn her nerves thin. It started long before that day, before Hero was even born, and he hated to hear her fret so much. She was too kind.

Heqet's voice lowered to its usual silky sound, her use of the Language of Ages alerting him to the surrounding danger. "*Vien'ou ya do, Hero. Quer vepa le renme.*"

'I'm so sorry, Hero. You were supposed to succeed the throne.'

"*Ven, Reinka. Me'em so osla, er noh quer nei pa.*"

'It's okay, Highness. Even if we don't, we'll be happy as we are.'

Heqet let out her stress in a slow breath, her aura radiating appreciation.

Hero chuckled, though there was nothing funny about the situation. "*Quos, er kul veia.*"

'That is, if we live through this.'

She gripped his arm tightly.

Once he realized his error, he consoled her again. "*Soel, igur fe irln nei kun eos osla.*"

'Right now, we must collect ourselves and learn what has happened.'

She conceded. "Ye.... Aurelius, please take Hero to the Conference Room and watch over him as you would me. If something happens, you must inform me immediately."

"With my life," Aurelius said. He patted Hero's arm and went a few steps ahead.

Hero mulled over the information as they walked down the long palace hallway. His thoughts traveled back to his childhood and up through the ages, piecing together the one person present in every case. From his father's death, to his mother's death before he was old enough to understand, one person remained a constant. She guided him through decisions, and each time moved both him and herself forward. *Isis*. She stood beside him and supported him, but for what reason?

His gut wrenched at the thought.

Isis now held his kingdom in her palm, the same way that she'd held him in her grasp since childhood.

He pressed a hand against the side of his head and tried to block out the distant sound of a door creaking open. Thinking about Isis and his mother's death made one of the seals unstable. He treaded upon a trigger that threatened to break open. *Just wait. I can't collapse now. I need to confirm these suspicions. I need Fate to know.*

Aurelius led Hero up the winding staircase to the second floor.

Outside the Conference Room doors, he and Aurelius paused. "The High King is approaching.

The High King's heavy steps trailed into the hall from ahead. He touched Hero's arm and greeted, "King Hero, it's a pleasure to see you."

Hero found it difficult to hide his distrust. "Hmm, yes, wish I could say the same."

"That sounds unpleasant. Is there something we need to discuss?"

"No, I came to speak with Isis."

The High King chuckled. "Praise be, you made it sound important."

Hero twitched. "Just a small issue about my kingdom's throne."

Khnum responded in a heavy voice, followed by a subtle exhale. "I see."

Isis stepped out of the conference room, her shoes clacking as usual. "Hero? What a pleasure! I'm so happy to see you!"

Hero listened more carefully in her presence. He'd missed so many details over the turns, but he saw more now that he'd lost his sight. "Do you have a moment to spare?"

"For you? Always. Please enter the Conference Room."

He turned towards Khnum. "With your permission, of course."

Isis opened the door. "Hero, really? No need to be so formal."

It stunned him that he had dismissed her conduct for so long. In the past, he'd mostly witnessed Isis's disregard of Niteo, which wasn't unusual since he was Rahma. However, in the presence of the High King, her actions came across as shocking and blatantly disrespectful.

Isis ushered him inside and closed the door. "Please, take a seat."

Hero swept a hand across the table and chose a seat close to the door.

"I'm sure you're here to ask me about how and why Neco signed over the palace to me," she said. The clicking sounds told him that she not only drank tea, but that she sat at his immediate left. "I made this deal with the High King and Neco a long time ago. If not, your father would have gained control over all of Nex."

"Why does it matter? You're a Council member and he followed your cause."

"Because if that happened, you'd have nowhere to go. I'm sure you've noticed, Mortis is Aska, like myself. He's a mercenary from my kingdom, sent by me."

He said nothing about Mortis's relation to Isis because he found it curious that she would reveal the detail herself. "Fate had trouble digging up information on him. This would explain why."

Isis set down her teacup. "I'm sorry about Abyssus. I sent Mortis to watch over Neco and to kill him just in case something went wrong. I don't know who tortured him, but it wasn't Mortis."

"I know that. Mortis isn't so precise," he said, insulted by how much she had underestimated his notations. It troubled him that she admitted she had sent Mortis. This didn't seem like something a criminal would do. Then again, she could be saying it as a distraction.

"There's a darker power in Mu," she said. "A third party is stirring in the shadows, and that man, Akira, is leading them. You mustn't trust him."

"What's wrong with the third party?"

"Every time he comes around here, something bad happens. You know, right? He became interested in Elaine before her death. She trusted him blindly. I'm not even sure he's a Caeles. Forget what Chi has told you. We have no proof that he's really who he says he is."

Hero leaned against his hand, sighing. "All he says is that he's her cousin and his name is Akira. That's not saying much now, is it? Don't tell me you're discriminating against him because he's tainted."

"Absolutely not. I don't discriminate, Hero. You know that. It's his aura. There's so much malice. Are you trying to tell me that a man with that much anger hasn't committed a single crime? What about that poor girl? What happened to her?"

Hero chose to respect his old friend. "You mean Lara? I have no idea. She didn't look the same."

A sense of urgency rose in Isis's voice. "If he's a representative for the Grim, he might be a Puppeteer. He might have made her into something else."

"Hmm, no. She specifically said—*you will bow down before the real Queen of Mu*—and I seriously doubt she was referring to herself." Lara had never possessed the necessary confidence to consider herself in that position. She admired those she considered prettier and wiser than her, and still viewed Ancients as superior beings. Even then, she seemed to be trying to convince herself that she was better than before. He shook his head. "I don't believe it."

"Then who? You don't think she was right, do you?"

"About what?"

Isis leaned closer. "Fate."

"That's absurd. The Grim brought Fate into existence to be the High Queen. There'd be no reason for her to go out of her way when she could just do exactly as she did and see Heqet for training. Not to mention, Fate wasn't alive when the first murder took place."

"To what are you referring?"

"Liulfr. His death took place long before Fate and I came into existence."

Isis sat in a long silence.

Hero heard her breathing.

"We don't even know if they were connected," she said at last.

"So, you think it's a coincidence that both of my parents were killed just turns apart."

Isis was the only person who really had something to gain, and who remained within proximity of the events.

Mortis, whom she had appointed, killed Abyssus when Hero refused to side with the Council.

Neco, who had kidnapped Fate and Abyssus, by some extraordinary means, signed over his kingdom to Isis.

Hero's seals were strong—strong enough to deter him until his adulthood—yet even he noticed the pattern. He just didn't understand why she would admit to sending Mortis. It didn't seem like an accident.

What is she trying to accomplish?

He stood and paced in a small circle, pondering. The details were not in alignment. Something was missing, and he couldn't decipher what. Again, he traced the hourglass, stricken with an idea. "Isis, do you know someone named Bedad?"

Isis responded quickly. "What? I don't. Why?"

"It's on my hourglass." He held it towards the direction of her voice. "I thought he might be the person who made it."

"Oh. Perhaps. Do you think that this person is important?"

"If I ask you to help me uncover the identity of this person, will you?"

Isis seemed focused. "If I do, will you join the Council?"

"Hmm...."

"I can't pilfer information for someone Tainted without good reason. You should know the kind of danger it poses for me as well, but I'm willing to bargain."

As he suspected, she was still trying to bring him over to the Council's faction. He turned fast and faced her. "Isis, you do know that the Council wishes to erase me, right? Why don't you just join the Rebellion?"

She replied tersely. "It would be against my beliefs."

"What *are* your beliefs then? The Council believes they should eradicate the Tainted and that light prevails above all. As far as they're concerned, people like me and Akira are disposable. If that's how you feel, why would you confide in me at all? Why not just capture me?"

Isis's aura radiated green light, swelling the more he prodded her. "It's more complicated than that, Hero. What about the Rebellion's beliefs?"

"They're fighting for equality, no? The way I see it, isn't the Council in the wrong?"

"There is no wrong or right. There is only balance or imbalance. Since the dawn of the Mortal Realms, our universe has lost its grace. We need only return to our roots to restore our grand Euphoria to its natural state."

Hero had her right where he wanted her. He weighed the results of this interrogation before proceeding. This reminded him of his childhood, when he used to prod at her for a reaction. It still amused him, only now the repercussions were more severe. "But I'm from the darkness."

"What?"

"Is that not true?"

"What makes you think that? Your ailment? Don't let the darkness fool you. Look at you, Hero, you are a child of light, no different than me. We can heal you. All you need to do is come with me to Thule. The Council Leader has assigned a research team to find a cure for the Taint. The Rebellion thinks we should simply ignore it and let the Tainted roam free. You know well the effects of the Taint—the harm it causes to those around you. Would you really wish that upon anyone? If it were so easy, the Crystal Empire wouldn't have collapsed, and your clan would not be facing extinction. These are trying times, Hero. I just don't want to see you fall to the same illness as that monster, Akira."

Monster....

"What makes him a monster, exactly? We suffer from the same ailment. I don't understand. If he's a monster, then so am I."

Isis's voice wavered. "Hero, your stain has grown worse. You are not thinking clearly. You need medical attention."

He tapped his fingers on the table. "Isis, are you willing to help restore Nex?"

"Of course. Why else would I go through these measures?" Her aura trembled. Whatever the reason, the conversation had upset her. "When I had Neco sign over Macellarius, I had every intention to secure the kingdom. Sooner or later, you'll be High King. We must plan accordingly."

"Since when did it become *we*? The only *we* here is me and my wife. When did I agree to partner with you?"

Isis's breath wavered as she inhaled. "What are you saying? I've supported you since you were just a child."

"So?" The objects on the table rattled. "What do you want from me, Isis?" Silence returned to the room.

Isis's aura settled as calmness swept through the area. She had managed to collect herself and laughed with slight delirium. "You're right. I think there has been a misunderstanding. I considered you my confidant. You've always been important to me and I've always protected you. I do feel sorry about what Mortis has done. I wasn't sure how to face you when it happened, but I can't undo the past. I can only move forward. It seems only right that he be imprisoned as the Lady Fate arranged. I will not contest that, but your mistrust hurts me deeply. Like you, I'm simply trying to find a balance in the chaos."

Hero questioned her state of mind. It sounded as though she was grasping at reasons for her behavior. "Right."

"I could ask the same. What are you trying to gain by interrogating me?"

Deadlock.

Shit. She's smart.

Hero sat down again. "I'm just trying to find common ground. We are in opposing factions, so how in the world can we get along? As you mentioned, my stain has grown worse. It's only a matter of time before they take me to Thule. What then? You're going to go to trial for your enemy?"

Isis's aura made him dizzy. She must have felt the same, since she was quiet for so long. "I would."

"What's the point?"

She made a sound that resembled a sigh, except it sounded more pained. "You're giving me a headache. What do you want? Macellarius?"

"Yes," he said.

"What else?"

"I'll go with you to Thule, but I want you to stop the Council from interfering with Fate's research."

"Why?" Isis had grown cautious.

Hero contemplated deeply. If he fell into the Council's hands, they'd have the next High King within their grasp, and Mu would fall to Council rule once more. He concluded that this was what Isis had sought all along.

If she had spoken to the Council, and known of their plan, she might have schemed as early as his childhood, and strategized.

His head rocked with realization.

She's their strategist.

He kept his aura steady as he closed their deal. "Will you be in Nex tomorrow?"

"Yes."

"Great. We can speak with Fate then. Most of the reformations were completely of her making. I'll meet with you again in the latter part of the afternoon. Please expect us. When we meet again, we'll discuss our bargain."

Isis tapped her finger on the table. "If that's so, I may be able to assist you in finding the information you seek. Understand that you are asking me to turn my brother over for vengeance."

"Vengeance? Justice."

Hero rose, ignoring the ticking sound resounding in his head—more like crackling. The seal weakened by the moment. His concern rose as he made his way for the door. If it broke, he'd die... or would he?

Isis called out after him, sounding pleased even though she agreed to such a dark arrangement. "I'll see you again soon."

Hero stepped out of the room and took Aurelius by the wrist. "I'm going to visit my aunt. Come with me."

The guard responded in his deep voice, "At your service."

Isis's footsteps passed him and continued echoing down the hall. From what Hero could perceive, she spoke with another guard in the distance, most likely on her way to report her deal to the Council immediately.

This gave him some time to return and inform Fate of his conclusion. He didn't trust Isis or his own perception. If she was an Aska, she knew how to create illusions and, with his senses weakened, she could have tricked him quite easily. When he thought back, he could easily decipher several times she used illusion for 'good intentions,' like creating Holly, the horse that never died, or hiding the potent miasma that plagued the palace and the constant deaths he'd caused. When it benefitted him, he looked the other way and pretended not to notice her meddling. For all he knew, she'd spun an illusion before he arrived and he lived it out, never stopping to consider when it began, until now.

The ticking sound in his head grew louder and louder the closer they traveled towards Chi's cottage. A chill in the air filled his lungs, making him feel as though a storm loomed not far off.

Chi stopped him outside the door. "Hero, are you going to visit with me before you leave?"

He gripped the side of his head. "I need to get home as quickly as possible."

"What is wrong?" She hovered around him anxiously.

"Please don't touch me. It's the miasma. I need to send a message to Fate."

"Yes, anything. Please come inside for a moment."

"I don't have time."

"All right. What message should I get to her?"

He fought to think over the crackling sound but eventually pushed his aunt inside her cottage, closed the door, and whispered, "Tell her that we guessed right. The answer was beside me all along. The answer is in the contract." He kept his message inconspicuous, hoping to safeguard his aunt from the chaos that he and his wife faced. The Spinner could defend herself better than anyone he knew, and he trusted her to interpret his report.

If Chi had any questions, she kept them to herself. "Consider it done."

Hero staggered out the door and to the carriage for the trip home, ailing from the breeding miasma. One of Kyou's protection bands broke off his wrist and crumbled.

"Praise be," Aurelius muttered.

"Leave, if you must," Hero said. "But the coachman will fare no better."

"I shall stay. It's my duty to the Queen."

"There's nothing to be done. The seal is breaking. I promised I'd return home. We still don't have any evidence."

"What are you saying?"

"Nothing. It's drivel. Sorry." He faded in and out of consciousness as the carriage hobbled through the forest path. Even though he was still awake, images flickered behind his eyelids of Priscilla and his mother, both covered in blood as they died, choking on something. He fought the visions as another wrestled him down. Fate also suffered, poisoned by flakes of crystal that entered her body through consumption. The clinking of porcelain caught his ear, but the sound emanated from somewhere in his memories. Priscilla sat down with Isis, accepting small confections—caramels, his mother's favorite and Isis's specialty. He had found it strange when he learned that Fate was poisoned by caramels, and now he knew without a doubt that Isis had plotted against them to attain the throne. She'd killed his parents, tricked Lara, attempted to poison Fate, and succeeded in deceiving everyone for personal gain.

Aurelius stressed. "We're almost there. Hold on."

Hero's chest ached. He clutched it and coughed, but the pain shot throughout his body and under his skin. All of his memories surfaced, making his head throb. He remembered his mother's death and the brazen woman who apprehended him when he tried to hide.

Isis turned him over to the Council, as a suspect in the murder of his mother, to hide her own ills. No sooner did she commit the crime than she framed him and suppressed his memory of her.

Aurelius gasped, crawling back on his seat. "Crystal. Your skin!"

Hero's hands and arms ached. A thin layer of crystal formed over his skin and jutted out from the carriage by his feet. "Get out!" The crystal grew rapidly, encasing him first in a thin layer and then spurting out around him.

Aurelius shouted.

The carriage shook, tossing Hero from the seat and against the side, and the horses neighed and stomped as the entire carriage turned onto its side. Bright golden light spilled across the damp soil. The warmth reached Hero's hand and stained the tips of his fingers.

Anima, the essence of light and life, appeared gold, and so did blood with the blighted Annulus Eye. More of the gold fluid trickled through the carriage onto Hero's face. He couldn't move. Parts of the broken carriage and the crystal pinned him down.

"Aurelius...."

He wriggled and pushed his arm free, then sat up, choking out a fluid caught in his throat. As it left his lips, it coated his hand in gold. If it hadn't already, the crystal would manifest after touching his blood. The asphyxiating pain induced a widespreading panic. He couldn't stop it anymore, and the breath left his lungs.

The coach and its driver, coachman, and passengers lay silent—dead silent.

Crackling reached Hero's ears, and then a sharp chime—the third seal broke.

Vien, Fata Miina.

When Hero awakened, he floated in the sea of stars. Moments later, he realized he wasn't floating but falling, as broken pieces of mirror drifted upward. Everything moved at half-pace, making the descent last for ages.

A woman spoke to him in his thoughts as he sank down into the nothingness, *"You seem to have forgotten something."*

The shards of glass reflected in the light, shimmering as they floated towards the opening far above, where the unknown woman peeked down at him.

What is this?

All at once, he was on his knees at the bottom of the Abyss. He pulled himself up from the ground, aching and stiff, and gazed up to where he'd fallen from. The woman still peeked at him, her eyes hidden in shadow as dark as the hair that swayed at her shoulders. As soon as he caught a glimpse of her, she vanished. He looked for a while longer, but eventually gave up trying to see her.

At his feet, crystal sand glistened in the starlight. A plucking sound startled him from his observation. *A violin?* As he turned towards the sound, he faced a strange creature, which sat and stared. Its misshapen body and dark form resembled a malformed person. Its mouth opened and closed, opened and closed... releasing the string-plucking sound.

Hero leaned closer to it, peering at the empty spaces where its eyes would have been. "What are you?" It should have frightened him, but he found it curious.

The creature chattered its sharp, pointed teeth.

"A... Shadow Creature." He glanced around the landscape. "Is this the Void?"

A shadowy figure stepped out from the clouds of dark smoke that wafted across the beach. "You shouldn't be here."

"What?"

"You'll go blind."

Hero tilted his head. "I'm *already* blind."

The stranger grasped his wrist and began leading him through the darkness.

"Hey! Can you hear me? Excuse me."

They walked up to a crystal door in the infinite space, and the person gestured to it. "Here. Go now. It may already be too late."

Hero frowned. "Am I losing my mind?"

The person wouldn't allow him to do anything else, so he opened the door and passed through to the other side.

19
THE EYES OF THE UNIVERSE

Hero stood perfectly still until the Dreamscape stopped rotating around him. He recognized the light flooding into his line of vision and discerned that the energy resonating must be from the last door. Something in here held more importance than Mu and its murders, but he sensed it would also lead to his death. The crushing pressure of the crystal dissipated, and he stared at the door, and his fate, contemplating the value of his life against the secrets hidden beyond the door.

He reached out and pressed on the handle, allowing the door to swing open on its own. Beyond it, darkness stretched infinitely into the distance. He put one foot in and checked inside before venturing any deeper, then entered. Several steps from the entrance, a pedestal stood containing the silver horse artifact. He plucked it from the spotlight, and it immediately resonated, taking him back to the moment he saw the horse fall to the ground at the feet of a striking woman with long dark hair and sad eyes.

Everything became perfectly clear to him inside that room. He cracked a smile as he recalled that day. "It wasn't a woman at all," he said, clasping the horse in his palm.

Footsteps trailed into the room behind him.

He turned, his smile growing. "It was you."

Jackyl blinked once, hard. "You seem to have remembered. It was difficult catching you away from Fate. We've been here so many times, but someone always manages to interfere. I know you're the Lord of Chaos but we should keep it within reason. The only way we could ensure we succeeded is if I did it myself."

"Lord of Chaos?"

Jackyl flinched. "So, we haven't quite remembered everything. Not to worry, I'll help you through it."

"Why would you put yourself through all of this... chaos?"

Jackyl nodded. "It's my duty and my pleasure. I am here because I choose to be."

Hero ruminated on the past and his mission to restore Euphoria's balance. How could he forget such a thing? All the fractured pieces of his consciousness came together.

Jackyl nodded his head towards something in the darkness, a chrysalis larger than himself.

Hero walked towards it and pressed his hand to the rough crystal, unable to see through the iridescent surface.

Jackyl joined him, keeping his hands back. "Do you remember the tale about the Chrysalis?"

Hero recalled the tale as he ran his hand down. "I'm inside?"

Jackyl pushed his mask to the side of his head, tangling up his dark hair. "The real you."

"Who is the real me?" Hero stroked the chrysalis with this new knowledge that it held the completed version of himself—his whole self, whoever that may be.

Jackyl gazed upward at the chrysalis. "The truth is that you already know but you don't want to accept it. Normal Ancients don't dream, but you do, don't you?"

Hero held no desire to lie to Jackyl because he instinctively knew how much he cherished their bond through all ages.

Jackyl continued. "What do you dream about?"

Hero's mind wandered to thoughts of the trees with books for pages, the shadow creature, and the beach in the depths of the Void. "I dream about darkness."

"Well, the dream isn't over yet," Jackyl said.

"What?" He looked down as a crackling sound caught his ear. Tree roots broke free from below and wrapped around his legs. He struggled to break free from it, but it soon covered his entire body, until he saw Jackyl from only a small opening between the branches. He strained to reach out, and the constricting branches filled him with panic. "Don't leave me!"

Jackyl smiled softly and took Hero's hand. "I won't. I never did."

"Nox!" Hero stared at him for a long pause, remembering their bond throughout the ages.

Jackyl's expression froze, holding a look of surprise as he disappeared behind the violent branches.

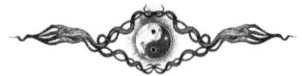

Hero stirred from his sleep at a sudden tremble to find himself face down on a cold translucent floor. Space whirled below in a kaleidoscope of colors. His mouth fell open as he tried to pull the collective of stars into focus. Once alert, he immediately popped up onto his hands and knees to view his surroundings. Scrolls fell off rows of skillfully crafted wooden shelves, the hanging light above swung back and forth, and a spinning wheel across the room spun with a ticking sound. He jumped to his feet to venture through the quaint building, a place he remembered as the Hall of Forgotten Memories.

A man spoke, his voice gentle and soothing. "Leoht."

Hero turned back towards the scroll room as the red-haired man strolled towards him, his long robe trailing behind in a cascade of silken coy. "Cas?"

Casluhim smiled. "You remember."

Hero surprised himself because it felt as if he'd always known.

"What else have you forgotten? Hm?" Casluhim waved a hand and the shelves twisted, revealing a long hall. They walked down the hall towards a room that Hero knew well. He once stayed inside as a resident of the halls after....

Hero stopped following, pressing a hand to his stomach in a failed attempt to quell the hole in the pit of his gut. His heart raced and one concern rang in his mind. "Where is my father?"

Casluhim turned back and tucked his hands into his long sleeves. "You know the answer. Isn't that why Nox was looking after you?"

Hero tried to remember what happened and what mission he had set out to accomplish.

"Come," Casluhim said with a wave of his hand. "This will help you remember." They continued their walk down the hall to Leoht's old room. Again, Casluhim gestured.

Hero reached out to the door. His head seemed to be full of memories but never the right ones. He hoped that this time it would be different.

Casluhim bowed his head. "I bid you well."

Hero opened yet another door. Once he stepped into the room, it closed behind him. Clocks and mirrors of all different shapes and sizes hung on a wall, all oddly colored a deep glossy burgundy.

Akira sat on a long, oval table set for twenty or so other people, kicking up one foot to look at the shine on his shoe. He hummed to himself while he inspected it.

Hero queried. "Why are you in here?"

Akira raised his head, his expression still. "Why not?"

Hero frowned. "You're not welcome here."

The sunny glint in Akira's eyes revealed the smile hidden behind his mask. He stepped down from the table and straightened his pants. "I don't need to be." He put out his hands to each side. "How long do you think you've been traveling the Dreamscape?"

"I'm not sure. Time here seems kind of irrelevant to the physical plane."

"Right. This realm has no regard for time at all. Must you loathe it so?"

"I wouldn't know." Hero's eyes traced the darkness bleeding into the room. Something about Akira had changed; his mannerisms came across far more flippant. He radiated pure energy. "What's going on with you? You're not being as obnoxious as usual."

"What is the meaning of *usual* in your realm? You don't know me."

"I don't but... I get the impression I understand you."

Akira smiled again, though this time, the subtle hint of malice crept into his gaze that unsettled even Hero. "Indeed, you do... albeit unpleasant for the both of us."

"Agreed. I would prefer we finish any business we may have quickly," Hero said, crossing his arms to block out the insufferable aura.

Akira gesticulated as he spoke, looking much like the conductor of a symphony. "Alas, you can't help the discomfort. We are of one mind."

He squinted, turning an ear towards Akira. "Pardon?"

The fox-masked man repeated himself with a fixed tone, pulling at his collar and then unnecessarily straightening his vest. "We are of one mind."

"How so?"

"We are both here to fill the same role, the role of Akira."

"You... are not Bedad."

"And neither are you, but we *are* nevertheless of one mind. It is a trait of all those who carry a specific spiritual strain."

"The Albedo Gene."

"See, you *do* remember."

Hero avoided any reaction that would give away his thoughts. "But who the hell are you?"

"I am Time," Akira said.

Hero knew to call him *'Akira'* though it seemed perfectly clear, by his perky and cunning persona, that he was not Bedad. He figured the answer must be a reference to the Lords but knew nothing about such a being. "Time doesn't exist in the Beyond."

"And yet I am here."

"Why?"

"To remind you of your purpose, Leoht Miina. It is high time you awaken. You've slept for far too long. Things will not end well if you can't learn to move with a sense of urgency."

Hero turned his head and glared from the corner of his eye. "This is a job for Bound and you're not my Bound."

"That's not important right now. It's unfortunate, but she can't be here to wake you, so I must be. You have forgotten your job and you must be reminded of what it is. Shortly, Bedad will be swept up by the Ripples of Time. We must proceed without alerting anyone to our plan or our shortcomings."

"Out of all the people in the universe, I'm supposed to awaken at the hand of someone I neither know nor trust?"

Akira gripped the end of the table, keeping a long silence.

Hero had begun to think that his comment was overlooked when the mirrors and clocks started to shake. At first, they shook subtly, but within a couple of breaths they appeared ready to fly off the walls, much like Akira, whose white hair stood on end.

"Listen, you little shit," Akira said. "I didn't come here to argue with you about whose job this is. You're going to wake up or I'm going to make you wake up. You are the one who forgot your mission, and I'm the one who has come to remind you of what it is. Every moment that passes in here is wasted time in Euphoria. I can't change or control how you perceive my element in your realm. So, act or be forced to act."

The realization of time distracted Hero from his inherent fear, something that didn't come easily to him. "How long has it been? What happened?"

At last, Akira's expression lightened, and the clocks and mirrors stopped shaking. "Fate is still alive and well. She's eluded the Council for the last turn and a half. Your son is five now. The battle for Nex hasn't gone swimmingly. War is coming and you are needed."

Hero had just been there to give Leon-Ru his name. He had left his family wondering whether he would ever return. "I have to go back. I can't leave them. I promised."

"You'll learn to thank me one day, Leoht." The hands of the clocks in the room spun faster and faster. "When you leave here, you must prepare yourself. They have arrested your wife for your murder. My accomplice, Besil, is in the middle of breaking her out. I can't gauge what will happen from there."

"With your abilities, wasn't there a way to avoid this battle?"

Akira gestured again with one hand as he answered. "I've tried everything. It took just about everything to get us to this point unscathed. There's something like a universal formula, a set of rules which much be followed. If you read the old scriptures, everything happens as described."

"What are you specifically referring to?"

"The first law of the universe. *Everything that has happened, is happening, will happen again.* History can and will repeat itself but there's more to it than that. The Universe is like this because it was designed to follow other sets of laws and rules, which are kept in line by—"

"The Watchers," Hero almost shouted, the memory returning in a flash.

"Correct," Akira said with a nearly imperceptible sigh. He hung his head forward and his hand went limp. It didn't take much to perceive the constant air of defeat and frustration that he felt towards Hero, to the extent that Hero felt a little guilty. Just a little, though.

Hero tried doing his own reflection to speed things up. "I'm still forgetting something important."

Akira nodded slightly as he leaned against the table again. "Every door in this place is a brand or a seal that was placed to keep you suppressed. The Council fears what you could become, but they also fear what might happen if they try to kill off the Lords... particularly you. This is an advantage. If mine is not existing, then yours is that you're virtually indestructible. However, they've still killed you once and that means they're willing to take chances to get what they want. The Guardians are in place to make sure that doesn't happen again." He trailed off for a moment. "...at any cost to ourselves."

"Oh, you were a Guardian. But aren't they in place to protect space *and* time?"

Akira smirked. "There are more precious things to protect, if you ask me."

Hero found it hard not to hold some sliver of admiration for this person who clearly hated him and still made sacrifices for the greater good. This trait reminded him of something important. He repeated from a memory, "Let's play a game...."

Akira raised his head like an animal who'd heard a suspicious noise. He and Hero finished the thought at the same time. "...to uncover the identity of the next Grandmaster."

Hero clenched his jaw and ground his teeth before continuing his thoughts. "The Game isn't over yet." He knew well enough that neither he nor this man before him had even existed when someone first spoke these words, but the Universe relayed them like a mantra or a puzzle to be solved.

Akira stood upright, swinging both his head and his hip to one side. He made many movements that differed from the Akira that Hero had encountered previously. "The truth is that no one knows for certain who it is. It could be you or me, or it could be a joke that the last Grandmaster is playing on everyone. He's trying to teach a lesson and I don't particularly care what it is. We all have something or someone we want to protect and, no matter what that is, we require a functioning universe to do so. Euphoria's balance must be returned, and the rightful rulers of the thrones of Universe and the Void must be returned to their places. We require the Lords of Light and Shadow to succeed."

Hero nodded. As everything came back to him, a deep sadness returned with those memories. He thought of his father, his real father who'd left him with this task, and of his mother, who'd left a very strong impression on him, probably even stronger than that of his father. "There's much to be done. Thank you for setting me straight."

Akira paused for an unusually long time.

Hero felt through some connection that this man deliberated on something severe and that the choice weighed on his mind. He also got the impression that he knew of his identity, but that bit hadn't fully surfaced and, even if he knew, saying so would only cause more harm than good.

Akira exhaled slowly and opened his hand to Hero. "Give me the horse."

Hero did so, sensing a deep purpose for it.

Akira's mouth set in a line, holding back either words or an emotion that he did a good job of concealing. He snapped his hand shut on the horse and crushed it with darkness.

Hero's heart gave a pang. He clutched his chest as he doubled over in pain and gasped at the inexplicable rush of terror and loss. As quickly as it came, it left. The fear and pain subsided, leaving behind a hollow and numbing sensation in his chest. He got back onto his feet, stunned. "What happened just now?"

Akira closed his eyes hard and breathed deeply again as he murmured to himself. "Please tell me I'm not going to regret this. Please tell me I'm doing the right thing."

Hero rested his hand over his heart. "What did you do? I feel so... so *liberated*."

"Without emotions to distract you, your memories should surface easily."

Hero turned towards the door, now aware of a clicking sound like the one that echoed over and over through his mind. "What's that sound?"

"The other seals are breaking. I need to you understand something vital. You have presently been stripped of your emotions and that means you ought to be aware of your behavior and its effect on others. This mission was imparted on me, though

I loathe it. Please don't make me regret any more than I already do. Don't make me hate you."

Hero gazed at his own hands, unable to feel any connection to himself or his body. In this state, he wondered why it would even bother him to be hated, because the guilt had fled his soul entirely. He could only rely on what he knew to be right, and hoped he wouldn't forget why he cared. "You did this to remove distractions. I'll do my best to use it wisely."

Akira nodded his head just once. "That's all I can hope. Just remember...."

Hero finished the thought. "...we are of one mind."

20
OUT OF TIME

A chime rang, stirring Hero from his sleep. A rush of icy air brushed against his face, and streaks of violet light coursed upward, winding through the new room. He pressed his hands around the place where he'd been resting—hard like stone, and cold to the touch. More importantly, he regained his vision. Even better than this, he gained heightened vision. He looked carefully at his surroundings. Gazing through the rocky matter appeared like gazing through a prism where the colorful light created a murky surface—the Chrysalis. He'd finally succeeded in evolving.

Jackyl inquired, "Leoht, are you awake?"

Rather than respond, he waited for the chrysalis to crack and break open. He then stuck his hand through it and kicked at the crystal until it fell apart and enabled him to climb out.

Jackyl offered his hand with a dimpled grin. When he had helped Hero out, the smile faded. "Isis has called Fate to trial."

Hero brushed off the particles of crystal, careful not to get any caught under his skin. "What for?" Flakes of ice floated in through the doorway of the family tomb, which he recognized from the Ancient statues that guarded the doorway.

"She has accused Fate of murdering you."

"That's right. And why would anyone believe that?"

Jackyl shuffled a foot. "The only way to hide the chrysalis was to hide you, so Isis has been making these accusations from the moment you disappeared."

"You faked my death?"

His voice grew shrill. "What else could I do? You told me to ensure your awakening at *any* cost, did you not?"

Hero vaguely remembered the conversation. The Echoes came too slow for his liking. If only he could remember everything that had happened. He contemplated the death of Elaine, which he now recalled clearly. Even before the Council placed seals on him, the blighted Annulus Eye had blinded his spiritual sight, and this made him less of a threat, especially as a child. Anyone could have deceived him with ease.

Elaine felt no connection to him after losing her Bound, other than her general will to physically protect her child, so he lacked a support system outside of Chi. "I was framed. That's why crystal was used in every murder."

In each scenario, crystal was used as a weapon. His aunt had spent most of her life devoted to protecting others from the effects of crystal, and he'd spent most of his trying to understand why it was harmful in the first place. In his research, he found that the crimes committed with crystal were streamlined.

Lara's tragic attempt to poison Fate stuck out among the other murders. The fact that she was a Rahma made it painfully obvious that someone much older, an Ancient, had manipulated the poor girl. Lara's outward fondness for beautiful Ancient women, and her desperation to try and follow in their footsteps, made her the perfect target.

Only one person had Lara's complete devotion and access to all of the victims.

He pressed on the bridge of his nose. By removing Elaine, Nex fell under Rahma rule, easy pawns for an Ancient Queen. That left Hero. Since she aided him and earned his trust during his early childhood, she managed to courage him to take the Capital Throne. If he made these deductions, it appeared like a clever chess match that she won. Hero had too many seals in place to distrust her or notice.

"Are you all right?"

"Yes, it's just... why and how she did it is all becoming clear to me now." Hero instinctively prepared to ask why Jackyl hadn't told him, but then remembered how much Akira had puzzled over this period in history. *Variables of chaos. My place in this timeline has made it too difficult to manipulate.*

Isis had found her way to prove that she deserved the Council throne by dragging down the rulers of Nex, but Hero now had the memory and the ability to block her checkmate.

"Where is she?"

Jackyl grasped what Hero meant with minimal effort. "The trial is being held in Inoue Palace."

"Then, we're going to the Capital."

"Allow me to take you," Jackyl said, wrapping his arm around Hero. "It would be better not to overexert yourself until you're in full form."

"Yes. Thank you."

Darkness plumed from the ground, stretched upward, and consumed them with one gulp. In this form of travel, Hero felt as though he were falling without any sense of direction.

21
ONLY TIME WILL TELL

The air around Hero rushed as he dropped down into the Centre with Jackyl, surrounded by shrieking, running people. A pulse of light shot across the sky from the palace, causing a tremor throughout the city.

Jackyl released him and sprinted towards the stairs. "Shit... they're still in the palace. We must hurry and find them!"

Hero took his time immersing himself in the view of the surrounding terror, and trailed behind Jackyl rather slowly. The world appeared in hyper clarity, every detail jumping out at him in an array of variables. He saw more than ever before with his new sight. As he made his way through the chaos, he noticed a curious overlapping of time. He saw clearly, with his new vision, the possibilities spread out before him like images on sheets of overlying papers. The timelines aligned before him, telling him about the number of attempts they made to correct history and the balance. He paused as civilians pushed past him, stumbling over each other. One man stood out. He saw the man flee but he also saw him lying dead on the ground, crushed by debris. The effects of time rippled, and he fully understood the consequences of each action, reflecting before him in trails — *these are Echoes.*

A whisper caught his ear. *'You're out of time.'*

Hero rushed up the palace steps and slid into the main hall. He needed more time to adjust to this heightened vision. Everything looked washed out and so bright that it hurt to look for more than a few seconds. He found his way up the steps and through the right corridor towards the Conference Room.

At the top of the stairway, a woman called out to him. "You're alive?"

He turned towards Isis and tilted his head. "Is that all you have to say?"

"I don't want to fight with you, Hero. There's still a chance for you to come to my side. Akira has already sealed his fate, but what about you? Don't you want to survive?"

He tried reading through her. All this time, she'd stood beside him and invested her time to make him something greater. "I trusted you. I wanted to. I guess, in the end, the only one who was honest with me was Fate."

"Is she really honest? Do you think she tells you everything?"

"She doesn't have to tell me everything, as long as she doesn't lie."

Isis snapped, "If that's how you feel, then you're a hypocrite. All you *do* is lie."

"I know," Hero said. "I guess we're both trash." He moved his hand to the side and amassed darkness until it formed a short blade.

Isis glanced at it, her eyes glassy as she asked what she already knew to be true. "Are you really going to fight me, Hero?"

He responded only by maintaining his stance at first. Then, as he advanced, the floor rumbled and a fissure ran beneath his feet.

She drew anima from everything around her.

The stairway vibrated then collapsed.

Crystal shot up from the level below, breaking Hero's fall. He slid down one of the massive shards to the first floor.

Isis released a violent pulse of anima, throwing him onto his back. She wasted no time advancing on him when he was down. In a flash, she pounced and mounted over him with her spear to his throat. She looked him dead in the eyes.

He lay completely still, waiting for her to do something. Whatever power slumbered within him continued to do so even though he felt it stirring inside. "Are you really going to kill me?"

Isis dislodged her spear from the stone and peered down the hall at a waiting figure. Before Hero could turn to look himself, she dispelled her weapon and rushed off with only one fleeting thought. "You'll regret choosing them over me."

He rolled over onto his hands and knees again. His weapon dispersed into particles of crystal as he stumbled back onto his feet. Truthfully, Isis's decision did little except prove that she needed him, for some reason. He let that thought stew in his head, and smirked. *Interesting.*

Jackyl slid around the corner at the other end of the hall. "Hero, they're headed to the Centre! Come quickly!" He vanished in a flurry of darkness.

Hero groaned and dusted himself off. His body still lagged from the effect of his slumber in the Chrysalis. It would be some time before he'd manage to use flash or shadow step as they did. He made his way towards the collapsed entrance, viewing the Ussan as he passed by the viewing window. Visions of the forest long before the time of Mu haunted him. He saw it set ablaze and collapse repeatedly in his mind. He wondered how many times he'd failed to arrive at this moment. Fortunately, he felt nothing, and without the despair of loss to cripple him, he remained focused on his current task.

Screams arose from the Centre outside, and he channeled his crystal inward and took a deep breath, painting an image of Inoue's Town Centre. The shadows stretched out around him like smoke, forming a cradle. The sound of his breathing echoed and trailed. When he opened his eyes, the Centre expanded around him and took form. He appeared at the end of the pathway, which led from the palace. In the distance, Fate sprinted across the Centre towards the Ussan, led by a tall, dark-haired man in a blue blazer.

Hero began treading down the community steps, surprised to find that in one step, he'd moved to the edge of the Centre. He folded space without even trying. He pressed his hand to his chest, confirming that his heartbeat remained smooth and calm, and realized that he didn't need to flash or shadow step—his ability exceeded those who'd mentored him. He felt his focus wane as he heard a commotion just ahead.

On one side of the Centre, Jackyl arrived in a flood of black smoke, forming a scythe. Swarms of Reapers burst through a portal at his flanks.

On the other side, Isis entered in a pulse of green light, her spear ready for battle, with an army of soldiers behind her.

Fate and the man in blue slid to a halt, trapped between the two armies.

Both the Reapers and the soldiers charged the Centre in a flurry of shouts and elements flying. A mass of ether lashed out from Jackyl's scythe and, simultaneously, a ripple of anima gushed out of Isis's spear.

The man in blue let out a shout as he grabbed Fate and shielded her.

The elements intertwined and spiraled at the center, creating a vortex in between. As they joined, they released a pulse of energy that surged through the Centre, knocking many off their feet. It lapped across the stone and threw Jackyl and Isis back several paces.

The man in blue gasped as the energy created a vacuum and tore Fate from his grasp, screaming.

Jackyl's voice broke across the Centre but neither he nor anyone else could move against the powerful current. "Close the portal! She's been caught between them!"

The force of the vacuum pushed the onlookers to their knees.

Isis shouted back. "I can't! She'll be torn apart!"

Hero knew that if she truly sought to destroy them and take the throne, she would do just that and rip Fate's soul in two.

Fate's shrill cry filled Inoue Community as trails of red and violet light streamed out of the vortex, causing a devastating wake of destruction. Those closest to the blast disintegrated instantly. Buildings and landscaping were blown apart.

Hero watched on, defending himself best he could from the pebbles and stones that shot past his face and left tiny cuts.

A massive figure zipped by, spewing ether as it went. It passed by so quickly that by the time Hero caught clear sight of it, he only saw darkness billowing out in massive plumes to form a skeletal figure. Looming clouds filled the sky, casting a dark shadow over Inoue.

A Grim.

The Grim's teeth chattered as rumbling voices emanated from its cloaked form. "What have you done?"

Isis and her soldiers gasped at the towering display. "A Grim!"

Hero blinked hard to clear his mind and his vision, seeing the true form inside the skeleton clear as day. *Ra Bedad, how did you achieve Grim status?*

The darkness melted away from Akira's skeleton form, like thick black paint dripping from a canvas, and reconstituted into a heavy smoke. Two enormous, bony arms surfaced out from under its cloak and stretched over the people in the Capital with a whoosh, sending a wave of darkness across the pavement. Reapers fled in puffs of black smoke. The current swept Isis, Jackyl, the soldiers, and the man in blue towards the funnel below the vortex. The quarreling parties shared a din of alarm as they were swept inside.

Akira faced the vortex that held Fate and opened out his skeletal hand, and then suddenly clenched it shut. A flash of blinding light shot out, permeating the atmosphere, and then diminished, revealing that the force had split Fate into two identical forms.

He bolted forward and caught one of the Fates, but faltered as the other Fate got caught in the wake and fell into the funnel. Darkness and miasma spilled away from his body like soot caught in the wind. He struggled to keep his grip on the Fate he'd rescued, and descended towards the funnel. Caught in the pull of the vortex, his skeletal form broke away piece by piece, unveiling the man beneath.

Hero fought against the current, repeatedly folding space to create more distance, but it proved too strong, and he slid across the Centre towards the growing darkness. He heard a shout and reacted in kind, reaching out and grasping Akira by the arm. Together, they stood against the current until another pulse knocked them off their feet and dragged them inside with the others.

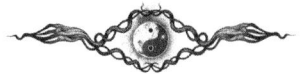

Orbs of light floated slowly up from the ground as Hero roused again. He noticed Akira's arm under his head. *He broke my fall?*

Akira still lay unconscious but seemingly calm in his slumber. What could be seen of his face from behind his mask appeared relaxed and in a deep, deep sleep.

Hero turned his head and saw Fate, also unconscious, only a few steps away. She looked gaunt but alive.

Everything was a mess. Inoue had fallen into war, and the conflict had torn everything and everyone apart and dumped them into the Abyss.

He rolled over, ignoring each ache and pain, so he could drag himself to Fate's side. He touched her cheek and felt her shallow breath against his hand. "Thank all that is."

He sat up and stared at the lights and phantoms that ebbed along the darkness. Stars twinkled above as they flowed like ocean waves. Phantoms swam through the air in all sizes, inching across the vast open space. The sight moved something deep inside his soul, reminding him of his childhood and something long lost. He wondered, if he still retained the connection to his emotions, if he would understand this sensation.

A small eel-shaped phantom zipped around the air in front of him and stopped as if to investigate his presence. He reached out and poked it.

The phantom vocalized, creating an echo from which the other phantoms mimicked across the landscape, creating a song of sorts—a choir unlike any other in the universe.

Akira spoke to him, so soft and low he was nearly incomprehensible. "Do you like them?"

As Hero glanced back at him, Akira shifted his multi-colored eyes and stared back, silently.

"They're phantoms, right?"

Akira repeated himself, sounding less inquisitive than before. "You like them."

"Of course. They're beautiful."

His eyes shifted forward again, and he lay still. Particles of light raced off his body, just as the darkness had in the Mortal Realm.

Hero needed to know. "Why did you come?"

"Because it's my duty."

"To whom or what? Saving her doesn't benefit you in any way."

"Save?" He muffled a sound that sounded vaguely like laughter. "Perhaps you're right."

Hero never really liked Akira. More specifically, he disliked the uncanny feeling that the man elicited. However, Akira had successfully led the Third Party despite his debilitating condition, and this made him likable in a sense—even respectable. At any rate, Hero didn't consider him deserving of erasure. "Will you be erased?

Akira heaved his body upright, hanging his head down in exhaustion. "What do you think?"

"I don't like this."

"I thought you hated me. Wasn't it mutual?"

"I don't hate you. You're just annoying. On the contrary, I admire you."

Akira snapped out of his droning trance. "What?"

"You say and do whatever you want. You travel all over the Universe, and even the people who hate you will acknowledge your wisdom and strength. Everyone talks about being superior, but to be truly superior, you must learn to control yourself. I always thought you were the type of person to wear a mask so you wouldn't hurt others, even when you were hurting. That's why I wished to be that kind of hero."

Akira squinted furtively. "You think too highly of me."

Hero continued his probing. "When did you become a grim? And how?"

Akira staggered over to Fate and took her up into his arms. "Stop asking me questions. I need you to go to Jax. You can throw the rest of your endless inquisitions at him. I have to go and search for the other half of Fate."

"You?"

"Unless you know how to traverse the depths of the Abyss and wrangle a Rogue Hunter."

"A what?"

"Exactly," Akira said, pointing. "Jax is straight ahead, tearing himself up about losing her. Go and comfort him. Tell him I wish for you to find your son in the Capital. He will take you."

Akira disappeared, so Hero climbed back to his feet and searched for Jackyl in the direction that Akira had pointed.

The Reaper stood with his face buried in his hands. Something had happened to his mask. It no longer hung on the side of his head. His clothes looked torn and dirty. When Hero approached, Jackyl jerked his head up. "I... I lost her... and Akira... he...."

There was nothing Hero could say. The words, 'It's okay,' served no purpose because he could see just as well that Akira's energy was almost completely depleted. He hugged Jackyl with a silent sigh.

Jackyl's body became rigid. "What happened to Bes? Where did he go?"

Hero figured that Jackyl referred to the long-haired man who had helped Fate escape the trial. "I'm not sure. He fell into the funnel like the rest of us."

Jackyl answered his own question, without much consideration to Hero's answer. "Wiser... he probably went to Wiser!"

Hero shook his head. "I don't know."

"What are we going to do? This is a mess. You're really awake, right? You're not going to vanish on us, are you?"

He avoided answering, though he realized that Jackyl's fretting would persist until he found an answer to his questions. "There's no way to reverse his condition? Will he truly be erased?"

Jackyl patted Hero's shoulder and grinned in a pained way. "We'll do everything we can to keep him safe."

"I see.... Then I'm glad. He told me to return to the Capital so I can find Leon-Ru."

"All right. I suppose he went after Fate. We can catch up once we get back. Hold on."

They held onto each other firmly, and Jackyl spun his scythe to accumulate darkness for their final portal jump.

22
THE FINAL HOUR

The darkness separated as Hero and Jackyl entered Chi's humble home, where the rest of the group waited for news. Chi held Leon-Ru close to her leg while she confirmed who had joined them. The Ignis Brothers also grew tense until they noticed Hero.

Leon-Ru hugged Hero's leg. *"Ba'ai."*

Hero pressed a gentle hand on the boy's shoulder and felt a jolt of anima.

The small boy twisted his head from one side to the other. "You can see me?"

Hero stiffened, having seen his son for the first time in his life. After being in the Chrysalis for a turn, he could now see a peculiar resonance in Leon-Ru's aura, unlike anything he'd ever noticed before. It took everything in his power not to seize up entirely. Everyone else would expect him to be emotional about this encounter when, in reality, it filled him with unforeseen terror and shock. It startled him even more to *feel* anything after having his emotions severed.

Amid his thoughts, it occurred to him that he'd been quiet for too long, and he finally patted his son's head full of stark grey hair, a trait of the Wolf Clan. "I'm relieved that you're safe."

Leon-Ru had grown immensely in a single turn, and his head now reached Hero's waist. The small boy stared up at his father with large lavender eyes, full of curiosity yet somehow vacant. He stared in the same way that a scientist scrutinized their subjects. In fact, he gave the impression that he could see through Hero.

Chi rose to her feet and gaped at Hero, covering her mouth. "Praise be."

Hero looked around the shocked faces.

Fortis leapt over the chair and scooped Hero into his arms with a bear hug. "By all that is! It's good to see you." He dropped Hero back onto the floor, where he scratched his cheek, wishing he had a proper explanation.

Jackyl stepped forward. "I'm sure you're all surprised.

"Firmus chuckled at them. "Surprised?"

Chi stammered, "Of course, we are surprised." She crossed the room and took Hero's face into her hands. "Do you know how thankful I am to see you?"

"Very much so, because I can see you too," Hero said, embracing her. His chest remained devoid of emotion but he knew exactly what to say.

Leon-Ru cast a shadow of doubt upon his father.

Hero may not know his son's facial expression, but the darkness in his aura rang out clearer than the Centre's warning bell.

"You should be prepared to say goodbye," Jackyl warned. "We need to review what happened in the Capital battle."

A banging at the door stopped the conversation.

Chi hurried to the window, then opened the door, allowing Kyou inside.

The instant that Kyou's gaze fell upon Hero, he stepped back, his words caught in his throat.

Chi patted him hard on the back. "...and he can see."

Kyou stood agape as Jackyl fidgeted with his cloak, his irritation bleeding out into the room. "Sense of urgency, please."

Chi's armor clanked and her aura crossed through the room towards the window. "Yes, of course. Continue."

Jackyl paused to check each person for their attention. "We secured the Centre and brought down Isis's army, but we failed to break Fate out in one piece."

Chi questioned him, a hint of suspicion creeping into her voice. "One piece?"

Hero rubbed his head as though it might remove the image from his mind. "It's true. She was caught in the crossfire."

Chi clenched her fists. "Crossfire? That ripped her in two?"

Jackyl answered. "Isis and I created a vortex when our elements collided. The force created a vortex that... split her soul in two. Akira has one half."

Hero broke in. "He's searching for the other half."

Jackyl winced. "We've lost one half of her to Isis. My Reapers saw her leave with the other half of Fate. There is no mistake."

Hero pressed a hand to his chin, feeling struck. "She planned it."

Kyou shook his head. "What do you mean?"

"Isis. This is what she intended all along. If she couldn't win the Spinner, she'd break her."

Firmus shrugged. "But why? She has control of Askadel, Rosetau, and now Nex. What purpose would she have for exposing herself in this way?"

Chi locked her jaw and ground her teeth. "The Spinner... Isis needed control. This is not about a couple of kingdoms, it must be about the entire Mortal Realm... or more. She wants Euphoria."

Jackyl waved his hands out to each side, frantic. "Fate could be anywhere by now. There's no time in the Abyss. She could do anything."

Hero scrunched his brow. "What will happen to her? Will she die?"

Jackyl hesitated. "I don't know. If she lives, she won't be the same. We would have to find both halves of her and reunite them before she runs out of spiritual energy. *Miina Feir* has already awakened, so her body won't be able to contain all of her aura."

She's awake and he knew? Fully awake?

Hero hid his skepticism to the best of his ability, especially feeling Leon-Ru's stare.

Chi's voice shook. "Will she be in pain?"

Jackyl answered again. "I don't know. We'll know what to do after Akira returns. For now, we should figure out what we should do in the worst-case scenario."

Kyou interjected. "Then let's decide what'll happen to Leon-Ru if Hero and Fate have to part from him. Children must be protected first."

No one commented.

Leon-Ru tugged Hero's shirt. "We'll have to be apart?"

Hero knelt and took his son's hands. "I don't know. We have to make plans to ensure your safety." He also tried not to shake, suddenly feeling duress from the immense energy coursing through his child.

Leon-Ru frowned. "I don't want to be apart again."

"I don't either, but I have to keep you safe. You're most important to us. No matter what decision we make, Leon, we'll always find you. We won't abandon you." He removed the hourglass from his neck and put it on Leon-Ru. "This artifact is important to me. I gave it to your mother when I left to travel Mu. I'll tell you the same thing I told her then."

"What's that?"

"This is a keepsake. Take care of it. I'll be wanting it back."

"I'll take care of it." Leon-Ru didn't smile too often. Sometimes it felt as though his son was the parent and he was his child.

Even as Hero tried to comfort him then, Leon-Ru fretted. "Who will watch over you if I'm not there?"

Hero laughed forcibly. "I can care for myself."

"But your middle is soft."

Kyou burst out, "Wow! What an old phrase!"

After hearing Leon-Ru say this, Chi's voice trailed in agreement. "Yes... it is quite old...." She wavered, then added, "I think Leon-Ru will do better in a setting where he can learn to fight. If Mu is to fall, he must be able to protect himself."

Jackyl stepped forward and muttered, "What if I take him?"

"To Niall?"

"If he's in Niall, then he'll have the protection of the Reapers and the Grim. I can be his guardian. After all, I'm his uncle. It would be strange to pass him to someone else when his immediate family is right here. Plus, we can put him through the Reaper's training, and I can help him find his parents if they're separated."

"That might be the best decision," Kyou said. "He should be away from Mu. The Shadow Realm will welcome him and, if he's with you, then we know he'll be in good hands."

Fortis choked back his emotions. "Will he be safe in Niall? There are portals and cavities that lead into the Void. Not to mention, Phantoms and Shadow Creatures. What if he's eaten... or worse?"

Kyou seemed at ease. "He's a smart kid. He'll listen to his uncle. Right, Leon-Ru?"

Leon-Ru lowered his head and shoulders. "I want to stay with *Ba'ai*."

Jackyl spoke even softer than before. "If I were being completely honest, I don't think that's possible. Fate is Hero's Bound. In order to sew her soul back together, the members of the Organization will need to seek out both halves of her. That could take time, and Akira might have to come up with another solution to this problem, which will most likely require Hero to leave. If they're separated, or their binding is fractured, they could both die, and then you won't have parents at all. I'm sure that if your dad decides to separate, it'll be because he wants to return to you when your momma's safe."

Leon-Ru's aura flashed white. This symbolized a rush of emotion, either rage or some other powerful force. He certainly disliked Jackyl's suggestion. Most of the time, it shone a multitude of colors, much like Akira's.

Kyou made a low sound at the back of his throat. "I hate to admit it, but he's probably right. Your mother is going to die if we can't sew her soul back together. I understand your distress. You're still young and you haven't been with your parents for long. This is going to be about trust, Leon-Ru. Do you trust your parents to do what's best for you?"

Leon-Ru grasped Hero's hand. *"Yu'un."*

Chi approached them with cautious movements. "Leon-Ru, where are you learning these phrases?"

Firmus interrupted. "Is this the time for that?"

"But they are—"

"We're trying to decide what's going to be in store for him. You can ask him about that later."

Jackyl broke the tension with another unrelated question. "Has anyone seen a Reaper in a cat mask?"

Hero caught himself squinting at Jackyl. The more he spoke; the more suspicious Hero found his friend's actions and behavior. *What are you hiding?*

"Something is coming," Kyou said.

The furniture shook and a cloud of darkness surged through the middle of the room. Tendrils of dark smoke whipped around and formed Akira. A black cat hung around his neck and shoulders, and Fate dangled from his arms, unconscious... or at least one half of her.

He immediately began talking. "As you can all clearly see, we have returned, but I still only have half of Fate."

Hero wondered if anyone else saw the energy leaking off Akira's body like an open wound. He suspected that Jackyl and Leon-Ru could, since they could both see into to the Ethereal Realm.

Akira spoke again. "Hero, come with me to the guest room. Everyone else, stay out here."

As soon as the door to the room closed, his miasma poured out and the area darkened. He panted slightly as streams of gold light whirled across the empty space.

Hero reflected on the incident in the Capital and the dying Grim who had shielded him. He and Akira were always at each other's throats. Deep down, he wished that they could get along and find a way to survive. The fact that Akira stood there emitting what remained of his energy hurt Hero immensely. "Why are you feigning composure? To keep the others calm?"

I really did admire you though.

"Wouldn't you? What'll they think if I'm in this condition? You saw how Jax reacted. I'll tell him soon, but the others mustn't find out."

"What'll happen if you're erased?"

"Hmm, my cycle might end, but it'll take time for the Ripples of Time to reach every part of the Universe. You'll see. I've completed what I set out to accomplish."

Hero sensed that Akira might be smiling for some reason. "What was your Soul's Purpose?"

"Should I tell you? What good will it do?"

"I want to remember you. Is that so strange?"

Akira murmured, mostly to himself. "Very. I wonder why I must be remembered by you. I feel like Fate might be right—I might be some kind of joke the Universe made up for amusement."

"Was the Universe so cruel? If you rebuilt the Mirror of Time and Space, wouldn't you have made it that way yourself?"

Akira answered with unexpected honesty. "No. I'm trying to make it possible for my vision of the world to come to fruition. This world... is not mine. That's why it'll keep moving even without me. It's the New World that'll fall apart."

"What would you like me to do?"

"I'm going to offer my services for a final time." Akira wavered and a moment of silence passed through the room. "I've made some mistakes—some selfish mistakes. I know that. That's why I want to correct them, if I'm able. I never meant for Fate to end up like this. I can offer your family protection and Organization support, under the supervision of Wiser and the Reapers of Niall. We can discuss the details with Wiser in person, but it'll most likely require you to part from your son to recover the other half of Fate's soul. What do you think?"

Hero hesitated to respond when he remembered Leon-Ru's desire to stay together. "Do you think we'll be able to return to him?"

"I do not know," Akira said, his aura expanding and then shrinking, like a flame that had been caught by a breeze. "It'll depend on you two and your ability to cope. I don't know what Wiser will suggest. We can meet with the Oracle as well. She has just been recovered by Besil and taken to Niall for protection."

Hero strained himself trying to dig up every little detail of his plans. He knew that Akira made the Organization for a greater purpose and that this man, Wiser, had helped him found it. However, he wasn't around during the formation of this Third Party and lacked information. Still, he feigned a greater understanding. "Is Wiser in Niall?"

"He is right now... looking for me, most likely. It'd be best for you to discuss these matters with the person with whom you'll be communicating."

This sounded surprisingly logical.

Hero had little choice but to agree. "Leon-Ru is going to Niall with Jackyl, so perhaps this will give us more time to resolve these matters without misunderstandings."

Akira paused again. "How nice."

"Um...."

"Yes, anyway.... We'll be going then. Let's collect Jackyl and Leon-Ru and be on our way." He left the room.

Hero lingered, observing the sickly haze of darkness that Akira had become. The memory of past Akira burned holes in his mind. It was almost as if Hero could see those images shriveling up inside a massive flame. He wanted to pull them out and pat out the fire until he could recover what had been lost.

I'm sorry we couldn't get along.

"Hero, bring Fate with you," Akira said from the front room.

Hero scooped up Fate in his arms and warily stepped out of the room towards Akira's rising darkness.

Chi and Kyou hugged Hero one at a time and offered their blessings, while the Ignis Brothers tried encouraging Jackyl about becoming the guardian of a young child.

No one said anything to Akira, and the cat didn't so much as flinch.

It's a marvel that he's still standing after using flash step in his condition.

Akira said softly, "Jax, if you'd do the honors."

Jackyl spun his scythe and struck the floor, conjuring his darkness beneath them and opening a portal below. "Leon, take a deep breath." Violet and fuchsia lights flashed past them as they fell through the elasticizing vision of space gaping below.

It drew closer and they burst through the cradle of darkness as though splashing in through a pool of water into Niall. Large, shadowy buildings stuck out along the darkness.

Phantoms floated through the sky, some so large that, even high above, they appeared larger than the buildings. They dropped down onto an expanse of craggy rocks. Close by, small steps led into a corridor that branched off into many hallways, covered by a low roof.

Akira beckoned Hero to follow with a wave of his hand. "Follow me closely." He walked with a swagger and his cloak waved behind him. For someone on the brink of death, he held himself well.

This ability to convey confidence in a moment of utter agony fascinated Hero, since he could still see Akira's aura pulling away from him.

They traveled down the long outside corridor overlooking a large chasm into endless darkness, where phantoms occasionally swam out, vocalizing. On the left side of the hallway were many doors, and Akira stopped at one, first opening it for the others, then entering last.

"This is an official's office," he said, "which I suspect will belong to Jax shortly. This is where he and Leon-Ru will be staying while we make arrangements with Mayuri."

Hero tilted his head as he laid Fate on a sofa in the room. "Mayuri?"

Akira stared back, wide-eyed. "I mean... Wiser."

Jackyl gazed at Akira, his expression full of concern. "Are you all right?"

"Yes... it's just a simple mistake. It happens to the best of us."

"Not to you."

Akira picked Besil off his head and passed him to Jackyl. "Take care of him. I'll be back once we've settled business with Wiser."

Jackyl nodded. "We're here if you need us."

"I know. Come along, Hero. This meeting will have to be private. It'll be our secret with the Wiser, especially now that you know his name, but you may not return here."

Hero examined Akira as he followed. At the door, Hero stopped and glanced back at his son. He flashed a soft smile as Leon-Ru dashed over to hug his waist.

"It'll be okay," Hero said, returning the embrace. "No matter what happens, I'll come back for you."

"You promise?"

"I promise."

Leon-Ru nodded and stepped back. "I'll wait."

"*Rurul mir ven,*" Hero said, stepping out of the office.

'*See you again.*'

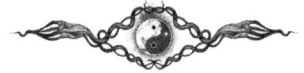

Time is a fallacy, albeit a part of our everyday lives. If I had a choice between a life with or without it, I'd choose to keep it. By measuring time, we measure the changes in our surroundings and those around us. By losing it, we lose sight of what's important and forget how to feel.

They wish to erase it, but it has earned its place amongst us just like everything else.

This story, sad as it may be from time to time, is about hope and survival. Even when odds seem bleak, do not forget that by pressing forward, you may yet live to see another day.

Follow closely. I have something to show you.

---THE STORY CONTINUES---

That's right... this is only the third book of this broad, sweeping, epic adventure. Be sure to move right on to *Prince of Shadows*, the fourth book (and the first book in the second arc) in the "Grims' Truth" series, which is now available.

Also, please continue for the Reference Guide, Book Club Guide, and more back-of-the-book extras.

CHAOS THEORY REFERENCE GUIDE

NOTE: We've designed the Reference Guides to be read *after* the book, or during the reading of the following book. Read at your own discretion. You can find a full version of these guides at **www.GrimsTruth.com**.

TERMINOLOGY

TAINTED/STAINED: A condition caused by a spiritual fracture. The term *Tainted* or *Stained* comes from a dark soot-like mark that appears on those who suffer from this ailment. The Council has deemed them *illegal*, by the notion that the Tainted are responsible for spreading spiritual blood called *miasma*, and causing the plague.

MIASMA: Sometimes referred to as *negative energy*, miasma is actually spiritual blood that causes ailment and/or pain to anyone in its presence for extended periods.

SEALS/BRANDS: Spiritual restraints that come in the form of accessories, ink, or burns on the skin. There are so many forms of seals that the temples keep books on them. Watchers have outlawed most forms of sealing, but the Council still practices them on the Tainted.

THE MORTAL AFFLICTION: Philosophy provided by the Grandmaster, the Ruler of the Universe. It is said that when he first brought mortals into being, he wished for the Ethereal Beings to learn what it meant to be mortal and to understand pain, love, and fear.

A SOUL'S NAME: A name given to new souls by the Universe. This name indicates a Soul's Purpose. Even if a soul is given a new name, their Soul's Name is branded on their spirit. This name can be used to erase, seal, or control another being, so they are often kept secret.

A SOUL'S PURPOSE: A purpose given to a soul when they're given their Soul's Name. Whether the being is mortal, ethereal, or a Doll, they must have a purpose. This purpose cannot be changed nor can a person deviate from their purpose without suffering severe repercussions.

FOLKLORE & HISTORY

THE BOOK OF BEGINNINGS: The oldest scripture responsible for shaping Ancient society. Like the Book of Ages, the stories are written as folklore. However, since no one knows the authors of these books, there are many who doubt their authenticity.

THE BOOK OF AGES: The second scripture of Ancient society and beliefs. The stories here are more prevalent in Ancient culture and viewed as common knowledge, but rarely referenced due to their fantastical viewpoints and questionable authenticity.

THE TEACHINGS OF GRIM: A collection of passages, proverbs, and teachings by the Grim. Many consider them warnings, but for the studious followers, it is pure wisdom for any who can read the Language of Ages.

ROTA FORTUNAE: A tale from *The Book of Ages* about a young girl, Fati, and the God who adopts her. She is said to be from the lower realm, and her soul's purpose is to weave the strings of the Kismet like the master before her. However, she is given the opportunity to choose her path, and thus change the way history unfolds. It is closely related, and mirrors, *The Story of Space & Time*. It also has two endings. This story turned out to be the basis for a children's game in Undal.

THE STORY OF SPACE & TIME (LEOHT MIINA): A story about a boy called Leoht, who is abandoned by his father and taken in by the red-haired God. Unlike many other tales from the Book of Ages, Leoht creates two paths—one in which he accepts a gift, and another where he refuses to make a decision.

THE MAN WHO STOOD AT THE EDGE OF TIME: Many people talk about this tale, but all they really say is that it's about a man who broke the Mirror of Space and Time, and then traveled to the Edge of Time.

SANDS OF TIME: A fiction novel written about two Bound lovers named Solaris and Ulnaire. They say that the characters were modeled after Leoht, Fati, and the Man Who Stood at the Edge of Time.

THE PRINCE OF SHADOWS: An old folklore from *The Book of Beginnings*, which tells the tale of Nox Daeleris, the ruler of Hell. According to the story, he was the most beautiful being in all creation... and also the unluckiest.

THE STORY OF NIGHT & DAY: Another folklore from *The Book of Beginnings*. This one weaves the tale of two star-crossed lovers, one from the light and one from the darkness, Luna & Syo. The red-haired God appears in this story, as well as a character called the Creator.

BENEVOLENCE OF QUEEN: A folklore from the *Book of ages* that features a beautiful and talented illusionist who brings the world to destruction by convincing everyone that she's doing what's best for them. The morale of the story seems to be that appearances are deceiving.

MAIN CHARACTERS
By order of appearance and importance....

*****CAELES HERO:** The main character of *Chaos Theory*. He's the King of Nitor, also known as the Stained Prince and/or Leoht

Miina. He is Tainted, and often tries to avoid the eyes of the Council. After winning the Astor Tournament, he earned the title of Future High King of Mu. Despite his skill and status, few hold him in high regard. After returning from his studies, he became the King of Nitor.

CRUENTUS FATE: Also known as Nuvem Fati and/or the Spinner. She was raised as a Doll in order to become the Future High Queen of Mu. Now, she's the Queen of Nitor.

ISIS: The Queen of Askadel. She helped raise Hero, and shares a close bond with him despite being a Council member.

JACKYL: Also known as Jax and/or Abyssus. He's a Reaper from Niall who wears a jackal mask... sometimes. He was once raised to suppress the Spinner, but died protecting Hero. Now, he travels through time as Akira's aide. According to him, he's also a Guardian.

AKIRA: Also known as Ra Bedad. He is rumored to have been adopted by the Council and taken in by the Grim. In fact, it would appear he's a Grim as well, but his staggering health condition makes him a difficult ally.

BESIL: Also known as Bethshan and/or Amaimon. He's a shape-shifter and talented Puppeteer from the Void. Usually, he takes the form of a cat or an adolescent to avoid drawing too much attention, but he pays little attention to anyone or anything, aside from Akira and his cats.

THE ROYALS

CAELES ELAINE: The late Queen of Nitor. She was murdered when Hero was a child, and reappeared briefly to help him retrace the events.

CRUENTUS NECO: The former King of Macellarius. After losing Fate to the murder of Prince Abyssus, he passed away alone in his palace.

CRUENTUS NITEO: The former King of Nitor. He was murdered by Sally, and no one has said much about him since.

GISHIAN UNA: The former Queen of Elysium. Also known as Witch Huntress Una, due to her habit of hunting her kingdom's children at night. They used to say that even a witch wouldn't dare tread upon her land. She was rumored to have a rare disease that made her sensitive to the light and have a craving for blood.

GISHIAN LUNA: The former Princess of Elysium. She and her twin brother, Syo, were named after the characters in the folklore, *The Story of Night & Day*. She once tried to marry Hero in hopes of them and her brother escaping their parent's tyranny. Unfortunately, he refused, and she burned to death in a fire with her mother.

GISHIAN SYO: The former Prince of Elysium. He was once an overprotective older brother and, allegedly, the food source for his twin, Luna. He died during the Astor Tournament while fighting Hero in the arena.

IUNU KYOU: The First Prince of Inoue, also known as the Wayward Prince. He raised Hero for a short time during his childhood, and has become a father figure.

IUNU HEQET: The High Queen of Mu. She spends most of her time battling against her husband and the other members of the Council. If not for her incredible strength and wisdom, the Empire would fall at the hands of the Council.

IUNU KHNUM: The High King of Mu. He's a Council follower rumored to have been infected by the plague. Khnum speaks very little, mostly observing wherever he goes, and he has a strong belief in restoring full power to purebred Ancients. Few trust him because he serves only the Council and his own interests.

THE GUARDS

IGNIS FIRMUS: Abyssus' former guard. After the death of his closest friend and lover, he moved to the Capital and received assistance from Akira. He spends a majority of his time working between kingdoms and assisting his brother, Fortis, on assignments.

IGNIS FORTIS: Niteo's former guard. He now serves under Hero and Fate's rule. His Ancient blood and Royal background prevent most from changing his decisions; therefore, Fortis does as he pleases and has even gained the title of the Royal Philanderer.

MORTIS: Neco's former guard. He speaks very little and has an uncanny ability to survive even the most brutal attacks. Most people try to avoid him and pretend he doesn't exist, including the Royals.

CAELES CHI: The High Queen's guard. She is also Hero's aunt, but rarely has the time or opportunity to meet with him. When she isn't guarding the High Queen, she is directing the Capital's soldiers and studying the Ussan.

BROTHEL

IGNIS FORTUNA: The Queen of Tir Na Nog, one of the leaders of the Rebellion. Fortuna spent many turns protecting and teaching Fate during her stay in Mu. Her inconspicuous nature and striking appearance deter many from her real strategy and ability to turn the tides in the Rebellion's favor.

MYRNA: Tori's lover. She left with Nigel after the auction, and rumor has it she assumed an important role with the Rebellion. Her ability to remain hidden fascinates many, especially the few people who see her working.

TORI: Fate's closest sister. Also known as Aeros Ianthe. She is one of the last surviving Oracles after an attack on her village.

Her brother is a trusted member of the Organization who recommended her to be their first Oracle. She moved away from Mu to accept the position.

OTHER

THE COUNCIL LEADER: The leader of the Council, as well as Akira's adoptive mother. She seems to be from the Iu Clan and is a devout follower of the Grandmaster's Scriptures.

MAYURI: Also known as the Wiser. He is rumored to be omnipotent and has strange connections to the Council and the Grim. He is also the co-founder of the Organization.

MYLES: Priscilla's younger brother. He died from miasma poisoning after his sister smuggled Hero out of Nitor Palace to live with them.

NIGEL: Fortuna's lover. He is a valued member of the Rebellion that often appears in the Madam's stead to relay messages. His role and capabilities are hidden so well, no one even questions his presence when he arrives.

PRISCILLA: A young violinist from Elysium. She once taught Hero how to play, and even helped him escape from Nitor Palace. However, her good deed resulted in the death of herself and her younger brother, Myles.

SALLY: Also known as Lara, Hero's childhood friend. Since her attempt to kill Fate, she has lived in the underground tunnels feeding off the people inflicted with miasma poisoning.

GROUPS

THE COUNCIL: A group of Ancient Elders responsible for upholding the preservation of tradition and Ancient clans. They are rumored to be a lesser form a higher power called the

Watchers. The citizens of Mu live by Council laws and scriptures. The Council believes that maintaining old tradition and preserving purebred Ancients is their most essential task; therefore, they have outlawed the Tainted and half-breeds.

THE REBELLION: The Ancient uprising against Council law. The members of the Rebellion are inconspicuous about their participation, and work in the shadows to return balance to the world they live in.

THE GRIM: A group of Ancients who present themselves in the forms of large skeletal beings. The majority believes they have transcended beyond a physical form, but supposedly, they just disguise themselves by wearing a uniform. They always speak in terms of *we*, so as not to disclose their identity.

DOLLS: The *Children of Grim*. Dolls are old Ancients' souls who have returned in the form of a vessel. Currently, the Grim are the only Puppeteers left in existence, as Puppeteering has been outlawed by the Council.

THE GUARDIANS: Little is known about them aside from what Jackyl has claimed. They are said to be the protectors of 'space and time,' but the meaning of this is unclear.

THE LORDS OF LIGHT & SHADOW: A group of all-powerful beings rumored to have the ability to bring balance back to the Universe.

BREEDS

ANCIENT: Often referred to as the supreme beings by lesser breeds, yet disregarded by superior beings. Each clan inhibits different elemental capabilities and strengths, and all of them display strong genetic traits that are reflected in their physical appearance. They can live tens of thousands of years, and some even live out multiple lives with a special mate called their Bound.

HALF-BREED: A being that is part of two genetic strains. The Ancients refuse to acknowledge them as true Ancients because they do not have pure blood, but most of them still have elemental capabilities. They live longer than the Rahma but not quite as long as pure blood Ancients.

RAHMA: A lesser group of beings that only live hundreds of years by the Ancients' influence. They are incapable of manipulating elements and possess no special endowments, except that they live longer than Human Beings. They experienced an influx of population when the Age of the Ancients started to come to an end. Although they worshipped the Ancients to a certain degree, many Rahma believed they were greater, and were detested by the higher breeds.

HUMANS: The weakest of the breeds. They did not come into being until long after the Rise of the Rahma had come to an end.

ANCIENT CLANS

FEH – Electricity: The Feh are smaller than other clans, but make up for their lack of stature with tremendous force. Although they have a wide variety of physical traits, all Feh are tiny—the tallest being no larger than a juvenile Ancient. Due to their curious and intelligent nature, the Feh found many uses for their element, and made Nysa one of the most beautiful and sought after kingdoms in the Empire.

GRIM – Darkness: Although they were one of the original clans, the Grim took their leave of the Mortal Realm, and chose to exist in the darkness of the Abyss instead of share a place beside the Ancients and the Rahma, but their reason for doing this is not clear. The large skeletal beings appear to aid in the growth of the mortals, and yet remain separated from them. In spite of this, the clan is at odds with the mortal realm and the Council alike, and no one is privy to knowing why and how they operate Niall.

-Sub. REAPERS – *Darkness:* Reapers are an unusual group of former Ancients, turned rogue, who work with the Grim for unknown purposes. They are able to fold space-time at will, which makes it possible for them to appear and disappear from mortal events on a whim. This creates an uncomfortable situation for the Ancients, the Rahma, and the Council, but that's exactly how the Reapers like it. They are identified by their cloaks of darkness and soul-sealed animal masks. The most frightening forms of Reapers carry weapons crafted from darkness, and are marked by "the hand of death."

VEM – Air – RARE: Vem are marked by their delicate frame, pale skin, dark hair, and vibrant blue eyes. They have innate spiritual manipulation capabilities, and are one of the only clans able to puppeteer. They are shy by nature and thus usually keep to themselves unless they develop a deep emotional bond — which they will keep until death.

RA – Time – LOST: Very little is known about this clan. Their disappearance from the Mortal Realm is one the great Ancient mysteries. They may have left of their own accord, much like the Grim, or some unfortunate events may have driven them to extinction. The only certainty is that they were the sole masters of time. They could stop and even reverse time at will. This fact makes it unclear as to how a clan like this could vanish without a trace, if not by their own choice.

IU – Body: All Iu carry the same traits — they are delicate but tall with pale skin, black hair and violet eyes. They are seldom aggressive but, if angered, their wrath is much like a dance with death. They are one of the masters of the "flash step" — a movement so quick that the eye cannot follow.

-Sub. IUNU – *Body:* There is little evolution between the Iu and the Iunu. They are one of the purest sub clans. It is more a shift in clan temperament than an actual sub categorization. After the Verna Conflict, the Iu were all but lost except the Iunu branch family. They upheld the formalities and policies of the Iu clan as a whole.

CAELES – Crystal – RARE: This rare and unusual clan rose in Undal with the reign of the Crystal Empire. They were reclusive and hostile towards outsiders, and were the only clan able to withstand the Igni assault during the Verna Conflict. Their Empire rose up out of the Ussan suddenly, and collapsed just as quickly, leaving them nearly one of the lost clans. The Caeles are broken into two factions—the Wolf Clan and the Fox Clan. If not for the cleverness of the Fox Clan, the Caeles would have been lost altogether.

---*Wolf Clan* are the leaders of the Caeles. They are tall, strong, and agile, marked with silvery hair and an abnormal grey tone to their skin without actually being grey. They have a variety of eye colors, including gray, silver, icy blue, and pale yellow amber. Their battle prowess makes them a terrifying foe, because if you see one Caeles, there is most certainly a pack nearby.

---*Fox Clan* are known for being compact and stealthy. They are petite in stature, much like the Feh, but much stronger and faster. Like the Wolf Clan, they travel in packs and are quite capable of taking down much stronger foes. Fox Clan is, above all else, highly intelligent. They are so pale they are considered the albino of the breeds. With icy skin, mint eyes, and white hair, it is hard to believe they are so skilled at disappearing into their surroundings, but they are deadly masters of stealth and cunning. Beware of what you don't see, because it can kill you.

-Sub. **CALLIDAE- *Water:*** A sub clan of the Fox Clan. The Callidae are known for pushing the boundaries of science and spirit. They chose genetic alteration as a way of leveling their inability to manifest crystal. They unfortunately did not possess the fortitude to use their element so they altered themselves to become water elementals. Water, being the lesser form of crystal, was the best alternative for them.

-Sub. **GISHIAN – *Blood:*** A sub clan of the Callidae. They are the result of genetic experimentation and have attained the ability to manipulate blood. However, with this ability comes great consequences. The women of the Gishian Family feed off their male counterparts in order to survive. Often times, this has resulted in extreme illness and other deterioration in the spirit, mind, and body.

NIS – Fire: The Nis are emotionally and sexually charged Ancients, that appear much larger in stature but remain lean and agile. They are easily recognized by their dark hair, tanned skin, freckles, and amber eyes.

-Sub. Ignis – Fire: The Ignis carry the appearance of the Nis but hold a special trait known as "The Cat's Eye." This trait gives them the ability to see more than most, such as sensing spiritual change and seeing across vast expanses without aid. In fact, these qualities are what brought the Igni into great power during the age of Undal. Even though the clan nearly met their end with the cataclysmic fall of Chien, their drive for sex and an innate need to immediately find their Bound, they recovered from the collapse and ended up being one of the strongest clans.

KA – Mind: Flaming red hair, intense green eyes, and sandy skin are the mark of the Ka. Their spirit burns much like their appearance. They are emotionally charged and passionate about everything they do.

-Sub. ASKA – Illusion: Aska carry the appearance of all Ka but they more volatile by nature. The passion of the Ka is always apparent; however, the Aska often turn to malice. Their feelings can drive them to commit personal acts of vengeance and/or spite. Their gift for strategy makes them formidable foes, so it is best to keep them from exploring deviant resolves.

LOCATIONS
In order of placement on the map....

MU: An empire where mortal beings live, both Ancient and Rahma. A majority of the kingdoms are Ancient-ruled despite the massive decline in their population. They encourage the union of Bound with the intention of bringing power back to their breed, but have faced difficulty in their endeavor. The Empire is vastly divided by the powers of the Rebellion and the Council.

INOUE CAPITAL: The Capital of Mu is a grand city that overlooks the sea. It is home to the largest population of Ancients in the Empire and some of the grandest celebrations. The Queen hosts regular parties, auctions, and events to bring the people together. It is also the political center for Mu, often called the Utopia of Mu for its magnificent view of the Ussan and its preservation of old tradition.

INOUE COMMUNITY: The community on the opposite side of the Centre between the Capital Palace and the beaches below. The people of Inoue live roof to roof on the slope, adhering to old tradition and gathering for celebrations held by the Royal Family living at the top of the slope. In spite of their spacious region, they prefer to remain close together, as a reminder to cherish their neighbors and their families. Children from this community gather in the Centre to listen to folklore told by the Elders.

USSAN: Rumored to be the only remainder of the once magnificent crystal empire. The forest is guarded by Capital guards at all times, because it is so dangerous, but many people from all around the Empire try to visit the Capital for a chance to see it up close. The citizens of Inoue say that the forest sings and chimes in order to tell the tales of the Old World. In some cases, they say that if you listen closely, you can hear it whispering.

NEX: A once luxurious region tarnished by the plague and Rahma rule. The two sides of the kingdom, Nex and Macellarius, were divided upon the coronation of the Cruentus Twins, Neco and Niteo. It is the smallest and coldest kingdom in all of Mu, and is often neglected by the higher powers due to its Rahma rulers. Even so, it is considered important because it is the only kingdom standing between the Capital and the rest of the Empire.

NYSA: The fifth kingdom of Mu—home of the Feh. Although they are few in numbers, they still hold a great deal of power and influence in Mu. With their intelligence and fantastic ability to manipulate their element, the Feh have created one of the most beautiful and peaceful kingdoms in all of Mu. Under the rule of their king, they also have sided with the Rebellion.

THULE: An island close to Mu where the Council established their religion and faction within a palace known as the Grand Acropolis. Rahma are prohibited from entering, as are the Tainted and Half-Breeds, because they are deemed a source of the Plague known as the Taint.

NIALL: A city of Reapers located in the Shadow Realm. Phantoms roam the shadowy landscape searching for sustenance. It is covered by strange glowing orbs and surrounded by space.

UNDAL: Often referred to as the Old World. Most people believe that it's a mythological world or theorist's tale about the world before Mu. However, there are a select few who believe in its origins and study its history and scriptures.

BOOK CLUB GUIDE

1. Based on what you've read so far, which faction do you side with and why? If not any, then what is your opinion on the battle thus far?

2. *Chaos Theory* restates and clarifies the purpose behind the Lords of Light and Shadow. Up to this point, who do you think the Lords might be? (Full list of lords at grimstruth.com for reference.)

3. Breadcrumbs tend to appear in the form of incongruity. What are some things you've noticed that might be hints in uncovering the mysteries of the series?

4. A lot of the First Arc takes place in the Dreamscape. The things inside each character's world are unique to their perspective and personalities, but what are some of the similarities between them?

5. Reading from various perspectives shines a light on the truths and lies of each character. Which lies or unconfirmed details have you spotted in the plot thus far?

6. The First Arc focused on the Tainted. Now that you've completed that arc, how has your opinion of them changed?

7. All three books in *Arc 1: The Tainted* use reference to the folklore from *The Book of Ages* and *The Book of Beginnings*. After learning new information in *Chaos Theory*, how do you think these stories pertain to the current events? If not at all, what do you think they mean?

What's Next?

PRINCE OF SHADOWS
Grims' Truth – Book 4
By Isu Yin & Fae Yang

Be swept further away into the world of Grims' Truth with *Prince of Shadows*, the fourth book (and the first book in the second arc) in this epic fantasy series.

~~~

After the collapse of Inoue, Jackyl finds himself leading the Reapers and shouldering the weight of the Guardians against his better judgment. Unfortunately, he already faces warnings of catastrophe as a dark force moves through the Reaper City of Niall.

With far too much too handle and a small boy in tow, he quickly stumbles into another perplexing conundrum—an imposter Akira. Jackyl forges ahead into the unknown as Mu falls apart. Feeling disparaged and frustrated, he struggles to overcome impossible hurdles with a hand full of people he trusts. Even against all odds, he must succeed or the war for Mu will be lost and the Guardians will cease to be.

~~~

For more information on this series, and to enjoy a variety of special content related to this sweeping, epic project, please visit the authors' website at the link below.

www.GrimsTruth.com

ACKNOWLEDGEMENTS

Hello, and thank you for making it this far into the series. Usually, the acknowledgements are full of names in our books, listing the specific people we know who have made it possible for us to continue writing this beast. This time, we decided to leave it more open-ended.

We honestly couldn't be more glad or excited to finish the first arc. It feels like we've crossed a major obstacle in our very long path to book sixty.

Our long term readers have stayed with us through this Arc 1 experience for a few years now, so we're excited to present *Arc 2: The Guardians* and finally answer some of the long-standing questions.

We are grateful to everyone who has invested time and money into *Grims' Truth* and has joined us on this journey.

Though, naturally, we always give a special shout-out to our editor, Lane Diamond, for making sense of our story.

We look forward to the launch of *Prince of Shadows*, and will continue to work hard to improve for future works.

Thank *you*, and we hope to see you next arc!

About the Authors

For as long as we can remember, we have been either plagued or blessed with dreams of the vast universe we call Euphoria. The fascination and devotion we share for these dreams, and all the people inside them, has driven our artistic visions for decades.

We have studied photography, linguistics, graphic art, video editing, traditional art, and literature, all with the intent of sharing this massive story and vision. Though many obstacles may lie ahead, we look forward to embarking on this journey with whomever may find a vested interest in our work.

For more, please visit Isu Yin & Fae Yang online at:
Author Website: www.GrimsTruth.com
Publisher Website: www.EvolvedPub.com
Goodreads: Fae Yang
Twitter: @DollsOfGrim
Facebook: www.facebook.com/DollsOfGrim/
Instagram: GrimsTruth

More From Evolved Publishing

We offer great books across multiple genres, featuring hiqh-quality editing (which we believe is second-to-none) and fantastic covers.

As a hybrid small press, your support as loyal readers is so important to us, and we have strived, with tireless dedication and sheer determination, to deliver on the promise of our motto:
QUALITY IS PRIORITY #1!

Please check out all of our great books,
which you can find at this link:
www.EvolvedPub.com/Catalog/

Thank you!

CPSIA information can be obtained
at www.ICGtesting.com
Printed in the USA
LVHW040610010423
743125LV00003B/393